A FALCON FOR A WITCH

When Margred leaves her home in the Welsh mountains and travels south with her dancing bear, she sets in motion events that will affect generations yet unborn, for in Elizabethan London she meets Sir Harry Falcon of *Kingsmead*. Their love is destined to yield a curse, and a tale of a forbidden passion and a macabre revenge unfolds, against the glittering background of the Queen's Court and the witch trials of the early Jacobeans.

Books by Catherine Darby
Published by The House of Ulverscroft:

FROST ON THE MOON
MOON IN PISCES

CATHERINE DARBY

A FALCON FOR A WITCH

Complete and Unabridged

ULVERSCROFT
Leicester

First published in Great Britain in 1975 by
Robert Hale Limited
London

First Large Print Edition
published 1998
by arrangement with
Robert Hale Limited
London

British Library CIP Data

Darby, Catherine, *1935* –
A falcon for a witch.—Large print ed.—
Ulverscroft large print series: romance
1. Love stories
2. Large type books
I. Title
823.9′14 [F]

ISBN 0–7089–3998–8

Published by
F. A. Thorpe (Publishing) Ltd.
Anstey, Leicestershire

Set by Words & Graphics Ltd.
Anstey, Leicestershire
Printed and bound in Great Britain by
T. J. International Ltd., Padstow, Cornwall

This book is printed on acid-free paper

1590

1

Now that she was fifteen the days seemed to fly past as swiftly as the birds winging their way to the south. Sometimes Margred tilted back her head to watch them as they passed over, black bodies sleek beneath the sky. Once she had asked Old Prys where they went when they reached the south.

'London, I suppose,' he answered, scratching his head. 'Or further still, to Spain or Africa.'

'Wouldn't you like to go there?' she asked.

'Went as far as London once,' the old man said, and his eyes clouded as if he looked at distant scenes.

'What was it like?'

She had heard the story many times, but knew he liked to tell it over and over.

'Big,' he said. 'Houses as high as ten men, and ladies with coloured stones in their shoes, and horses with ribbons on their saddles. And people talking English as fast as we speak Welsh.'

'And the King? You saw the King, didn't you?'

'As real as life, with his hair gold as the

3

sun, and diamonds on his doublet. Old Harry Tudor himself! Mind, he was a youngling then, about my own age; but he rode on a horse and I stood with the groundlings. Wasn't anyone to touch King Harry, but then wasn't he of good Welsh stock! Wasn't Jasper Tyddyr his own great-uncle, and didn't they march into England, bold as brass, to take the throne!'

'Yes, Prys. Didn't they though!'

'Wonderful times for the Welsh, clinking coin in the taverns, bussing the wenches, but it's gone now; all gone.'

'But King Harry's daughter is on the throne now, isn't she?' Margred said swiftly, to cheer him.

'Aye, Tudor Bessie. But she's an old woman now, near as old as I am; and that's too far to count.'

He was past ninety, he believed, but he looked ageless, his leathery skin stretched tightly over the jutting bones of his skull, his hair yellow-white like the fleece of the little sheep rubbing themselves against the rocks.

'Reckon she'll be dead soon,' he said gloomily. 'Reckon I won't last long myself after that.'

He had been prophesying his own death for as long as she could remember, but in

4

sudden terror she threw her arms about him, hugging him with all the strength of her thin little body.

'You won't ever die, Prys. Promise me you'll live for ever! Promise!'

'I'll be squeezed to death in a minute if you don't leave off,' he said irritably, but his glance was tender.

Prys ap Prys loved his grand-daughter more than any living being, more than the memory of his dead son.

Ieuan ap Prys had been a lusty babe, so big and strong as he came howling into the world that he had killed his mother, that slim, silent girl that Prys had married and taken back to his cottage. It had been a late wedding with Prys near fifty and not interested in a wife until he saw Mair at her spinning. Well, she had only lasted a year, but she had left him a fine son.

Ieuan had taught himself to add up coins on his fingers and to trace the letters of his name. He had listened to the English who came over the border to buy cattle and practised their tongue, even persuading his father into the speaking of it. They had been content, just the two of them, until Ieuan came home one day with a black-haired girl and told Prys that her name was Margred and that he had married her.

5

Prys had never been able to discover exactly where she came from, or of what stock she was sprung. She spoke the dialect of the south, larded with words of another language that was not English. Ieuan had seen her at the cattle-fair, weeping because somebody had stolen her purse, and the beauty of her had chained his heart.

She was quite useless in the house for she could neither spin nor weave, nor bake bread without scorching it; but she had a sweet smile and wide, wild eyes of a strange yellow colour like no eyes Prys had ever seen in a human creature before. Once she had told him that her mother had bedded with a fox and she was their child. It had been a jest, he knew, but she had flung back her hair and whined, deep in her throat, like a vixen in heat, and he had felt uneasy as if the moon cast long shadows.

But she had been human enough, poor soul, to catch the sweating sickness and die of it, just two days after he had buried Ieuan from the same cause. That had been a bad season with many new graves and the bells constantly tolling and the gorse turning the fields yellow.

It was cruel that Prys, who was old and past use, should escape the sweat and Ieuan, who was young and strong, should die of it.

First Ieuan and then his wife, pouring out
the last of her fevered strength to give birth
to the child in her swollen belly. And when
the child was an hour old, the yellow eyed
girl had died, one hand stretched out as if
she implored pardon.

The babe was a girl, small but daintily
made and unblemished save for a blue mark
on her tiny hip. A little moon-shaped mark
that never faded but remained like a dark
stain on the white skin. Her mother had
had a similar mark. Prys had not been able
to help noticing because her skirt had ridden
up during the birth struggles and there was
the mark, the colour of the dark violets that
nestled in the hollow of the hills. He had
buried her deep and laid heavy stones over
the turned earth and gone back into the
cottage to tend the child.

There had been no wet-nurse, for the local
folk were too busy with their own buryings,
and Prys had always been a reserved man
who made no friends and seldom troubled
his neighbours. Instead he had soaked rags
in cows' milk, and the baby had sucked
greedily, then opened eyes so yellow that
Prys had forgotten his intention of naming
her Mair and named her Margred instead.

She was fifteen now and still small, with
breasts that strained against the red wool

of her gown and hair that fell, blue-black and shining, to her waist. She was not as lovely as her mother had been, for she had Ieuan's tip-tilted nose and wide mouth, and her white skin had long since been tanned by the wind and sun to a hazel-nut brown, but her teeth were pearl perfect, her ears set close against her head, her eyes dancing amber between long lashes.

Prys thought she was the most beautiful creature who walked God's earth, and considered it a mystery beyond understanding that nobody had made an offer for her yet. She was not only pretty and healthy and sweet-tempered, but when he died she would have the cottage and the land that went with it. Despite his frequent words of gloom, Prys was privately convinced that he was immortal, but he had taken the precaution of walking down into Caernarvon to have the notary draw up a proper Will.

It was a good cottage too, stone built, with a roof made of slates, and two rooms, and a hearth sunk deeply into the centre of one of them, and wooden shutters at the two windows. There were two pallets with covers of wool and sheepskin, a table and two stools, and a cupboard where the dishes were kept. At the back of the house was a well that sent up sweet water and a shed where he kept the two milk cows and a yard where the hens could scratch. The rest wasn't much, petering out into thistle and scrub, but there was an apple tree and a patch where Margred tended herbs, and he had about a dozen sheep.

Yet nobody had made his grand-daughter an offer, nor came sneaking round the house hoping to snatch a kiss. It was very confusing, thought Prys, happily unaware that his dead daughter-in-law had told others the sad, mischievous tale of her fox-father, and that nobody fancied a yellow-eyed wife wife with a slanting smile and a passion for brewing up concoctions from the herbs she grew.

Weddings were the last thing in Margred's mind as she ran through the fields. It was enough simply to be alive on this golden October day with a sharp breeze giving an added zest to the warm sunshine. She ran without heed, bare feet flashing under her red kirtle, her hair bouncing on her shoulders. There were times when she wanted to run to the edge of the world and stand on tiptoe, crying, 'Look at me, God! Look at me! I am Margred, and I am fifteen years old!'

She preferred talking to God when she was in the open air. Neither she nor Prys felt comfortable in stuffy churches, though they went to service now and then, to avoid paying the recusancy fines. But it was better to be in the fields, or down on the shingle beach that stretched along past the bulk of the great castle towards the coast villages.

That castle had dominated the town since Edward of the English had conquered the Welsh lords. The weekly market was held in its shadow, fishermen launched their boats under its frowning eminence; from its corroding battlements one could look out across the tossing straits to the flat, mist-wreathed isle of Anglesey, last stronghold of the Druids.

One or two lads catcalled after Margred as she went swiftly along the broad walk between postern gate and stone-walled quay. As usual the harbour was full of little boats, bobbing at anchor on the little, sparkling waves. Trading vessels called here often, some from Ireland, others from Brittany. These latter spoke a bastard Welsh and had cheerful faces and bright caps pulled down over their ears. Margred had often watched them and wondered how they could regard their sea journeyings so casually. She had never been further than the outskirts of Caernarvon in her life, and the shining water and the gay boats beckoned her away.

'When I am a woman grown I will go to London,' she said aloud, resting her elbows on the low parapet and breathing in great gulps of the salt-laden air.

The man who leaned against the wall some feet away never turned his head, but he answered in English.

'There's nothing worth seeing there.'

'There are houses as high as ten men and ladies with coloured stones on their feet. Prys told me so.'

'Prys is a liar. London is filth, disease, the stench of burning flesh.'

'That was long ago. I heard of that.'

'I saw it.' For the first time he turned his deepset, brooding eyes upon her. 'I saw the flames leap high and my mother writhing, blackening. In those days they tortured Protestants. Today they torture Papists.'

'But not everybody,' she objected, 'else there'd be no people left.'

'You're a fool,' he said flatly, and turned his head towards the sea again.

Margred doubted if anybody had ever heard his name. Perhaps he had forgotten it himself, for he had lived alone for as long as anybody could recall. If he had a trade nobody knew it, yet he was always decently dressed and had never been whipped for vagrancy. There were periods when he seemed to lose his senses altogether and went up and down in the narrow streets

11

roaring psalms at the top of his voice. Most of the time, however, he was completely rational, hidden within some deep, soul-searing bitterness that made the brightest day dim.

'Not such a fool,' she said with spirit. 'I can speak English.'

'With an abominable accent,' he growled. 'Up and down, up and down, with your voice on a seesaw and your words back to front most of the time.'

'All the same,' she persisted, 'if I can speak the tongue, it's a pity not to be seeing the land.'

'Stay safe,' he advised curtly. 'There's no virtue in travel. Look what happened last night.'

'There was a high wind. We bolted the door, and sat close to the fire.'

'There was a boat ran aground at Allalas.' He jerked his shaggy head to further along the harbour where the shingle began. 'A Breton boat. All drowned, save one, and him they thrust back that the sea might not be cheated of a life.'

'Was there much booty?' she asked with interest.

'Bales of lace, stained with the salt water. Some casks of malmsey.'

'I'll go and see.'

She liked poking about amid the rocks and there was always the chance the townsfolk might have overlooked something from the wreck.

'Go where you please,' he said indifferently. 'But stay away from London. It's full of dead martyrs and devils' children, and the coloured stones are only glass.'

Margred made a face at his averted profile and hurried past him, picking her way carefully from tufted grass to flat stone. Fingers of sea-heather clutched at her ankles, insistent as the fingers of drowning men, and the wind whipped her hair into a tangle.

Bits and pieces of shattered wood lay high above the tidemark. It had been painted in red and blue, but the colours were already running together as the water seeped through the bark. There was not a scrap of lace nor a cask of malmsey anywhere to be seen. Neither were there bodies, but then they would have been weighted with stones and thrown back into the harbour to nourish the fishes.

Margred sat down on a rock and dabbled her scratched feet in a little pool. Nearby a jellyfish lay in abject surrender. She wrinkled her nose at it in distaste, knowing the spitefulness of its paralysing tentacles. Within reach of her hand a tiny crab took fright and scuttled to safety.

'If I went to London, I would see all the things Prys talks about,' she said aloud.

Like most solitary children she had early invented an imaginary companion with whom she could discuss things that couldn't be talked about with her grandfather. This companion had neither shape nor sex, but she thought of it as Mott. Mott was privileged to hear many things about Margred that nobody else began to suspect.

'I will buy a silk gown and a white pony and watch Queen Bessie ride past,' she said. 'And I will go down to the harbour and get on a boat and sail south, following the birds.'

As if in mockery, a white-winged gull swooped low, its beak open in perpetual hope. Hope deferred, it called aloud in frustration. Margred called back to it, laughing as it skimmed the surface of the water.

'Go south, like the other birds!' she called. 'Go where it's warm and the fish sleep on top of the waves!'

There was a low, answering growl so close behind her that her voice froze in her throat. Infinitely slowly, the hair at the nape of her neck prickling, she turned her head.

It stood, squat and brown with bits of

seaweed clinging to its thick fur, its little eyes blinking at her. It must have crept into some hollow of the rocks and slept there until her voice had encouraged it to venture forth. Margred knew what it was. Some tinkers had passed through the town four summers before and they had had a bear which did tricks and danced to the fluting of a reed.

This bear had a collar about its neck from which a short length of broken chain dangled. Obviously it had escaped from the Breton boat, and equally obviously it was her duty to hit it over the head and push it back into the water. She looked at it doubtfully, wondering what she could use as a weapon and if she would have the strength to hit hard enough.

The bear whined and dropped to all fours, shambling towards her and sniffing. Her hand reached out to touch the matted, salt-encrusted fur. Something was growing in her — a kind of recognition as if she and the bear belonged together.

'Mott?' she questioned. 'Shall I call you Mott, then?'

The bear whined again, licking her hand. It was very tame, she thought, and felt a little surge of gladness as if she herself had taken the wildness out of it.

'Can you dance, Mott?' she questioned. 'Can you dance like the tinkers' bear?'

The bear sat back on its haunches and whimpered.

Margred began to hum, the sound warm and sweet in her throat, swelling out into a wordless song that reflected the waving sea-heather and the glint of the sun across the brown rocks. The bear backed off a little and rose on to its hind legs, its head moving from side to side, tentatively at first but then more surely as the rhythm became more insistent. Clumsily the animal began to move, lifting its feet, its head high, its muzzle thrust forward.

'You're dancing!' Margred cried in delight. 'You're really dancing!'

As she ceased the tune, the bear dropped to all fours again and shuffled up against her, obviously seeking a tit-bit. Margred delved into her waistband and fished out a piece of marchpane. She had already nibbled the edges of it, but the bear accepted it gently from her outspread palm.

'I'll take you home with me,' she told it. 'You can have something to eat there, but you must leave the hens alone.'

Did bears, she wondered, eat hens? She knew that foxes and wolves did, but at this time of year the wolves seldom came so near to the town or the outlying farms.

She reached down and picked up the end of the chain. There were deep scratches around the collar where the animal had evidently torn itself free.

'We won't go back through the town, Mott,' she said. 'People will stare at you and question. They might even want to drown you, but I'll not let that happen. We'll wait until dusk and then we'll go back through the fields.'

It was already cooling perceptibly, the wind rising, the rocks purpling. She drew back into the shelter of a higher crop of stones and sat down again, watching the sea. At her side the bear crouched, bewildered and submissive. She had talked to it in Welsh which was close enough to Breton for it to understand. Obviously it was a Breton bear, or its owner had been.

'Drowned dead,' she said without much real sorrow, for she had never known its owner. 'Drowned dead, and you without even a grandfather! Poor Mott, poor bear!'

It was dimmer now, rocks and sea and tufted grass merging together as the faint outline of a Jacob's ladder shone across the water.

Margred rose, taking a firmer grip on the chain, and went further along the beach past the jagged line of rocks to where an untidy group of pines straggled up towards the common. Several paths wound their ways across the green — deceptive green, for in many places marsh, black and treacherous lay beneath the sweet grass. An unwary step might bring one floundering up to the waist in thick, sucking mud.

Margred knew the path in every mood, in bright sunshine, in driving rain, in the mist that swirled up without warning after a hot summer day. She followed its twistings out of a force of habit, the bear pressing close against her legs.

The darkness was falling quickly, pressing down over the land, enclosing the landscape. Little trails of vapour spiralled up from the moss and bubbled down into the deep pools beneath. The birds were darting low to snatch and savour the insects, and here and there a thorn tree leaned sideways as if it paid homage to the range of mountains that encircled field and river, town and castle, and shingle beach.

A light flickered beyond the marsh, dipped and swayed, moved onwards following a line roughly parallel to the path. A group of fireflies, wing to wing, blossoming in the evening air? Or the death-candle which hovered ahead of one who would either die or suffer the death of a loved one within a twelvemonth.

Trickles of fear shivered her spine. The blue flame of the death-candle was something to be dreaded by all sensible folk; dreaded even more than the little people who lured maidens into the fairy ring. If one were tempted by the little people there was always the chance that one could come back after seven years in their dim, green world. But with the death-candle one had no chance at all.

The bear, sensing her fear, stopped and growled, its hackles rising. She bent swiftly to soothe it.

'Hush, Mott. We'll be home soon. Over the rise and across the field. Then we'll see Prys.'

The light flickered again and was lost in a bank of cloud. Unreasonably her panic suddenly overwhelmed her and she began to run, slipping and sliding in and out of mist, the wind slapping her cheeks.

A rushlight gleamed through the unshuttered window of the cottage. In the little barn the cows mooed as if they guessed at her coming. Panic was replaced by the excitement of being back in her own place, back at home. It was always like that when she returned from one of her solitary rambles. There was

19

always the last, breathless little rush up the slope and then the cottage was there, with its field around it, and the barn, and the two graves with the slate headstones, and the patch of garden where the herbs grew thick and sweet. And when she saw all that, the world was safe again. But when she was home she looked outward, longingly beyond the mountains to the city where ladies had coloured stones on their shoes.

She paused for an instant and then ran down the slope past the apple tree and the well with its flat slate cover, and through the open door.

Prys lay on his pallet against the wall, his hands clutched to his thin chest, a bubble of blood at the corner of his mouth, his eyes open and filled with disbelief as if he could not credit that his own prediction had come to pass.

Margred stopped as if invisible cords had checked her. Bread and cheese were set out on the table, and a stew simmered in its pot from the tripod over the fire. The rushlight dripped tallow into its shallow saucer and made tiny shadows against the wall. She saw all that, without realising that she saw it, and then, unwillingly, inexorably, she looked at her grandfather again.

He was dead. Instinct told her that, told

her too that his old heart had given out at last, and that nothing she could do would alter that. For a moment a cold, sick feeling of betrayal rose up in her. Prys had never been going to die. In her world the old man was always there, talking of the long ago time when he had visited London, preparing supper for when she came home.

The bear padded in and laid its head on her knee, its little eyes sorrowful. Margred stroked its matted fur, while some part of her mind thought, coolly and practically.

We'll be alone now. Prys will have to be buried, but I can't do it. He's too heavy for me to lift. And he died with his sins on him, and no minister near. Ninety years of sinning is a long time.

It would be a wise precaution to send for the sin-eater, who would eat a meal from the corpse's chest and so take upon himself the sins of the one who had died. But the sin-eater lived a day's walk away and there was no certainty he would be at home. He was greatly in demand around the local villages even though the ministers drove him away with blows and curses. And Margred herself shrank from the filthy old man whose very presence seemed to whisper of evil.

'We can't stay here by ourselves,' she told the bear. 'It's lonely here with no neighbours and only the graves for company. We'll leave, you and I. We'll go south before the winter starts. We'll go to London. That's what we'll do, Mott! We'll go to London and you can dance in the streets. People will give us money, and then I shall have my silk gown.'

All the time she was talking she was moving aimlessly up and down the little room, picking up things and setting them down again. Her eyes returned constantly to the still figure on the pallet.

Ninety years old and nobody to eat his sins, unless — her glance rested on the bear. A moment later she was smearing honey on a chunk of bread and laying it on the chest, motionless and concave under the faded smock.

'Come, Mott. There's food there. Eat it.'

Her voice urged gently, her fingers tugged at the chain. The bear whined, dragging back with a strength that almost lifted her off her feet. But desire for food had the mastery over fear of the smell of death. Mott lunged at the sweet bread and ate it noisily, scrabbling for crumbs.

'Please God put my grandfather's sins on Mott and let him rest easy when he's buried,' Margred gabbled, closing her eyes.

She would set rushlights burning at the

head and feet, and at first light she would go to the tumbledown shanty where the Englishman lived. He would not want to take Mott away from her nor be interested in her plans to move south, but he would see that Prys was decently buried and that the right people were informed.

She would give him the hens and the two cows in return, for she would have enough to do with looking after Mott. All she would take with her were her thick shawl and the good leather shoes she wore in the winter, and some springs of green from her mother's grave. She had noticed the little shoots only a few weeks before, pushing their way up through the moss-grown mound. The leaves had been a queer, brownish-red veined with purple, and when she crushed a leaf between her fingers a sharp fragrance assailed her nostrils. She would take some of the shoots with her in the leather pouch where she kept dried seeds and a bit of coral that Prys had given her to protect her against the evil eye.

But Prys was dead and would give her no more things. He would never crouch by the fire, warming his mottled hands, talking about the days when he had been young and seen the Tudor King.

Tears misted her eyes and rolled slowly

down her cheeks as she sat down on the little stool. After a while the bear padded over and sat by her side, his head nuzzling her skirt, one blunt paw curved about her feet.

2

Spring sunshine gilded the roofs and lit the little courtyards into a brief and quivering beauty. This was the best season of the year when the ice of winter melted, before the heat of later months brought the sweating sickness and the plague to the city's narrow streets and huddled houses. On this day housewives had opened their doors and windows and were sweeping the stale rushes into the gutters. It was not hot or dry enough for linen to be washed, but blankets were being shaken from upper windows, and the last of the salt meat would soon be eaten.

Margred came into the city with all the eagerness of young sunshine seeking to illuminate a gloomy corner. The months that lay behind her seemed in retrospect a gay and exciting adventure. It was difficult now to remember the nights when she had lain down hungry on cold straw in an alien barn, the time a farmer's wife had threatened to set the dogs on her if she didn't leave. On the whole she had been fortunate. Her ignorance of the world prevented her from realising just how fortunate she had been to arrive safely at the capital.

She had laid a cloth over her grandfather's stiffening face and open eyes — she could not bring herself to close them — and before first light she had wound her way over the marsh path to the shack where the Englishman lived. He had glanced up with no more than a flicker of interest as she approached, with Mott padding at her side.

'Prys is dead,' she said without greeting. 'Will you bury him for me and tell the minister? You can have the two cows and the hens.'

'Where will you be, then?' he asked.

'I'm going south,' she said firmly.

'With that?' He nodded towards the bear.

'I found him,' she said, quickly and defensively. 'He was saved from the wreck, and all the people in the ship were drowned, so he's mine now.'

'You're welcome to the creature.'

'I'm going to London,' she said with weak defiance, but it was wasted on him for he merely nodded.

'I always knew that you would.'

'They burn Papists now and I'm not a Papist,' she said.

'Hang, draw, and quarter them,' he corrected absently. 'Suppose you get there and find they're killing Protestants again?'

'Then I'll turn Papist,' she said.

He gave a shout of harsh laughter that ended as abruptly as it began.

'I knew you'd make out,' he said. 'Have you any money?'

'The bear can dance.'

'You'll need some coins if you're not to be picked up for vagrancy.' He dived into his pouch and brought up a couple of sovereigns. 'Keep to the main roads and don't try making the bear dance if there are constables about. You've no licence.'

'Where would I get one?'

'Wait until you reach London. Then apply to the nearest magistrate for one, and save some coin to pay for it.'

'And you'll bury Prys?'

'I'll see him under.'

He dropped the money into her hand and threw a piece of wood on to the fire.

'Won't you wish me God speed?' she asked uncertainly.

It was a desolate feeling, to leave a place where one had spent one's whole life, with nobody to grieve.

'You don't need it,' he answered curtly. 'You're one of those who carry their fate in their eyes, and Heaven help the man who crosses you!'

She had gone then, leaving him gazing into

the fire with the haunted look on his face that told her he would soon be roaring out psalms again.

From the beginning she had tried to be sensible, to conserve her strength by walking no more than ten miles a day until her legs swung into the rhythm of the road and she was able to make fifteen miles in good weather. She made a point of stopping whenever she passed through a hamlet or village, and making the bear dance to her singing. There were always a few coppers earned that would buy her food for the day, and sometimes sufficient to provide a lodging for the night too. At other times she made use of barns and hedgerows, grateful for the warmth of the bear as frost hardened the ground.

Perhaps it was the presence of the bear that saved her from molestation. Mott had accepted her completely as his owner, or possibly regarded himself as her owner, for he growled threateningly if anybody came too close, and his teeth and claws were formidable.

But now the discomforts and occasional terrors of the journey were past, and she came slowly into the sunlit city, limping a little for her cracked and broken shoes had raised a blister on her heel. She had seen the tall spires and high walls of the city from afar off since dawn, and walked steadily towards them, her heart bumping a little with excitement.

Her way ran through small villages that merged into larger ones until she found herself in a maze of streets with high buildings all about her, and realised she was actually in the city and not viewing it from afar. For several minutes she stood motionless, filled not with wonder but with dismay. Prys had never made it clear that there were so many people in London, or that they would be so noisy. Already her ears ached from the cacophony of sounds — hucksters crying their wares, a chiming of bells from the nearest spire, a dog barking furiously about the legs of a drayhorse, two women leaning out of their upper windows and engaging in a loud and incoherent gossip, three men haggling over something or other.

Pressed against the wall, Margred thought in panic that all these people seemed to know exactly where they were going, Their faces were confident, their voices loud and quick so that it was hard to follow what they said. Nobody took the slightest notice of her. Why, she might stand here until she died and then be shovelled away into the pile of filth that smelt so rank at the corner of the street.

'Come, Mott.'

She spoke firmly, gripping the chain tightly, and began to elbow her way through the crowds as she had seen others doing. She would find an inn that looked respectable and take a room for the night. On the following day she would have to discover how to go about getting a licence so that she and Mott could earn their living.

A little of her fading confidence returned when she rounded another corner and found herself in a courtyard teeming with ostlers and pack horses. Set back from the cobbles a handsomely proportioned building announced on its gilded sign that it was *The Travellers' Rest*. Margred was unable to fathom the letters, but the place was obviously an inn, and a respectable one.

She was almost at the door when a heavily built man, with shirt sleeves rolled up over his jerkin, barred her way.

'No thieves, vagabonds or players!' he said briskly.

'I wanted a room.' She stopped and looked up at him shyly, hoping her English had come out clearly.

'We don't have rooms for females,' he began, but she interrupted, eagerly.

'I can pay for it. I have three shillings.'

'And what am I supposed to do with that?' He pointed to Mott.

'He's very clean and gentle. If you had a place in your stable, we could make do with that.'

Out of the corner of her eye, she could see a small crowd collecting. One man, with a brand on his cheek, called out, 'Have you a licence for that animal?'

'I mean to get one,' she said earnestly.

'Does the bear fight well?' somebody else called.

'He's a dancing bear.'

'A dancing bear!' The man with the branded cheek reached out and flicked a whip skilfully around Mott's hind legs. 'Let's see him dance then! Let's see him perform!'

'Don't! He's not used to ill-treatment,' Margred pleaded.

'Beg the wench's pardon!' some wag cried. 'This is obviously a very superior bear!'

They were hemming her in now, jeering, pointing. Mott was shivering and growling, his teeth bared. She turned from side to side, seeking a friendly face, and, glimpsing a little way beyond the menacing circle a man on horseback, called imploringly.

'Oh, please, sir! Make them let me alone!'

'What ails the wench?' The man was dismounting and striding towards her, the crowd parting to let him through. The man in shirt sleeves tugged at his forelock and spoke respectfully.

'If it please you, Sir Harry, this wench asked for a room.'

'I can pay for it,' Margred said, 'if they won't take Mott — '

'Is that the bear?'

'Yes, sir. He's a dancing bear, but he's not used to the whip and we cannot perform until I get a licence and we have walked all winter to be here.'

She stopped, feeling an unaccountable desire to burst into tears. Blue eyes looked down at her from a healthy, high coloured face.

'Walked from where?' the man asked.

'From Wales, sir. From the north. My grandfather died and I had a great desire to see London.'

'Wales, eh? Your voice sparkles like a rainbow. Do you have a name?'

'Margred, sir.'

'I'm sorry you should be dragged into this, Sir Harry,' the shirt-sleeved man said apologetically. 'You know I try to keep a decent place here, to attract the better class of customer — '

'Give the wench and the beast a room and a meal,' the man said. 'I'll pay for it.

And take care of my horse! Yon whip would be better employed on some of those idling grooms.'

'Yes, Sir Harry. Will you be having supper here yourself?'

'Aye!' The man turned and shot over his shoulder; 'With the wench!'

Margred stood still, her bewildered gaze following the tall, broad-shouldered figure in the mulberry doublet and sleek grey hose. The man, in her inexperienced eyes, was splendidly attired, his bearing godlike, his voice displaying none of the quick, slurred syllables that made the other people so difficult to understand.

'Get a move on! Sir Harry wants your company at supper,' the man in shirt sleeves said.

'Is he — is he an important man?' she ventured, falling into step beside him as they crossed the cobbles.

'Sir Harry Falcon pays his bills and a mite more beside, if we treat him right,' was the reply. 'No, not through the front door! You'd best come through the side passage.'

'Is he a lord?' she enquired.

'A knight. We have many gentlemen of quality as patrons. In there!'

He had pushed open a door and she was thrust into a hot and steamy kitchen where a great flurry of activity seemed to be taking place. Maid servants were bustling up and down, passing tureens to a perspiring young fellow who darted between table and passageway. In one corner a half-naked boy was turning a spit on which chunks of meat were deliciously browning. Margred's mouth watered at the smell.

'You can wash yourself, if you've a mind,' the man said gruffly. 'There's hot water in the pantry. Sir Harry likes his women clean. You'd best chain the bear up in there, too. I'll see it's fed and not teased.'

It had begun to seem like a dream. Watched by the man, who was studying her with unflattering interest as if he were trying to discover why she had taken his patron's fancy, Margred splashed hot water on to her grimy face and hands and rubbed them dry on the towel he indicated. She had no comb, but used her fingers to some effect in the tangles of her hair.

'Leave the bear here. Sir Harry will be waiting.'

The man gave her a little push out of the stone-floored alcove in the direction of the passage. Mott, secured to the leg of a heavy stool, growled and she paused, briefly, to soothe him.

They went, not in the direction of the

public rooms from whence she could hear laughter and the clattering of tankards, but up a narrow flight of stairs and along another passage to a door at the end.

It was partly open and through the gap she could see the man in the mulberry doublet sitting at a round table, near a fire which was not blazing on a central hearth but tucked into the wall in a manner that fascinated her so much that she was inside the room before she knew it.

'Two capons and a duckling with sweet parsley, Jake,' the man was saying, 'and some quince tarts and a dish of comfits for the lady. You know my taste in wines.'

'Indeed I do, sir. You have an excellent palate.'

'I know when my sack is watered,' the man said. 'Bring the meal yourself and then see that we're not disturbed.'

'I'll see to it at once, sir.'

The door was closed and blue eyes twinkled at her across the width of the table.

'Sit down, girl — I forget your name.'

'Margred, sir.' She sat down, easing her blistered feet out of the cracked and stained leather.

'And you're from Wales; from the north.'

'Yes, sir.'

'Call me Harry. Harry Falcon,' he invited.

'And you're a knight.' She smiled at him timidly, showing her pretty teeth. 'I never met a knight before.'

'My father was dubbed knight by King Henry,' he said with a tinge of pride.

'Then that's *very* good,' Margred said with enthusiasm.

'You speak English very well,' he approved.

'Prys — my grandfather — could speak some, and I learned more from an Englishman who lived in the town.'

'And you've come to London to seek your fortune?'

'To buy a silk dress,' she said dreamily, 'and shoes with coloured stones on them. Mott can dance and I can sing a little and brew herbs into tisanes. We'll earn coin.'

'In that way, or another.'

The blue eyes hardened imperceptibly as they rested on her breasts upthrust under the faded red woollen dress. Then his smile flashed out again as Jake came in, bearing a laden tray.

'The best sack and a jug of malmsey to wash it down, sir,'

The landlord set down pewter dishes, flicking away imaginary crumbs with the end of the towel over his arm.

'Is Mott all right?' she enquired anxiously.

36

'One of the girls is feeding it now. Tame, isn't it?'

'Very tame.' She eyed the crisp meat and buttered parsnips.

'That'll do. We'll serve ourselves.'

Harry Falcon waved his hand on which a handsome ring gleamed.

'Thanking you, Sir Harry.'

Jake withdrew, with one last, puzzled glance at the girl. All skin and bone, he decided, with tangles of heavy hair and those odd yellow eyes — not the sort of armful he'd expect a man like Sir Harry to relish.

'Eat up. You're probably hungry.'

Harry Falcon set the example, seizing a capon and tearing it apart. As he ate he watched the girl covertly. She was not the sort of wench for whose services he usually paid on his rare trips to the city. His taste ran to plump and obedient blondes, but this one had something about her that fascinated him. Her skimpy gown outlined thin hips and legs that were long in proportion to her height. She was making pathetic attempts to eat daintily, taking little snatching bites and closing her mouth carefully as she chewed. He wondered if she might possibly still be a virgin, and the thought excited him.

'Do you live in London, sir — Harry?' she asked politely.

'On the Kentish border. I have a small estate there.'

'A farm?'

'A sort of farm. Not very big — about five hundred acres. The manor was built by my father.'

'It sounds big,' she said. 'Do you have cows and sheep? Is that why you come to London — to sell them in the market?'

'I leave that to the steward,' he said, a trifle piqued. Did she take him for a farmer? 'I come to London to attend the Court.'

'To visit the Queen?' Spoon midway to her mouth, she stared at him.

'To wait upon her,' he said, and thought wryly of the long corridor where the lesser nobility whiled away tedious hours in gossip, ears pricked for the clash of steel and the high screech of a trumpet that would warn them the Queen was approaching. Bend the knee! Bow the head! Be alert for the tap on the shoulder and the command.

'Rise! Her Grace will speak with you, grant your petition, refuse your petition, accept your gift, listen to your suit!'

Men had grown old, waiting in that corridor. Others, like Raleigh, had risen to the dizziest heights.

'Do you — have you ever spoken to the Queen?' she breathed.

He shook his head, adding hastily, 'But she speaks to very few. She did smile at me once.'

He remembered that tight, closed little smile and the swift, flashing glance that took in every detail of his appearance. Then she had passed on, enormous ruff like a nimbus behind her curled wig, farthingale shimmering with silver butterflies.

'I would like to see the Queen,' Margred said wistfully.

'She comes sometimes to the tournaments at Whitehall,' he said.

'I never went to a tournament,' she confided.

It was on the tip of his tongue to tell her that anybody with a shilling could get a seat in the public gallery, but he shrugged instead, casting her a sidelong look.

'Perhaps I can arrange to take you to one.'

'I'd have to get my gown first. This one is too old.'

'I'll have to buy you a gown then. Silk is costly, but dimity or sarcenet would suit the spring.'

Margred's smooth little face was quite blank as she stared at him. Behind her untroubled brow her mind was working furiously. Innocent but not ignorant, she was wakening slowly to the fact that young gentlemen did not ask strange girls to have supper with them nor offer to buy them gowns unless they expected something in return.

Instinctively she was responding to his kindness, to the terms of equality on which he was treating her. No man had ever behaved with such flattering attention before, nor looked at her so warmly.

'If you please,' she said at last, clasping her hands tightly before her. 'If you please I have never — I am still a maid.'

There was a touching simplicity in her manner at that moment, a gentle dignity that called out some deep, protective strain in him. For an instant he was tempted to give her a sum of money and let her leave. Then his imagination stripped the dirty gown from her shoulders and his mouth grew dry.

'Then it is best,' he said softly, 'if you lie first with one who loves you.'

She had not thought of love; had not connected the stirring within her to an awakening desire for passion. Prys had seen her grandmother spinning and loved her. She had been told how her father had seen her mother in the cattle market and loved her.

Evidently it happened as quickly as that when it happened at all. And now it had happened to her. A gentleman had looked at her and loved her, and wished to lie with her. The same sequence of events occurred in the countryside, and at some stage in the proceedings the minister was called in.

Thoughts of right or wrong never entered her head. It was sufficient at this moment that she had found a friend. The Englishman had told her that her fate was in her eyes, and now those eyes rested on a tall man with a broad face and close-curling nut brown hair.

'What about the room you told them to make ready for me?' she asked shyly. 'Won't it go to waste?'

'Jake never expected it to be used,' he answered easily, and rose from his place, snapping his fingers in casual invitation.

To his surprise, instead of giggling and running into his arms, she continued to sit quite still, her hands clasped against her thin body, her eyes clear as water. He could see twin images of himself reflected in the pupils.

The thought that she might not be as easy to tame as he expected afflicted him with a pleasurable shudder.

'I am not,' he said carefully, 'a man of

many words. You must forgive me if I sing our love in actions.'

'No man ever courted me in any way,' Margred said simply.

A dart of unease pricked him. In the firelight her skin had a translucent quality as if it had been fingered by moonlight, and there was in her stillness something of the waiting quality of some forest creature. Then she rose in her turn and stood close to him, laying her small hands between his own, in a gesture that both demanded and conferred a loyalty.

'The bed is in the next room,' he told her, and cursed himself for having nothing more romantic to say, but with her strange blend of wise child and practical woman she appeared to take the remark as a natural progression in their relationship and went ahead of him to the inner chamber.

'I saw a bed once,' she told him, fingering the carved posts that supported the embroidered canopy. 'Shani had one left to her when her father-in-law died, and everybody went to have a look at it. Prys and I had pallets, of course.'

'Your grandfather?'

'He died before the winter came.' She shivered, not wishing to talk of death in this elegant, oak-beamed room, and said, without looking at him, 'Is it true that you love me? In so short a time?'

'Between one step and the next,' he told her, and she drew a deep breath as if some danger had been averted and burrowed suddenly against him, her face pressed against his doublet, her black hair falling over his arm.

He could have taken her there and then, but he forced himself to move slowly, to disrobe neatly, to lift her politely to the high coverlet. He was not prepared for her response, for after the first moan of triumphant pain she yielded herself to him with an intensity that had in it something of desperation.

It was a long time since he had taken a virgin and he had forgotten, or never realised, that they could be so sweet. She was light and boneless beneath him, almost like a child, and then her lips fastened upon his mouth and he heard her groan deep in her throat as if some primaeval anguish sought to escape her.

He heard himself, as if from a distance, whispering love words.

'Pretty one; lovely girl; delight of my heart.'

He had used the words before, many times, but now he felt the power behind their meaning, and it was as if he had never spoken such phrases before.

She laughed suddenly, all child again, and flung her arms about his neck.

'I was so miserable before, so much afraid of the strange people, so sick for home.'

'Is it beautiful there?' He spoke thickly, dragging his senses back to reality.

'It is home,' she said, a little puzzled, for it was not in her power to describe the spirit of a place. 'There is the sea, and the mist rising from the marsh, and the walled town, and the mountain that is all snow with its sister hill. It is home.'

'But you came to the city.'

'To buy a gown.' She sat up and looked down at him in the dim light. 'Do you think a green dress would look well on me? Prys would never let me wear green. He said it was the colour of the little people and not fitting for humans, but 'tis a brave colour.'

'I like you best with nothing on at all,' he said lazily.

'But wouldn't that look very odd at a tournament?' she demanded.

He had forgotten the tournament! In dismay he stared up at her as she went innocently on.

'I never thought, not in a thousand years, that I would ever see a real tournament! At fair time, the lads have mock battles with wooden swords, but the real thing must be much more exciting. Perhaps the Queen will be there, and smile at you again. You are going to take me, aren't you?'

Her voice rose into anxiety as if some doubt had crept into her mind.

'I'll take you anywhere you want to go,' Harry Falcon said.

He had spoken those words before too, but now, tracing the outlines of her body with his fingers, it was the first time he had ever meant them.

3

Harry Falcon woke to a shaft of sunlight falling across his face through the unshuttered window. For a moment he lay supine, his eyelids flickering under the light, his body relaxing consciously into the softness of the feather mattress. It had been, he was beginning to remember, a splendid, enchanted night. There had been a wench — his eyes flew open and he raised himself on his elbow and looked down at her sleeping. Her face was half hidden by the covers and her own hair, but he could glimpse the tiptilted nose and the faint sprinkle of freckles across the bridge. She was curled into a ball, her thumb in her mouth, seeming so young that a pang of tenderness went through him.

So often he had woken on these occasions with the sour taste of stale wine in his mouth, and seen the beauty of the previous night coarsened into a cheap harlot. This girl, this Margred, looked as childish as if she still possessed her maidenhood.

'Margred.'

He had spoken the name aloud, and she

was awake, leaping the gap between dream and consciousness with no more than the briefest of yawns.

'Good morning, Harry.'

She used his name without constraint, leaning up to kiss him, shaking back her hair in a little, feminine gesture that roused in him an echo of desire.

'You slept well,' he remarked.

'As sound as a bell!' She jumped lightly from the bed and stood naked in the patch of sunlight. 'I must go down and make sure that Mott has been fed. He will be fretting about me.'

'Put your dress on first.'

'It looks as if it didn't belong to me any more,' she said wriggling into it. 'It looks worn out, like a yesterday person.'

'Send Jake up to me when you go down,' he said, 'and I'll see about a new dress for you. Breakfast too.'

This was a wonderful world! A world in which a handsome man said that he loved you and with a casual word could produce dresses and breakfasts from nowhere.

'And then we'll go to the tournament? How will we get there?'

'By river, and disembark at the watergates. You'd like a trip down river, I daresay.'

'I was never in a boat in my life before!'

She came back to the bed and kissed him again.

'I'll tell Jake to send up hot water and a comb too,' he promised.

She was a sweet wench; it was pleasant to give her things, to watch her pointed face light into loveliness as she thanked him.

Harry Falcon lay back on the pillows and decided that she should have the green dimity. He was aware that it was the custom for many of the fashionable ladies to sell off their dresses when they had worn them a little while. Jake would be able to get something suitable.

Glimpsing his face in the mirror of polished steel, Harry Falcon decided that generosity became him. He was, in fact, by nature a generous man, but he had inherited from his father the sound business sense that prevented him from becoming a spendthrift.

Harry Falcon, the elder, had been a small farmer, who having educated himself in languages, and law, had sought service with Thomas Cromwell. His report on the conduct of the monks in a wealthy local priory had led to the speedy dissolution of that particular foundation, and though King Henry the Eighth had granted the actual building to one of his own favourites, Harry Falcon had gained a knighthood and five hundred acres of sweet orchard and meadow. He had built a manor house there and reared his only surviving son to have a due respect for land and titles.

But it was pleasant to be generous, and a gown and a tournament were little enough. Harry, overlooking the fact that he had never, in his thirty years, ever given such expensive presents to a wench before, raised his voice and yelled in high good humour for the landlord.

In the pantry Margred was feeding Mott who seemed inclined to reproach her for her desertion. Somebody had spread out a blanket for him but his eyes were sullen. With her arm about his neck she coaxed him.

'Everything is so wonderful now. The gentleman who stopped them from whipping you in the courtyard has fallen in love with me. We're going to the tournament today but you must stay here. And, oh Mott, there won't be any need for us to get a licence now.'

'The gentleman says you're to go up,' a maid servant informed her from the doorway.

'Sir Harry? I'll go now,' Giving Mott a final pat she said, 'Will you see the bear is fed again before night? And will you talk to him a little? He doesn't speak English, but he likes the sound of a human voice.'

'I've better things to do than talk to bears,' the girl began scornfully, and paused, seeing the smile fade on the other's face, the yellow eyes slant. 'I'll probably find a minute,' she said, and wondered briefly why, just for a moment, she had felt cold.

'It would be a kindness,' Margred said gently, and then the little thrill of power which had run through her as she sensed the girl's uneasiness was swept into a rush of excitement as she recalled Harry's promise of a dress.

Of Harry there was no sign, but a jug of hot water stood near the basin on the table, and a green dress was spread out across the bed. Margred touched it with reverent fingers, her eyes darting to the kirtle and the farthingale beyond. She had never seen such a pretty garment before, never dreamed that she would ever be given anything so fine. There was even a little cap with a short veil hanging down behind.

When she had washed and used the wide-toothed comb on her hair, she put on the garments one by one, relishing their softness against her damp skin. The shift was of white lawn, and the farthingale — she had never examined one closely before — evidently laced over it, holding out the dark green of the low-necked kirtle at each side of her waist. The overdress was of a paler green, sprigged with tiny white flowers. Its bodice ended in a V-shape and was cut away to show the darker shade of the kirtle. The sleeves were tied to the shoulders of the overdress with green ribbons, and were finished at the wrist with a narrow band of lace.

Both Harry and Jake had gauged her size well. The dress was only a little loose and the low-heeled shoes that went with it fitted her narrow feet exactly. Final glory was a green cape with slits in the sides through which she could put her arms.

Harry Falcon, having argued the price of the dress successfully, came back into the room to find a leaf-green wench waiting for him. In the modest farthingale, with her hair drawn back smoothly under the little cap, she was a thing of brightness and grace. He stood staring at her, deriving much of his pleasure from the knowledge that she was, in a way, his own creation.

He had expected a rapturous embrace and a flood of gratitude, but she stood motionless, her eyes shining, and spoke with the odd dignity that sat so touchingly on her slim shoulders.

'Dear heart, you are so very good to me.'

'Have you eaten?'

He had devoured an excellent breakfast while she was fooling about with the bear.

'I'm not hungry.'

'Then we'd best start. The boats will be filling up.'

He took her arm and ushered her down the stairs.

This time she went through the front door with nobody to impede her, and then she was in the narrow streets again, clinging tightly to Harry, her eyes bright as she looked about her. The crowds were as thick as on the previous day but this morning they had lost their menace, and were ordinary good-humoured folk, intent on their own concerns.

'We must go to the landing wharf. You will see the Tower from there,' he told her.

She had heard of the Tower, but her grandfather's description had not done justice to the frowning bulk of the dark walls. It surprised her that people should be hurrying down to the river with no more than a passing glance at the great fortress.

The river itself was so crowded with boats that she had a moment's qualm lest they be overturned into the grey-green water, but Harry swung her expertly into the rocking vessel and the leather-coated waterman winked in friendly fashion as she sank, gasping, on the bench.

At her side, Harry pointed out the sights with the faintly self-conscious pride of a man who knew the city well and enjoyed showing it off to a visitor.

'This is London Bridge. There were three Jesuits topped last months. There are the heads.'

She grimaced, turning her eyes from the almost fleshless, decaying heads, and then clutched at Harry's arm as the boat lurched forward.

'The rapids are tricky here,' he reassured. 'One has to catch them on the tide.'

The bridge, with its grisly trophies, was receding and she looked with more pleasure towards the crowded banks, the high buildings beyond seeming to stand on tiptoe as if they craned to catch their reflections in the water.

'We are coming to Whitehall now,' Harry said. 'We go up the steps at the watergate. The tiltyard has enclosed galleries on three sides, so even if it comes on to rain we won't be wetted.'

'Which is the palace?' she asked in bewilderment as they stepped out on to damp stone.

'Why, all of it is, I suppose.' He gestured vaguely towards the huddle of buildings beyond a series of alleys and courtyards towards which groups of people were strolling. 'The royal apartments are separate from the public rooms; the galleries are open to the public. The gardens too, on certain days.'

'It's a big place for one queen,' she said, impressed.

'She has others,' Harry told her. 'Westminster is further down river; and St. James's is beyond Whitehall. Then there's Richmond and Nonesuch, and Hampton Court and Windsor. She moves from one to the other as the fancy takes her, and sometimes she goes on progress to the houses of her courtiers.'

'Has she ever been to your house?'

'Not yet, and God grant the idea never enters her head!' Harry cast her a daringly mischievous glance, lowering his voice. 'It's said that a visit from Her Grace can cripple a man. Royalty, you see, never pays for its board and lodging. Good Lord above!'

He had stopped short, his face lively with astonishment.

'Is it the Queen? Has Her Grace come?' Margred asked.

Harry Falcon was striding up the broad avenue, hand outstretched, his expression an incongruous mixture of surprise, pleasure and embarrassment.

'Roger! Roger Aston!' he exclaimed. 'Where the devil did you spring from? I thought you were in the Low Countries!'

'Dropped anchor a week ago. Good to see you, Harry! How's everything and everybody?'

'Fine, fine. I'm only here for a few days.'

'On business?'

The newcomer, who was short and broad, with a pleasantly plain face, cocked an eyebrow towards Margred.

'A friend of mine, from Wales,' Harry said. 'Mistress Margred.'

'Delighted to meet you.' Roger Aston bowed politely. 'If I had known that London was grown so attractive I'd have left the Low Countries sooner.'

'Are you a friend of Harry's?' she enquired, as they fell into step beside him.

'My family and the Falcons are neighbours,' Roger told her. 'My brother, William, has the estate. I, as a younger son, must earn my bread, alas.'

'It suits you very well,' Harry said over his shoulder as they began to mount a covered flight of steps. 'You would go mad if you were forced to stay at home as William does.'

'I'm due for a visit in a month or two anyway,' Roger said airily. 'I'll ride over and take a cup of wine with you before harvest.'

'I leave tomorrow,' Harry said, protecting Margred hastily as a crowd of younglings bustled past, swords clanking.

'I'll see you then!'

Roger Aston raised his arm as they were borne upwards among the spectators struggling to the tiers of seats.

'Is that a close friend of yours?' Margred asked, as they wedged themselves on to the bench. At her other side an amply proportioned matron was complaining bitterly.

'Three farthings for an apple pasty! It's a crying shame, and a scandal the way prices are rising!'

'We grew up together,' he said. 'The elder, William, inherited Aston Manor when Sir Thomas died. Roger has little interest in the place, though he keeps on good terms with his brother and visits his mother there once or twice a year. He was apprenticed into the cloth trade, but he's a pirate at heart. At one time there was talk of his marrying Alys, but the Prescotts and Astons are cousins, and it was thought best not to proceed.'

'Who is Alys?'

'My wife,' he said, and gave her a quick, half-shamed look of apology. 'You did not think I had reached the age of thirty without a wife, did you?'

She was staring down into the sunlit green of the tilting field with such concentration that her eyes ached, and it was difficult to speak over the lump in her throat.

'Is — your friend married?'

Harry shook his head. 'Roger isn't the marrying kind. I told you he's a pirate at heart. William did his duty though. His wife died in childbed six months ago. But Eleanor is a pretty babe.

'Does — have you children?'

They were sounding trumpets and heralds were marching out, crying 'Largesse! Largesse!' but they were blurred and shimmery.

'Alys is barren,' he said in a hurt, harsh voice, 'and as far as I know, I have sired no children either.'

The stout matron called, on a high note of excitement, 'Her Grace is come! The Queen is here!'

The railed gallery opposite them had been empty, but now it began slowly to fill with ladies and gentlemen in such rich and dazzling colours that the heralds were eclipsed. The spectators were rising and applauding and then a tall figure moved slowly down to the carved chair set apart from the others.

She was not like a woman at all, Margred thought. She was like some strange, unearthly being who visits from another world. Her gown was of stiff white stuff, covered from neck to hem with golden moons and suns, each secured to the material beneath with seed pearls. Larger pearls edged with lace the fan and ruff, diamonds outlined the pointed bodice and sparkled along the seams of the hanging, sapphire blue sleeves. Above the high ruff, a face as smooth as an enamel mask looked out under close-curled red hair.

She stood as straight as a larch, then raised her hands to acknowledge the applause, and the sunshine drew fire from the gems with which her fingers were covered.

It was impossible to realise that she was close on sixty. Such a being was ageless, immortal. Her hands made a brief, hushing gesture and then she sat down, a gentleman in dove velvet coming to kneel at a footstool close to the great chair.

'Sir Christopher Hatton,' Harry indicated under cover of the general bustle as the audience reseated itself. 'He has stayed a bachelor all his life for Her Grace's sake.'

Two contestants were entering the lists

now — the one in white armour with fleur-de-lys on his standard, the other in silver.

'Visiting knights, who have the honour to joust first,' Harry said. 'The seeded contestants will come later. That is when the biggest wagers are laid.'

Margred heard him only vaguely. The excitement of the Queen's arrival was draining away, and the misery of Harry's information had overwhelmed her. She had never thought of his already having a wife, had never really thought of marriage in connection with him at all. She had assumed that sooner or later he would put a ring upon her finger. Yet he had said that he loved her.

Under cover of thundering hoofs and the clash of lance against lance, she asked urgently, 'Do you have an affection for her?'

'For whom?'

'For Alys; for your wife.'

'She does well enough, I suppose,' he said absently. 'Oh, a hit! A hit against our French friend!'

The man in white armour was on his back, struggling to rise. A group of squires ran up to help him to his feet.

So Harry didn't love his wife. And she

59

was barren. Poor soul, Margred thought, and then triumph diluted her sympathy. I could bear him children, she decided. Oh, they would be bastards, but among gentlefolk it's not so important to be wed. And I wouldn't be taking anything away from her. If she loved him she would have come up to London too, and be sitting here, in my place. And I do love him. It happened with me suddenly and strongly, as it did with my parents and grandparents.

Suddenly her misery was lifting and in its place was creeping a passion of desire that trembled along her nerves. I will never marry, she vowed silently, unless his wife dies, of course. And I don't wish the poor lady any harm. I shall be close to him all my life, closer than his own flesh, and nobody will ever know what lies between us. And I will give him children, fine boys and a pretty daughter, and bind him so tightly he will never want to say farewell.

A mock joust was taking place now, between four young pages mounted on ponies. The tiltyard was all brilliance and confusion, and her head ached with the noise. A stir of excitement rippled through the close-packed spectators as the boys rode off, and a knight in black armour on a coal-black horse rode alone into the lists.

' 'Tis Essex!' Harry told her. 'The Earl of Essex will joust against Sir Christopher Blount. They are both rivals for the Queen's affections, but everyone knows she can deny Essex nothing, even though he wed without permission.'

The black knight was saluting the royal gallery. The Queen had leaned forwards, her stiffly clothed body tense with yearning, her hands curving slightly. Another knight, vivid in gold, rode up to join Essex, and the Queen, a smile quivering on her mouth, glanced between them.

'Raleigh is not here, else we should see good sport!' somebody exclaimed.

'I thought the other gentleman was her favourite,' Margred said.

'Hatton is sick. He has attacks of the stone,' Harry explained. 'In his youth they say he was the best dancer at court.'

'And now must kneel on a stool while others enter the lists.'

Margred felt sorry for him, even while something in her appreciated the arrogance of the coal-black knight.

How wonderful, she thought, to be a royal queen and have handsome men vying for one's favours! Then, looking at Harry as he leaned eagerly forward, she knew that she would not wish to change him.

He was, she decided, much younger in his ways than she was. Although something in her responded to the colour and pageantry, the actual jousting had begun to bore her a little. It seemed so foolish for grown men to spend a beautiful morning knocking one another off their horses. Yet Harry, in common with all the people around him, was on his feet, shouting odds, as if nothing in the world mattered beyond this present test of skill.

'Blount falls! Blount is down!'

The golden knight was rising dizzily as the black knight, lifting his vizor, rode to the royal gallery. In profile his features were as delicate as a girl, strands of auburn hair curling from beneath his close helmet.

The Queen rose, drawing a ring from her finger, and tossed the jewel to him. Then she turned and went slowly to the back of the gallery, pausing once to raise a hand in farewell before she disappeared through the double doors.

'Her Grace goes to dinner,' Harry said, sitting down again. 'They will bring hot pies and comfits and spiced ale round in a few minutes. You must be hungry!'

'I have been thinking,' Margred said, 'that your lady-wife must not find out about me.'

'Alys find out? Lord, no!'

'We must devise a tale that will content her,' Margred said thoughtfully, 'else she will not look kindly on me when I go into Kent.'

'Go into — ?' His attention now caught, he stared at her in dismay.

'If there is a hut or a cottage on your land I could live there quietly and never need to meet her,' Margred said. 'I can live on very little, you know, and then you could visit me when the fancy took you.'

'But, my dear love, you could never hope to live undiscovered!' he said.

'Then tell her that you met me in London and saved Mott from those who were beating him, and that you were sorry for us both and granted us a place to live.'

The notion was so simple, so daring, that it took his breath away. And it would be only a little less than the truth.

'You would not leave me alone here, in the city?' she questioned.

It passed through his mind that she had made the long journey alone without mishap, but then her wide and frightened gaze caught his eye. Certainly London was no place for so young and tender a creature. She would, if she were fortunate, find another protector, who would pass her on to a friend when he had grown tired of his sport. If she were unfortunate, she would drift into the stews and end in ten years raddled with disease.

'I could never gaze upon another man with love-liking,' she said intensely.

The thought that she had even considered such a possibility brought jealousy boiling to the surface. The vehemence of his own feelings surprised him. He could not remember ever having felt this way about any woman before. The ten years of his marriage to Alys had been peaceful, unmarked by great love or great hate on either side.

Perhaps matters might have been different had there been children. As it was, Alys had her household duties, her charities, her needlework and feminine gossip. He had devoted himself to the care and management of the estate, and his London adulteries had been fleeting affiars, to be briefly regretted in the morning.

But to take home this black-haired girl, to set her up on his own estate — temptation whispered sweet as honey.

'Near the river there is a little house. My mother lived there after my father died. She thought it wiser for mothers to live separate from their son's wives. We called it the Dower Cottage, but it is very small and it has been empty these two years.'

'If there is room for a bed,' she said with a swift, upward look that promised much, 'it will content me.'

Commonsense nudged a last warning, reminding him that there would be gossip, that he was now committed to a double life. But Alys was the least suspicious of women, and the Dower Cottage was a long way from the main house.

'We will have to be circumspect,' he said. 'I would not mar my credit in the district.'

Margred nodded gravely, though for her part she would have been happy to shout out her joy to all the neighbours. But a knight must not cause scandal, she supposed.

'Shall we eat now?' she asked, with the practical sense that contrasted so piquantly with her romantic fervour. 'And can we go down to the water to look at the swans?' He put his arm about her shoulders, touched suddenly by her childish trust, and was startled by the blaze of desire in her yellow eyes.

Amid the clatter of spectators coming to and from their seats, the cries of the apple sellers, the blaring of trumpets as the next contest was announced, she said, for his ear alone, 'I will never leave you now, nor think of any place as home unless you are there.'

4

Lady Alys Falcon had begun the day in a mood of serene good humour. She had woken to sunshine and the whistling of a blackbird from the tree beyond the latticed window. For a moment she was half-inclined to whistle back but the impulse died with the reflection that her maids would certainly think she had run mad if she did anything so ungenteel. There had once been a time when she had answered the birds and sat by the river fishing with an old rod, but those days were long past and never to be thought of; now she was thirty years old with the management of the household on her shoulders. Yet the feeling of joy persisted, and she greeted Agnes with the warm smile that redeemed her plain features.

'I will come down in an hour to oversee everything,' she told her, glancing with pleasure at the laden tray on which bread and cheese and lean beef and a tankard of ale were carefully arranged.

When Harry was in the city she liked to eat breakfast up in her room and then make a leisurely toilet. It gave the servants time to get the rest of the manor into a semblance of order before she made her daily inspection.

Alys took her duties as mistress of *Kingsmead* very seriously, partly because she had been trained from childhood to take her place as a lady of a prosperous establishment, partly because she loved *Kingsmead* with a fervour she might have bestowed upon her children had she been blessed with any. As it was a stillborn daughter and two miscarriages were the nearest she had come to producing a family. Her failure was a constant shadow over her placid contentment, though she never spoke of it. It only prevented her from complaining aloud when Harry came back from a London visit with perfume on his breath and a guilty satisfaction in his blue eyes.

Alys had never been a pretty woman, but maturity had given her a certain staid charm. With her pale hair rolled artfully over small pads and her rosy skin enhanced by a light dusting of rice powder, she might even have been called comely, save for a figure thickened by too much nibbling from the comfit dish. This morning, however, her appearance pleased her.

Her open fronted gown of black velvet revealed a shift of pleated yellow silk and a kirtle of the same shade edged with green.

The puffed yellow sleeves were decorated with green flowers and ended at the wrist in narrow frills of saffron lawn which matched the small ruff beneath her chin. Her hood of black velvet was trimmed with borders of yellow silk. At her waist hung the bunch of keys with which she could lock or unlock any cupboard in the house.

The putting on of each garment banished a little further the memory of the girl she had been, so that by the time she had sprinkled lavender water over her hands she was the image of a perfect gentlewoman whose only reaction to the blackbird was a vague hope that it wouldn't tear at the cherry blossom.

At the top of the wide stairs she paused to look down into the hall. This central apartment rose up through two storeys to a vaulted roof from which two huge iron chandeliers were suspended, each spiked circle holding fifty wax candles. Harry's father had built in stone, intending his house to last through generations of his descendants. He had built bricklined chimneys and bought Flemish tapestries to hang against the walls, and employed the best local craftsmen to carve the dark oak furniture. After his death Harry had installed clear glass in the latticed windows and put up screens to mitigate the draughts from the huge door, but nothing further had needed to be done.

On this morning sunshine flooded through the glittering panes turning the rushes golden and casting a patina upon the polished oak of the long trestle table with its attendant benches and the two carved chairs at its head. It glittered too upon the dresser with its rows of pewter and silverplate towering up towards the hammerbeams. Apple logs were laid in the two hearths at each side of the foot of the staircase, and the smell of cooking wafted through the open door on the left which led into the big, stone-flagged kitchen.

Kingsmead had been built on traditional lines, old Sir Harry having had little use for Grecian columns and such foolishnesses. The manor itself was a solid rectangle of stone, with a front and a back room at each side of the main hall and four corresponding apartments above.

Alys moved into the kitchen where the three maid servants were already toiling over the charcoal range and the table on which a heap of chickens lay limply, waiting to be plucked. These maids came in daily from their homes in the village. The cook slept in, as did the steward and the two boys who served the meals and worked in the garden, the latter three above the stables, the

69

cook in one corner of the kitchen between the fireplace and the stone basin where the dishes were washed.

'Is everything in order, John?' She addressed herself to the steward who gave the formal reply.

'All in order, my lady.'

'Phyllis has the toothache,' Cook said.

'Is it very painful?' Alys turned to the smallest of the maids whose heavy eyes and lopsided jaw bore witness to the cook's veracity.

'It hurts terrible, my lady,' Phyllis said dolefully.

'You had best pack it with cloves and bind her face with flannel,' Alys said sympathetically. 'If it is no better by tomorrow, you had best take her over to the toothpuller at Maidstone.'

'There's nothing better for an aching tooth than a jug of cold water poured over the head,' Cook declared.

'Let us try the cloves first,' Alys said, patting the afflicted Phyllis reassuringly on the arm, and moving into the adjoining apartment.

This room was probably her favourite place in the house with its shelves of preserves and candied fruits and flower wines, its big copper vat where the fruit was boiled and stirred, the deep chest where the soundest apples were kept for the household's own use. Each jar was labelled in Alys's neat script — bilberry wine, cowslip wine, dandelion wine, blackberry preserve, cherry and quince preserve, elderflowers steeped in malmsey. Her practised eye ran over the shelves, noting where gaps meant replacements needed to be made.

'We will have some of the blackberry preserve tonight,' she said to the attentive steward. 'Sir Harry is very fond of it.'

'If he gets back safely from the city,' John said gloomily. 'It seems all wrong to me that a gentleman should travel alone without a regular servant. It's not safe, my lady, as I tell him.'

'Frequently. I know. But the roads are quiet enough these days, and he often hires escort if there is any danger of his being delayed after dark. And it is not for us to question Sir Harry's habits.'

Her voice was pleasantly firm as she left the stillroom and passed through the kitchen again. At the other side of the hall a door led into the parlour whose windows faced the stables at the back, and thence into the solar whose windows faced the courtyard. These two rooms were family rooms, affording some measure of privacy in long winter evenings or sunny afternoons.

Harry's fowling pieces were here, and a few leather-bound books, a lute on which she practised dutifully to little effect, her tapestry frame with its box of assorted silks. On the inner wall hung the two portraits of Harry's parents, commissioned as a finishing touch when the house had been built. They did not, Alys decided, look very much like either of them. Sir Harry's dead white face and lashless eyes stared down at her in a manner that suggested he was avoiding the gaze of the doll-faced woman in the gable hood.

'When we have our first child,' Harry had said, 'I will have our portraits painted too.'

That had been ten years before when her waist was still narrow and her heart had been breaking because they would not let her marry her cousin, Roger, but had betrothed her to Harry Falcon instead.

'You and Roger are within the fourth degree of kinship. It would not be wise for you to wed,' her mother had said.

'Weakens the stock. I've seen it happen again and again with brood mares and longhorns,' her father had agreed.

She had longed to cry out to them, 'Am I not more than a horse or a cow? And do you think me a fool that you lie to me? Roger is only a younger son and must make his way in the world, but Harry Falcon will be master of *Kingsmead*, and that is why you want me to marry him. So have done with this talk of cousins!'

She had said nothing, of course, To have done so would only have brought a rain of blows about her head. But she had slipped out into the garden when the moon was risen and sobbed out her despair in Roger's arms.

'We will run away together,' he had comforted. 'We can find somewhere to be together, some minister to marry us. Harry is my friend and would understand. He would never force an unwilling maid into his bed.'

They were talking nonsense, of course. Roger was already apprenticed to a cloth merchant and dare not break his indentures, and Harry had as little choice in the matter as they. Her parents had saved and scrimped all their lives to provide her with a handsome dowry, and Harry would have the manor and five hundred acres of land.

They had been married in autumn, at the dying end of the year, and the one bright spot in that miserable day was that Roger had not been there to see her misery. Harry, who was good-natured but not analytical, assumed her tears on the wedding night were due to maidenly reluctance, and had treated her kindly. That her love for Roger had ever been more than a passing fancy never entered his head.

And, of course, he was perfectly right, Alys consoled herself. Her feelings for her cousin were no more now than the mildest affection, and on the rare occasions he visited them he was treated as a valued friend. Yet he had never married nor settled down, and sometimes she wondered if it were for her sake.

'My lady, Mistress Aston is here with the babe.'

John's voice broke into her reverie. Alys went eagerly into the hall to greet her aunt. Eleanor and Jocasta Cuthbert had been sisters, the one marrying an Aston, the other a Prescott. Eleanor had always been a sweeter, more pliable character than the sterner fibred Jocasta. Alys suspected that she had been disappointed when her younger son and Alys were not wed, and that she had been more than a little afraid of her elder son's wife. But Ann was dead now, and Mistress Aston had charge of her little granddaughter.

Nell was swaddled tightly lest her limbs grow crooked, and her plump baby face beamed out of the cocoon of linen. Her grandmother panted a little as she clambered down from the high cart and mounted the shallow steps leading to the front door. Like her niece she was overfond of the comfit dish.

'Alys, you are prettier than ever,' she said, with such evident sincerity that Alys was moved to hug her heartily.

'Let me take the babe. Come into the solar. Such a long drive as you've had!'

'But safely travelled, thank God!'

The old lady, having offered thanks for being preserved alive at the end of a three-mile drive, unwound herself from her voluminous cloak and took the proffered stool.

'Such good news!' she said, rocking back and forth. 'We had word this morning that Roger is back from the Low Countries and intends to pay us a long visit some time in the summer. Only think! it is two years since we saw him. He came home just before Harry's mother died.'

Alys's face which had flushed and softened, hardened a little. Though they had been on outwardly cordial terms there had been little love lost between Elizabeth Falcon and herself. She had always sensed that the older woman had guessed her initial reluctance to

75

wed Harry and resented it accordingly, and although she had insisted on moving out to the Dower Cottage, she had managed to convey the impression that she was only moving because Alys wanted her out of the way.

Well, the woman with her sweet smile and martyred airs had been dead these two years, and the Dower Cottage stood locked and empty.

Pouring wine carefully, Alys said, 'You will be happy to see Roger again.'

'Happy? I cannot tell you — not that I don't think the world of William, but he is rather — pudding natured!'

Mistress Aston gave her niece a mischievous, guilty glance.

'I know what you mean,' Alys returned the look with a conspiratorial one of her own, and proffered the dish of comfits.

'Just one. I promised myself I wouldn't stuff. You would not believe it, but I have had to let out all my kirtles!'

Hand hovering over the dish, she finally selected two and crunched with relish. Eleanor Aston enjoyed eating with the same frankness as she enjoyed gossip and playing at spillikins. Alys ate because there was deep within her a gnawing hunger that could not be satisfied.

'I expect Harry home tonight,' she said. 'Will you stay for supper?'

'Lord, I could not!' Mistress Aston looked horrified. 'The night air would poison the poor babe. Such a good little soul as she is, but then I was fortunate in the wet-nurse. Maggie is a clean, healthy wench, with enough rich milk to feed all of Marie Regina.'

The village of Marie Regina which crouched in a hollow on the other side of the highway took its name from the old monastery on the hill beyond. The building was no more now than a blackened shell, though folk swore they had seen lights moving about within the gaping walls and heard the sound of chanting. All the surrounding land had been church property until the monks had been driven out and their broad acres divided among those who had helped in the sacking.

The women chatted comfortably while the baby, Nell, dropped into a sleep interspersed with brief hiccoughs, for like her grandmother, she was inclined to over-indulge herself. At eleven, John tapped on the door to tell them dinner was ready, and the babe was borne off to Maggie in the kitchen.

The Falcon household ate, according to custom in the main hall, Alys taking the head of the table with Mistress Aston at her right. When they had helped themselves to the meats and breads and spiced sauces the big serving dishes were sent down to the end of the trestle where the servants sat, with the exception of Phyllis who sat by the fire, holding her face, and sipping hot broth through a straw.

In Harry's absence, Alys recited the Grace, folding her hands and bowing her head, her voice clear and self-possessed beneath the echoing rafters. For Alys, the Grace before meals, the household prayers after supper, weekly attendance at the parish church, were all part of the ordered scheme of life at *Kingsmead*; all the more precious because when she and Harry had gone, there would be nobody left to carry them on.

Mistress Aston left shortly after midday, bearing a recipe for almond cream and a bag of marzipan, lest her strength should fail her on the way. Her visit, pleasant as it had been, had set Alys behind. There were the account books to be made up, and money for John's trip to Maidstone to be taken out of the great iron chest stapled to the floor of Harry's bedroom.

The Falcons slept in adjoining chambers, a habit that had caused some comment, but Alys slept lightly and often whiled away the night hours in reading. Harry could not close his eyes unless every particle of light was excluded from the room.

At the other side of the house, over the kitchen and stillroom, were the two guest chambers. Once she had imagined them filled with children, but over ten years the dream had tarnished. A carved cradle and a pile of lovingly worked baby clothes were all that remained of that dream.

Quickly she reminded herself that the borders of the herb garden were in need of weeding, that her blue cloak had a rent in it, that she must make out a list for John to take into Maidstone. She needed fresh sewing needles and more tapestry canvas.

Harry was a little later than she had expected. The spring afternoon was fading into dusk, and she had twice told Cook to keep back the meal, when he rode into the courtyard and she went out with the welcome cup.

'I thought you delayed by footpads!' she exclaimed scoldingly. 'Did you hire escort?'

'No need. I've nothing on me worth stealing!'

He drained the wine and kissed her, his eyes not quite meeting hers.

'Was your visit a success? Did you see Her Grace?'

'At a distance only.' He threw his cloak vaguely in John's direction and strode into the hall.

As usual, his coming back into the house subtly reduced her authority. Already he was shouting to the fuming cook that he would eat in half an hour when he had washed off his grime, and his tread on the staircase was heavy. Alys trailed at his heels, questions on her lips.

'Was Her Grace in good humour? What did she wear? Did you notice if farthingales are wider this season?'

'Her Grace looked splendid. I never noticed the colour of her dress. The ladies seem to be wearing farthingales of every size and shape.'

He stripped off his doublet and unfastened the small ruff at his neck. Harry was unusually fastidious for a man. He changed his linen every fortnight, washed himself every day, and took baths three times a year though John warned that it weakened the spine.

Now, splashing cold water over his face and neck, he said, 'Have matters ridden well here? Did the lads catch that fox?'

'A week ago. The whole village turned out. Parson Grimshaw fell off his horse into the mud.'

'Serve him right! He'd best stick to

preaching! You'll never guess whom I saw in London.'

'Roger Aston.'

'God's death, but now you go about to read minds!' He towelled himself vigorously.

'Aunt Eleanor drove over this morning. She said they'd had word he was back.'

'I met him as we were going into the tournament.'

'We?'

'Five thousand and me,' he grinned. 'They'll have to extend the galleries if the joust becomes any more popular. Hand me a clean ruff, there's a good wench.'

'Is Roger well?' she asked.

'You know Roger — he never changes. Mind, I had only a word with him before the crowd parted us. He'll be over to see us before the summer is out. Perhaps we'll have a masque or a mumming, break open some of my father's sack. Would you like that?'

'Very much.' She gave him a fresh doublet and hunted under the bed for house shoes.

'There's a present for you in my bag,' he told her. 'See if you like it.'

'That was kind of you. I asked for nothing.'

Her fingers pulled at the straps of the leather bag. When the present was in her hands she gave a little gasp of pleasure and surprise. The broad ribbon of cloth-of-silver was sewn with thick clusters of tiny green stones.

'I thought it would serve as trimming for a cap,' he said, unable to resist adding. 'Those are chips of emerald.'

'It must have cost a great deal.'

'I don't grudge it,' he told her. 'You are a good wife, Alys.'

'Thank you.'

She gave him a puzzled little smile, for though they rubbed along well together, endearments and praise were rare between them. Certainly he had never brought home so expensive a gift before.

'And there's to be no selling off the stones for charity,' he said. 'Indeed, I have just indulged in a little charity of my own.'

'Oh?'

'I found a tenant for the Dower Cottage,' Harry said, sitting down to pull off his boots. 'I've thought for a long time what a pity it is to let the place fall to ruin.'

'Who is the tenant?'

'A wench out of Wales, if you please. A wench with a dancing bear. They had no place to go.'

'There are many in the land with no place to go,' she said. 'Why did you choose this one?'

'If I had fifty dower cottages I could lodge fifty tenants,' he said, 'But as I only have one then I must choose one.'

'A wench with a bear. Has she a name, this wench?'

'Margred. Some such name. Her people are dead and she is newly come into England.'

'She is young, I take it?'

'Oh, fifteen, sixteen years. Half-starved from the looks of her,' Straightening from his task, he began to bluster. 'I tell you, I scarce noticed the girl, but some louts were teasing her bear, and she was weeping. I was sorry for her, all alone and weeping. Then I remembered the Dower Cottage and thought to settle her there. She can keep the place sweetened, and pay peppercorn rent. God's blood, it is my property, and you've been saying for months that something needed to be done with it!'

'Dame Sudbury would like a little place of her own,' Alys said. 'She was telling me after service on Sunday that her old house is so ill-repaired it will likely blow down in the next gale.'

'I cannot turn the wench out now,' he said sulkily. 'I hired a horse for her and the bear to ride upon. Lord! but they made an odd sight.'

'Where are they now?'

'At the Dower Cottage. She wished to go straight there, not wanting to cause any nuisance by stopping off here. I warrant you'll not see her above once in a twelvemonth. She's a shy, wild creature.'

'But not too shy to ride off into Kent with a strange man,' Alys said.

'As to that she was at her wits' end, having no money and no performing licence. And she's not the sort to take a man's fancy.'

'She's not pretty?'

'I told you, half-starved and speaks English with an abominable accent. Now you'll not rail at me for showing charity to a fellow creature?'

'No, of course not.'

She forced a smile, but the muscles of her face felt stiff.

She had always known, without being told, that Harry's solitary trips to London were not solely for the purpose of hanging about in the corridors of Whitehall. The knowledge had never troubled her for, not being in love with her husband, she suffered no qualms of jealousy. But then he had never brought any woman back to his estates before. Instinctively Alys felt her own domain threatened by invasion.

'Pin the band to your cap. Let me see how it looks,' Harry was saying.

She went obediently to the mirror, her fingers clumsy as they fixed the jewelled cloth-of-silver. In the darkly silvered surface her skin was drained of all colour, her eyes pale holes.

'Wear it at supper,' Harry said. 'I vow I'm hungry enough to set about my own horse.'

'Shall we have music later?'

'Not tonight. I have to ride over to the Wainwright's to put some business his way.'

'John can go,' she could not help saying.

'Tush, give John an evening's respite. I don't expect to be very late.'

'But you don't want me to wait up?'

She dropped her hands and stood, thick-waisted, looking at herself in the mirror.

'No need, sweetheart, unless it pleases you. I hope the meal is good.'

'There's blackberry preserve,' she said dully.

In her own stomach the hunger had begun to gnaw at her again.

5

Margred stood, hands on hips, and contemplated the newly whitewashed cottage. She had been in possession for almost six months, but merely to look at the little house raised in her such a warmth of happiness that she suddenly clasped her arms about herself as if she sought to contain her abundance of joy.

All her life she would remember that late afternoon when she had jogged along the road, with Mott at her back, and heard Harry say, 'The gates of *Kingsmead* are on the left. My land extends to the banks of the river and the Aston estate begins on the other side.'

The river bisected the highway, dropping down towards the huddle of houses that was Marie Regina. The road narrowed at the water's edge into a sturdy, wooden bridge and then at the further bank it widened into a road again, leading upwards towards ruins that crowned the green tor.

It was a gentle landscape, the long grassed meadows undulating between forests of pink and white blossom, primroses starring the tangled hedgerows.

'We'll take the short cut across the fields,' Harry said. 'The Dower Cottage is near the river. The wood has grown up around it, I'm afraid, but there is some furniture there, linen too. The place was locked up after my mother died, and so far nothing has been done with it.'

He had not suggested taking her to the manor house and she had been glad of it. From now on the cottage would be her world, and he had explained that he would visit her whenever he could.

'Husbands often have to go away for a spell,' she nodded, and she was not thinking of Alys, but of herself waiting in the cottage for Harry to return.

He left her hastily after unlocking the door and handing down the bread, apples and ale they had purchased along the way. For a moment she felt a pang of hurt that he should be so eager to leave, but he had other duties, other responsibilities, and she must learn to accept the situation.

The little house was of stone, its windows latticed, bindweed and thistle growing almost up to the sills. All around it whispered the green wood, but a narrow track wound down to the river. It was, thought Margred, a most secret place in a wild corner of a tamed and cultivated estate.

Within was more luxury than she had ever known, even though everything was covered with a thick layer of dust. The front door opened directly into a long, low room which ran to front and back, and a door on the right revealed a smaller apartment. Both rooms had wall hearths, and out of the main one a staircase spiralled up into two similar apartments above.

Harry's mother must have felt like a queen here, Margred thought, innocently unaware that the old Lady Falcon had taken a perverse delight in exclaiming in sweetly martyred tones, 'Of course, it's terribly cramped, but I didn't wish to get into dear Alys's way up at *Kingsmead*.'

The rushes on the floors stank, and clouds of dust rose from the wall tapestries when she brushed against them, but there were stools and two tables and a dresser stacked with pewter and a chest of yellowing linen, and two four-poster beds. In another chest shifts and bodices and kirtles were folded.

'His wife must be very careless, not to have done something with all this,' she said disapprovingly to Mott, and the bear growled in agreement.

Alys had, in fact, been so relieved by her mother-in-law's death that she had not yet ventured to sort out the contents of the cottage for fear of reviving her own bitter dislike. There was even a half-finished piece of embroidery, and a crumpled nightcap on the bedpost. It was, Margred thought, as if the Dower Cottage had been waiting for her.

After it was dark, Harry came back with candles and helped her gather sticks to start a fire. He seemed anxious on her behalf lest she be lonely or frightened, but solitude had been her natural condition for as long as she could remember, and the night held no terrors.

'I have told Alys that I gave you this shelter out of pity,' he told her. 'She seldom goes beyond the house and gardens, except to go to church, so you are unlikely to meet her.'

'Must I go to church too?' she asked.

'To the second service. Alys goes to the early one. If you don't, you may be accused of Papistry.'

'And end up with my head on London Bridge? I'll go to church,' she said, so promptly that he burst out laughing and put his arms around her, saying she was the only wench who could make him laugh; and from laughing they fell to loving and the fire collapsed in a little heap of ashes without either of them noticing.

That had been six months before, and in

89

the time since, she had settled into her corner of the world as comfortably as a mouse into its skin. She had scrubbed the cottage, and washed the linen in the river, spreading it over the bushes to dry, and beat the dust out of the tapestries, and laid fresh-cut rushes over the floor. Apart from clearing a narrow path to the front door she had left the overgrown wood exactly as it was. The tangled briars and vine-tendrilled trees gave her a feeling of security; of power too, for in this place she was as absolute a queen as Elizabeth could ever be in her galleries in Whitehall.

She had walked into the village a few days after her arrival and been surprised by the friendly nods with which she was greeted. Even Mott acquired a circle of admiring small boys before they had gone many yards.

It had been Harry, coming to see her that night, who had explained. 'Alys told the servants about you, gave them the impression it was her desire that you stay here. She knew there might be talk else, and she wished to save my reputation.'

'And bolster up her own,' Margred said with a quick flash of dislike.

'Alys is a good-hearted woman,' Harry said stiffly.

Margred heeded the unspoken warning. Her lover had a regard for his wife and so she, Margred, would be wiser not to criticise her. Indeed it became easier not to mention her at all; to greet Harry with such love that when he was there the Dower Cottage became his home and his life elsewhere ceased to exist. And he rode over once or twice a week, usually with a present of game or fresh-baked bread.

Living was an easy matter, for apart from Harry's regular gifts, the villagers gave her pies and jellies in return for Mott's dancing, and no question of a licence was ever broached. As for fruit, one had only to reach up a hand to pluck down apple, pear, quince or cherry, and the river was full of fish.

'This is the garden of England, sweetheart, and you are its fairest flower,' he told her.

She smiled at that, feeling herself become beautiful in his arms, but then she pulled away, frowning.

'Flowers die,' she said, and the sharpness of fear was in her voice. 'Flowers grow brown and dry and their petals wither.'

'Everything dies,' Harry said comfortably, but she held on to him tightly again.

'Not us, not us! We were made to live here for ever!'

Now, in a golden October, she stood outside her trim and shining little house and felt her happiness stripped from her as if a chill wind had gusted through her tree of joy. The vivid scarlets and yellows of the falling leaves mocked her with the reminder that branches would soon be etched bare against the sky. Already the salting of beef had begun, and Harry had said he would arrange for somebody to cut a pile of logs for her winter use. And one day her season too would end and dust would lie thick in the silent rooms.

'If I had a child,' she said aloud, 'some part of me would remain.'

Harry was lusty, yet neither she nor Alys had quickened. The fear that she too might be barren had crossed her mind, but she had dismissed it. It was more likely that Harry's seed was weak. She had heard of such a thing, had heard too that the matter might be remedied; but she was not certain which herbs to use.

It occurred to her that she might gather some and dry them and try various infusions. The little room at the side of the living room had shelves fixed against the wall, where she could store roots and flowers. The task would occupy the long winter days, and Harry, to save his masculine pride, need only be told that she was trying her hand at brewing cordials.

For her own part she had little interest in, or desire for, children, but men set great store by families. How she would explain the existence of a babe to the villagers never troubled her. She would deal with it when the time came.

Although she had not told Harry, Margred had already contrived to see Alys, by the simple expedient of hiding in the hedgerow when the other woman rode to church. A very plain woman, Margred had decided, with her light hair rolled up in a fashion that made her broad face broader. After seeing her it was easy to forget her.

Mott growled, the fur on his back stiffening. Someone was approaching; a stranger, for he never growled at Harry's step. She turned and saw the plain faced gentleman whom they had met at the tournament. Harry had mentioned that Roger was come home, but she had not expected him to seek her out.

'Master Aston? Good-day.'

She was the first to speak, profiting from the expression of surprise on his face.

Roger Aston had, in fact, been almost convinced by Alys's words.

'Did Harry tell you that we have a tenant

for the Dower Cottage? A poor orphan girl with a dancing bear whom he ran across when he was in London.'

Only her voice, pitched a shade higher than usual, had caused him to stroll in the direction of the river. He recognised the girl at once. Even a fleeting glimpse had impressed on his memory that pointed face with the yellow eyes that should have been ugly, but was somehow enchantingly pretty instead.

'We have met before,' he said.

'In London, when we saw the Queen. You were just returned from the Low Countries.'

'And you are — ?'

'I am Margred. Will you not step in for a cup of wine?'

He nodded, trying to smile, but feeling an uneasiness strike through him. Despite her youth and slenderness there was a disturbing quality of self-possession in the wench. She had neither blushed nor curtsied, and her gaze was frank, as if she addressed an equal.

The house was sparkling, every pane of glass rubbed to perfection, sweet rushes laid on the floors, the hearth laid with logs. The whole ought to have been welcoming, yet the room seemed subtly to withdraw from him, to bind itself about the girl and the animal. Not being an imaginative man, he was a little alarmed at his own reaction.

'You have done credit to the house. It had been locked up since Lady Elizabeth died.'

'I know. Her clothes were still here, so I made them over for myself.'

She was wearing a russet kirtle with bodice and sleeves of green — a modestly charming outfit, but his uneasiness increased. She spoke, he thought with a pang of indignation, as if she had every right to use the clothes.

'I have proved very neat at stitching,' she said cheerfully, 'but Harry says my cooking is a disaster.'

'How then do you earn your bread?' he asked, more bluntly than he had intended.

'I keep the cottage aired and sweetened,' she said simply, 'and sometimes Mott dances in the village, and the people give me things. But Harry comes over with foodstuffs. Will you take some wine? It is brewed from elderflowers, with just a hint of ginger.'

'Thank you.' Watching her as she poured the liquid, he asked, 'And Lady Alys? Does she bring you things?'

'We never meet. It would not be fitting,' she said quietly.

So she was Harry's mistress as he had guessed. Sipping the wine, he admitted to himself that he had come this way to inspect this threat to Alys's happiness. He had vowed ten years before when she had been married off to his best friend that he would always stand her true friend and protect her from harm, and he had never forgotten that vow.

Neither had he ever seriously contemplated marriage with anybody else, even though the boyish ardour of his devotion had matured into an unspoken warmth and desire for her comfort. That Harry, of whom he was genuinely fond, should take the occasional light o'love bothered him little. But this girl was settled here on the estate, and her pretty manners and charming house were a threat he sensed without comprehending.

'Have you no people of your own?' he enquired abruptly.

'I have Harry,' she said, and her little face lit suddenly into such loveliness that he was astonished.

So the wench loved Harry, he thought in confusion. This was no light-minded girl, taking favours from an older, richer man, but a young woman whose feelings would endure.

Against his will he began to admire her, and to pity her, for he could not believe that the situation could continue indefinitely. Sooner or later Harry would tire of her, or Alys would assert her rights.

Impulsively, he said, 'If at any time you need a friend — '

'I have Harry,' she interrupted, adding politely, 'But I thank you all the same.'

'Well, I just felt — if anything ever happened,' He broke off lamely, noting with relief that she had risen from her stool, and was moving towards the door. 'I shall be away again soon,' he said. 'There are profits to be won if one is in the right place at the right time.'

'Will you go to London?'

'Until the spring, anyway. Crossing the Channel in autumn or winter is not to be recommended.'

'And will you see the Queen?'

She had never forgotten that lonely, splendid figure.

'The Queen grieves for her favourite,' he said, ducking beneath the lintel. 'Sir Christopher Hatton died of his kidney complaint.'

'Poor man!' Her eyes widened in sympathy.

'She has Raleigh and Essex still,' he told her.

'If Harry died,' she said simply, 'I would have nobody at all.'

He should have felt pity, but there was something in the finality of her tone that chilled him. It was not healthy, he thought, to feel so intensely. Then he reminded himself that she was still very young, and that with age came a cooling of the blood.

'Well, if there is ever anything I can do,' he said uncomfortably and bowed, perceiving amusement behind her steady regard.

'I thank you again,' she said, and stretched out a hand towards the bear as it ambled round the side of the cottage to join her.

As he made his way along the narrow track which led to the main road, he was conscious of relief all through him, as if he had just escaped from some danger.

It was his mother who brought up the subject of the girl when the Astons sat about the parlour fire after supper that evening.

Aston Hall was built on a much more modest scale than *Kingsmead* — hall and kitchen occupying the ground space, the parlour being a tiny apartment squeezed in between William's room and the one where Mistress Aston slept with Baby Nell. During Ann's lifetime, Roger, on his visits home, had made do with a pallet here. Now that William was a widower he shared his brother's bed, muffling his ears against his elder's snores.

Tonight they sat at ease, Mistress Aston chewing marzipan, as her foot moved slowly, rocking her granddaughter's cradle.

'Dame Pierson saw you on your way to the river today,' 'Did you have a good catch?'

'I wasn't fishing.'

'No, but I am,' she returned smartly. 'Did you see the girl?'

'I saw several,' Roger said innocently, 'but they were all promised or pockmarked, so I'll stay a bachelor.'

'Don't be tiresome, Roger! I mean the Welsh girl whom Harry has planted in the Dower Cottage. The one with the bear. Oh, Alys assures me that she persuaded him to it, but I know better!'

'Haven't you walked down to the river yourself during these past six months?' he enquired.

'Mistress Aston flushed slightly. 'William said that I must not,' she admitted.

'The girl dresses respectfully, goes to church every week, and keeps herself to herself,' William said.

A thicker-set, slower-spoken version of his younger brother, he was the only man of whom Mistress Aston had stood in awe since the death of her husband.

'Alys is my niece,'the old lady persisted. 'It's hard that Harry should make a fool of her. Indeed, I think he has behaved very badly.'

'I hope you didn't tell him so,' William remarked.

'As if I would! Why, it's none of our business,' Mistress Aston said virtuously.

'Exactly, so let it lie!'

'But did you see her, Roger?' She turned eagerly to her younger son. 'I caught a glimpse of her in the village once, but she goes there seldom and never stays long.'

'I met her and talked with her.'

'And what is she like? Is the pretty? Is the bear very large and fierce? She's a light wench, of course.'

'No, I think not.'

'Not? Oh, but surely — ?'

'What lies between her and Harry is their business. Theirs and Alys's, and if Alys chooses not to complain we should respect her silence. But the wench is no light wench, I'll swear.'

'Is she pretty?'

'Young,' he said, considering. 'No more than sixteen or seventeen. Long black hair and eyes — like cat's eyes, but yellow and not green. Her skin is dark, like a gypsy, and her teeth are very white.'

'How was she dressed?'

'In a made-over gown of Lady Elizabeth's. She told me she had altered the clothes in the cottage to fit herself.'

'Bess will be spinning in her tomb like a top,' Mistress Aston said with satisfaction. She had always cordially detested her niece's mother-in-law.

'Was the Dower Cottage in good repair?' William enquired.

'Clean as a new pin. She had scrubbed and polished everywhere.'

'And Harry goes over twice a week with foodstuffs,' Mistress Aston said. 'He rides over after supper, stays for an hour, and goes home again. I had it from John.'

'They are very discreet,' William said, half-approvingly. 'I've heard no talk in the village.'

'So the girl is a good girl,' Mistress Aston said. She sounded faintly regretful.

'No, not good,' Roger said, and bit his lip as his mother and brother stared at him. 'She's young and pretty and modestly mannered,' he said, 'and her little house is a picture, and yet — '

'And yet what?'

'I was ill at ease,' Roger said, 'as if — as if underneath the sweetness was something cold, something held in check. I don't mean that the girl herself was evil, not that. But it was as if she had some capacity for evil — I'm not sure what I mean.'

'It sounds to me as if you left your wits in

the Low Countries,' William said, to mark his disapproval of a conversation in which he was out of his depth.

'You were not beguiled by her yourself, were you?' his mother asked anxiously.

Although Mistress Aston would not have admitted it for the world she took a certain doleful pleasure in her son's broken heart. That he should remain faithful to the girl who had been denied him struck his mother as romantic and proper. She would have been secretly disappointed had he arrived home with a wife.

'You are not taken with her yourself, are you?' she asked again.

'I was glad to be away,' Roger said frankly. 'And yet I pitied her too. Indeed, I offered to stand her friend.'

'You had best leave well enough alone,' William said severely. 'And you, my lady-mother, should not seem to condone whatever is happening by wandering down to the Dower Cottage. For my own part I shall simply behave as if the wench is not there.'

'You were always so strong-minded, William,' his mother said sadly.

William was pleased by her remark which he considered showed perception. He had, he thought, been strong-minded since he was a boy and had put aside the paints and brushes and canvasses on which he wasted hours of his time in order to prepare himself for the task of supervising the estate.

No titles had come the way of the Astons and their holding was a modest one, but it would be William's when his father died. He would be better employed in overseeing the crops than in splashing brilliant designs on canvas. It had cost him a pang to give up the art which he had enjoyed so much, but he had ignored the pang, just as he had ignored the pretty daughter of the wheelwright and married Ann Temple, who was sharp-nosed and sharp-tongued, but had a handsome dowry. He had hoped for a large family, but after years of disappointment she had finally died in producing a daughter.

Glancing across at the tiny child, William felt a stirring of parental affection. He loved Nell far more than he had loved Ann, and was quite unaware that she reminded him of the fat little cherubs he had painted with such pleasure during his youth.

Now, following some train of thought of his own, he said slowly, 'It seems clear that Roger is a committed bachelor. And Nell will marry one day, so unless I take another wife, the Aston name will die.'

His mother's mouth fell open in dismay. For one moment she feared lest he had taken it into his head to court the Welsh girl himself.

'In a year or two,' William said, 'I may look about and pick another wife. A young, healthy wench with a little bit of property of her own.'

Mistress Aston relaxed slightly. She might have guessed that he would do nothing rash or ill considered. And a year or two was a long time.

'I shall look out for a plump little Dutch widow for you,' Roger said to his brother.

'Best find one for yourself first,' William said equably. 'For me a good English wench will suit very nicely.'

'I will ride over and visit Alys,' Mistress Aston announced. 'She and I will put our heads together.'

'Beware! they will either find fault with every woman in Kent or have you halfway to church before you can blink,' Roger teased.

'Get along with you!' She shook a playful finger at him. 'Alys and I would not dream of interfering.'

'She would have to be kind to Nell,' William said, his eyes brooding upon his daughter.

'As if anyone could ever dream of treating her harshly,' she reproached.

The conversation moved on to the charm

and good nature of the baby. Harry's involvement with the Welsh girl was set aside.

Roger thought of her again as he undressed that night. The room which he shared during his visit with William faced the side of the house, and far off he could see the river glinting among the trees. Margred would be in her little house on the farther bank. He wondered if she lay in Harry's arms and if Alys, like himself, stood sleepless at the lattice.

Harry was a fool to neglect a good wife for a yellow-eyed nobody from the back of nowhere. Even as the thought crossed his mind he was aware of a prickling uneasiness as if something dark had laid briefly across the moon.

6

Margred was taking a bath. Although she imitated Harry in washing herself every day it was rare that she immersed herself completely, but on this particular afternoon the sun was so warm and the river so inviting that she had pulled off her kirtle and overskirt and stepped down into the green translucence.

The water was cool, rippling against her skin, the bottom sandy and yielding under her bare toes. The river was running low, the current scarcely perceptible. She moved cautiously, spreading out her arms. It reached to her shoulders only, and the sensation of water washing over her slender limbs was exciting. When she glanced down, her body, seen beneath the tiny waves, had a dim and mysterious quality.

'I shall learn to swim,' she called out to Mott, who crouched on the bank with a disapproving look on his face. 'I shall swim all the way to Africa. And you ought to try it yourself! It would wash some of the fleas out of you.'

Mott dipped a paw into the shallows

and withdrew it hastily, shaking it in consternation. He looked so comical that she burst out laughing, and under the impetus of her own gaiety began to run, splashing through the water, clutching at the reed fringed bank, her long hair streaming down her back, tiny drops of moisture running down her arms and legs.

Overhead the sun blazed out of a blue sky, and at the edge of the water little golden-hearted lilies spread white petals among tall iris and intricate fern. In sheer joy of living Margred rolled over on to her stomach and pulled a stalk of sweet grass, nibbling the nectared end.

She had been more than two years at the Dower Cottage and each month that passed rendered her more secure. The people of Marie Regina took little notice of her. Themselves insular and distrustful of strangers, they approved her shyness and if they had a fairly shrewd idea of what passed between her and Sir Harry Falcon they held their tongues. Sir Harry was a lusty man, and if Lady Alys raised no objections then it was best to leave well alone.

As it was the wench caused no trouble at all, and her bear amused the younglings. She went to service every week, and her herb potions were very good, better than the apothecary's at Maidstone. She had offered one diffidently to Mistress Truman when the latter complained of stomach ache and Mistress Truman declared the pain was wonderfully eased. After that, whenever Margred was within earshot, people would make a point of mentioning their ailments in the hope that she would turn and offer some remedy.

Susan Hammond had actually ventured to the door of the cottage once, intending to ask for a poultice for boils, but the bear had crouched in her path showing his teeth, and Margred had stood at the door with her yellow eyes narrowed to slits, and told Susan to go away.

Margred herself had no need of her own remedies. At eighteen she was as healthy as a sound russet apple, her flesh firm and golden brown, her hair thick and vibrant as it sprang from her scalp. She had not grown an inch, which was a grief to her, but Harry said the most precious things were often the smallest. And when he said that he looked at her as if he could not believe his good fortune.

Margred, chewing her stalk, was filled with her own joy. Life for her was a series of small happinesses — the pungent smell of the great armfuls of herbs she gathered in the dark places of the wood, the roughness of Mott's fur under her hand, the smiling blue eyes of her lover as he bent beneath the lintel to greet her. Nobody, she thought, could possibly be as happy as she.

In that she was wrong, for William Aston was, at that moment, strolling through his acres, deciding that he was probably the most fortunate man in Kent. His daughter had grown from a plump baby into a plump, lint-haired child with such a gentle nature that sometimes he feared she would not live; but his mother assured him that the child was healthy and never ailed.

His brother, Roger, had returned to the Low Countries from whence he sent occasional letters giving scant news of his doings, but so cheerful in tone that his family worried less than they might have done. He was still a bachelor, but a year earlier William had begun to pay court to Mistress Stone who lived just outside Maidstone in a charming house bequeathed to her by her first husband.

He had fixed upon Betsy Stone after careful consideration. Of respectable parentage, she had been wed at eighteen to a much older man, who had trained her in the duties of a thrifty wife and died, leaving her a considerable property. It was the sheerest chance that she had not been snapped up again before he'd had a chance to enquire into her circumstances. But Betsy Stone was a shrinking mouse-like creature who behaved more like a spinster of forty than a widow of twenty-seven; and William's slow and careful wooing had been more to her taste than the speedier tactics of other gentlemen.

Betsy, he considered, would make a docile, good-tempered wife. It was a pity that she dressed so badly and that her only reaction to an attempted embrace had been an embarrassed giggle, but she would make a kind stepmother for Nell and her nature was so timid that his mother would continue to have her own way.

It was then that he saw the girl. She was lying on her stomach with her legs in the air and her black hair streaming over her naked body. She looked, he thought bemused, like some pagan nymph risen from a deep and secret pool. His eyes grew hot, his mouth dry, and a throbbing began in his loins. He had kept away from the cottage and avoided any place where he might be likely to meet the wench, and now he was come upon her so suddenly that his breath caught in his throat and he felt an abrupt and fierce dissatisfaction with his whole life.

Margred was scrambling to her feet, her breasts twin globes under his hungry regard.

She seemed unaware that she was naked and his heart recognised her innocence even as his mind screamed that she was evil.

'You trespass!' he said thickly, and his hands opened and closed convulsively. 'I could have you whipped at the cart's tail for wantoning so shamelessly!'

The veins on his forehead were bulging and flecks of red dulled the white of his eyes. He shouted, to quieten the clamouring of his desire.

'God forbid that any decent woman should see you! Cover yourself and begone!'

Margred turned and fled into the water, splashing through it in clumsy and terrified haste. She had never seen such anger in a human being before and she could not fathom how she had caused it. Granted that she had unthinkingly trespassed and that she had been wearing no clothes, but she had believed herself to be private.

On her own side of the river she looked back briefly and saw him still watching her. An irrational fear that he might wade after her seized her, and she zigzagged among the trees, snatching her garments from the branches as she went.

William Aston was shaking with an emotion which he consciously identified as rage. The wench was a strumpet, an abomination! He would speak to Harry, make him realise for his own good that the girl's presence could not be endured. He went on staring across the river but the slender, golden brown figure had gone and only the reeds quivered a little as if they shook in silent mockery.

His opportunity came sooner than he expected, for he reached home to find Harry waiting for him. For the first time his neighbour's appearance irritated him. A man who consorted with a harlot had no right to look so prosperous, so much at ease with his conscience. He contrasted his own plain features and stolid frame with the other's crisply curling hair and bright blue eyes.

Harry sat at his ease, with Nell perched on his knee. The child adored the big, smiling man whom she had been taught to call 'uncle', for he generally had a pouch full of sweetmeats and a story to tell. At that moment her smooth, round cheek was bulging and her dimpled hand lay confidingly in his.

'Nell, get down and go to Maggie,' her father said, so sharply that her blue eyes filled with tears.

Harry slanted a puzzled look but set her down, arranging her long skirt and tapping her small bottom playfully. He was fond of children and often silently regretted that Alys was barren. That Margred might ever become pregnant was a possibility that had never entered his head.

'She's a pretty wench,' he said, watching her with approval as she trotted off with bent head.

'She eats too many sweets. They will ruin her teeth,' William said coldly. 'Have you had refreshment?'

'Your lady mother provided me handsomely and then had to rush away — a domestic crisis in the kitchen. I came over to see you about that mare, to advise you not to buy. I had a look at her myself and detected a weakness in the forelegs.'

'I had already decided not to buy,' William said stiffly. 'I thank you, however, for the advice and would offer some of my own.'

'I am not adding to my stables,' Harry began, but the other interrupted almost violently.

'Women, not horses! You must do something about the lewd wench who lives at the Dower Cottage!'

Sheer surprise held his mouth open. Neither he nor William had ever been close personal friends, for Harry preferred the easy amiability of Roger, but they had been congenial neighbours. Certainly

113

Margred and her status in Harry's life had never been mentioned.

'She's a good girl,' he said.

'Aye, so good that she flaunts herself at me in nakedness!' William cried, his rage returning. 'And on my own land, for she had crossed the river. Naked as sin she was, and not ashamed of it!'

'You must be mistaken,' Harry said blankly.

'I saw her, with my own eyes!' William's heavy face was purpling. 'She stood, not two yards from me, displaying herself!'

'You lie! She would never behave so!'

'I will prove I am no liar! There is a mark at her thigh.' He had noticed it without realising the fact. 'A purple mark in the form of a crescent moon.'

Harry flushed deeply with anger and embarrassment. Endlessly fascinated by his young mistress he had assumed that her charms were solely for him. That she should attempt to catch another man's eye was something he had never even considered.

'I'll deal with her,' he said curtly.

'If my lady mother had happened that way, or my daughter! God knows, I never meddled in your business, Harry, even though your wife is my cousin, but this is a decent neighbourhood,' William said, in agitation, and was, by this time, firmly convinced that the girl had glimpsed him approaching and had deliberately tempted him.

'I'll deal with her,' Harry repeated.

His colour had faded slightly but there was an ominous white line about his mouth. He had, he thought, been generous to the girl, saving her from the degradation of a beggar's life in the city, settling her in a house, even letting her use his dead mother's gowns to furnish her own wardrobe. He left the hall without farewell, and rode away in frowning silence.

Mistress Eleanor Aston, one plump hand clapped to her mouth in dismay, stood at the other side of the kitchen door. It was not her habit to eavesdrop upon conversations but her son's angry voice had stayed her return to the hall. So the girl was not only wanton, but faithless! She was not content with stealing Harry from poor Alys, but was now luring William who was almost married to that neat, docile little Betsy Stone. Well, she had kept silent for long enough.

Drawing a deep breath, she entered noisily, exclaiming, 'Oh, but has Harry gone? I forgot to tell him to remind Alys I would be riding over tomorrow afternoon. Never mind! you can drive me to *Kingsmead* yourself, can't you? Usually he sends John to escort me.'

'Take one of our own lads,' William said absently.

There was the shine of sweat on his brow and his hands were twitching.

'Giles has a strained back from lifting that heavy chest,' Mistress Aston, who drove her servants crazy by periodically rearranging all the furniture, said sympathetically. 'And Piers is due to take those heifers to market.'

'Very well, I'll drive you,' he said abruptly. 'I have an errand myself, so I'll call back for you later.'

'And remind me to take some of that quince jelly. Alys particularly liked the last jar.'

She chattered on, while gradually William's trembling ceased, and the vivid desires that had flamed in his soul were thrust beneath habit and duty.

Margred was in the herb-room when she saw Harry arrive. The shock of having been discovered had passed, and she was half inclined to grin when she remembered William Aston's furious face. Rumour ran in the village that he intended to take another wife. Well, Heaven help him if the sight of a naked wench sent him gibbering! Then he passed out of mind as she hurried to the door, wondering why Harry should break his invariable rule and visit her in daylight.

'Has something bad happened?' she enquired anxiously, for he put her from him when she would have embraced him.

'You were on Aston land today!' he said curtly.

'I was taking a bath,' she said promptly, 'but how did — oh, of course; that Aston man has been tittle-tattling!'

'You had no garments on.'

'Well, who takes a bath with clothes on?' she asked reasonably. 'It was hot and sunny, and the water was cool, and nobody was there.'

'William Aston saw you.'

'Only because he chanced that way. I wouldn't have trespassed if I'd feared discovery.'

'He told me that you flaunted yourself at him, like a harlot.'

'That's not true!' she cried indignantly. 'It was he who startled me and yelled at me, calling me strumpet. I was so frightened that I ran back into the river.'

'William Aston is an honourable man and a truthful one,' Harry said unwillingly.

Margred seemed so innocent and yet a maggot of distrust nibbled at him. After all, she was a woman and Harry had been reared to believe them more vulnerable to temptation than men. That was why

117

daughters were kept at home, while sons were sent out into the world to make their fortunes.

'Perhaps it was a mood of mischief, a whim to tease him and make me jealous,' he suggested.

Margred's little face had grown hard and cold, and she flung back her head proudly as she stood before him.

'I do not have moods and fancies,' she said in a clear, cold voice. 'When I followed you here I gave my whole heart into your keeping for ever and ever. There will be no other man for me.'

'But William said — '

'Then believe him if you choose,' She shrugged as if indifferent even as tears ran down her cheeks. 'He is a gentleman and I am only a poor, ignorant girl who cannot read. No doubt he has described me to you in great detail. As for him, I cannot even tell you the colour of his doublet. I only know his face got redder and redder, and his voice louder and louder, and then I ran away.'

He hesitated a fraction too long, not knowing that the pause would affect the lives of those yet unborn.

'William was mistaken, or over-zealous. But it was foolish of you to behave so recklessly, sweetheart. Why, anyone from the village might have seen you!'

'I was very foolish,' she agreed, 'but no harm was done.'

'I hope not, though I doubt if William will gossip. But we have worked so hard to keep our reputations unblemished, it would be a sad pity to ruin all.'

To keep your reputation safe, she thought in deep bitterness. I would walk barefoot at your side through a hostile world. I never cared what people said, so long as you loved me. But with you it has to be a secret thing, because you don't wish to lose the good opinion of the world.

He had the best of the bargain, a placid wife in a lovely home, a pretty mistress near enough to visit twice a week. Not for him the long evenings with only Mott for company, nor the hours of waiting. Basically he was a selfish man, but knowing that made no difference to her feelings. She loved him and that was her reason for living.

'It grieves me,' she sobbed aloud, 'that you cannot believe me!'

'Sweetheart, I do, I do.' He put his arms around her, holding her tightly. 'William misunderstood the situation, that's all.'

But it wasn't all. With bleak perception she knew that part of him would never be quite certain of her again, that something sweet and true had gone from their relationship.

'If you did not believe in me,' she whispered, 'I could not endure to stay. I would have to leave, to go back to my own country.'

For the fraction of a second, relief flared in Harry's mind. Had he been forced to answer the question he would have said that he loved Margred passionately, and it would have been true. But something deeply conventional in his nature shrank from her occasional strangeness. Alys would as soon have cut off her head as jumped naked into a chilly river. In all their married life he had never seen her completely nude, and while consciously he found her shyness dull, something within him approved such modesty.

Certainly he could never imagine Margred as a wife. There was something untamed in her nature that both repelled and fascinated him. And it was a constant strain, always wishing to be with her when he was at home, and when he was with her always a little uneasy for fear of discovery. If she were to leave, it would break his heart, of course, but — his eyes fell upon her upturned face, the eyes blurred with tears, the full lower lip moist, red, trembling.

'If you left me it would be death!' he cried,

and kissed her as if he were trying to crush his own treacherous thought.

It was the first time they had made love in the afternoon, and there was an urgency in their embrace as if both had drawn back from a chasm and clung together to avoid falling.

While he was dressing, he said, avoiding her eyes, 'It would be wise if we stayed apart, just for a week or two.'

'You said that William Aston doesn't gossip.'

'No more he does, but others may be watching, and be less scrupulous about telling Alys.'

'Surely she guesses.'

'Alys would not have such thoughts of me,' he said loftily. 'Even if she did, she is a gentlewoman and would keep them to herself. But it would hurt her cruelly if others came to her with some tale.'

'By all means let us be discreet then,' Margred said lightly.

'It will be harvest soon anyway. The fields will be crowded with labourers from dawn to dusk.'

'I agreed,' she said, irritated that he should feed her excuses as if she were a child.

'You're a sweet wench,' he said, and kissed her with less urgency than before, and went out into the twilight.

Long shadows purpled the wood, and the Dower Cottage gleamed like a pearl set in green velvet. Margred whistled and Mott padded from the vastness of the trees.

'You've enough wood and provisions in?' he enquired as he mounted his horse.

'Plenty.'

She waited for something more, for some declaration that never came.

He only said, 'I'll be over as soon as I possibly can,' and was riding away.

'He thinks me light and foolish,' she said in Welsh to the bear. 'William Aston poisoned his mind against me, though Harry doesn't realise it himself yet.'

She was filled with such rage against the Astons that she felt physically sick. She knew them all by sight, of course, although until this day she had only spoken to Roger.

'I hate them,' she told Mott. 'I hate William Aston because he has a lewd and dirty mind and sees evil where there is none. I hate Mistress Aston because she is fat and wears satin kirtles and acts as if she's a great lady when all the time she's spoiled and silly with a face like a doll. I hate Roger Aston because — '

She was not quite certain why she hated Roger, except that he had once loved Alys.

Hatred coursed through her veins, not warm and red like blood, but cold and black and strong. For the first time in years she thought of the mother she had never known, of the strange, wild girl who had exerted her last strength in giving birth to Margred. Prys had been kind, but his had been the kindness of an old man, of a grandfather.

'I want my mother,' Margred whispered, and self pity mingled with her hatred. Mott whimpered, and the trees stirred as if something listened. In Margred's head a sentence was shaping itself, over and over.

'Destroy the likeness and you destroy the person. Destroy the likeness and you destroy the person.'

Moving slowly, as if she were in a dream, Margred went back into the house. On the window in the herb-room a bowl stood, filled with misshapen lumps of tallow, ready to be shaped into candles. A small paring knife lay near at hand.

Shaping the wax into four tiny, crude figures, it was as if she remembered what needed to be done. There was the biggest for William Aston who had spoiled the trust that lay between her and Harry. She drew a long pin from her head-dress and stabbed the figure through its centre.

The fattest piece, at the top of which she

had carved a bulbous little head was silly Mistress Aston. She stabbed that one too, grinding the steel through the wax. Two pins and two figures left, but her fingers ached and the power was draining from her.

She thrust one pin into the head of the smallest figure, the last pin into the leg of the fourth effigy. They had neither feet nor hands, and their eyes and mouths were only scratches on the surface of the tallow, but laid in a row each bore a sinister family resemblance to its fellows.

Margred dropped the knife and contemplated her work with dreary pleasure. She had never done anything so wicked in her whole life before. One part of her mind told her firmly that this was no more than childish spite and that it was mere superstition to think anything could possibly result. The darker side of her nature exulted in a vindictive triumph that was almost like pain.

She wrapped the objects in a length of silk and laid them at the bottom of her spice chest under muslin bags filled with lavender and rue. Then she went to the door to call Mott.

The bear came reluctantly, slinking down from the shadows, his little eyes sad and wise. The moon had risen, draining colour from the world, and the trunks of the trees were corpse-green, the bushes crowding about the house as if they sought to enter. It was cold, so cold that she felt it in the very marrow of her bones.

'Supper, Mott. Time for supper.'

She dropped the latch and shot the bolt into its socket, lit candles, stirred up the embers of the fire. Mott crouched on his haunches, watching her shadow.

In the midst of slicing bread, she heard herself say, 'Oh, Mott, who will eat my sins when I die?'

7

Mistress Eleanor Aston had possessed her soul in patience for nearly two hours. She had inspected the orange marmalade over which Alys had been labouring and had presented her own gift of quince jelly. She had debated the respective merits of green broadcloth or blue velvet as a new gown for Yuletide. She had remembered Nell's latest funny saying and told Alys about the cook having threatened to resign unless Piers left off swearing in the kitchen. But now her tongue ached with the need to say what she had really come to say.

William had left her and ridden off on his errand. Harry was over at Marie Regina and wouldn't be back until supper.

'And you must certainly stay for that,' Alys said. 'We are having goose done in the new way, and a raspberry sauce. If William calls for you in time he must join us, though I suspect his mind may be more on flirting than food. Do tell me when the wedding is to be.'

'Spring, I think. William never rushes. Alys.'

Mistress Aston paused, wondering how to begin, wondering too if it might not be best to forget what she had intended to say and leave well alone.

Alys set down the headress she was trimming and smiled across the sunlit room.

'Aunt, ever since you arrived you have been big with news,' she said. 'Now what ails you?'

'It's the wench with the bear,' Mistress Aston said clumsily.

Alys's expression didn't change, but she seemed to draw herself up slightly.

'You must make Harry turn her out!' her aunt said shrilly.

'The Dower Cottage is Harry's property,' Alys said quietly, 'and it is his business whom he chooses as tenant.'

'He makes a mock and a shame of you,' Mistress Aston burst out. 'And she is making a mock and a shame of him!'

'How so?'

'Yesterday, William was down by the river. The wench was there, on our side. Alys, she was stark naked! As bare as the day she was born. William was so startled that he couldn't think of a word to say, and then she flaunted herself at him. God knows what lewdness was in her mind. He shouted at her to begone

127

and she ran back into the water and among the trees. William was shocked to the soul!'

'I can imagine it,' Alys said dryly.

'He tackled Harry at once, warned him to get rid of the girl. Harry said he would deal with the matter, but it's my belief the strumpet is still there. Depend upon it, she will have coaxed him into believing it was a mistake.'

'Then what am I supposed to do?'

'You must put a stop to it,' Mistress Aston said firmly. 'You have been very patient, Alys, very forgiving, but there is a time to stand your ground and fight. Men are weak, silly creatures at the best of times, and it does no good to encourage them in their foolishness. It cannot be easy for you, knowing she is here, knowing that Harry visits her.'

'I put it out of my mind,' Alys said in a low voice. She looked down at her large hands and gave a little quivering sigh. Her eyes, when she glanced up again, were very clear. 'I never was pretty, aunt,' she said. 'Harry never loved me and I never loved him, though I have tried to be a good wife. But I don't have the right to stop him from seeking love.'

'Seeking it indeed!' Mistress Aston's plump little bosom heaved with indignation. 'He has planted the whore practically on your doorstep!'

'Down at the river's edge,' Alys corrected. 'I have never laid eyes on the wench, nor been near the Dower Cottage since it was locked. Harry has not altered in his manner to me — he was always kind. I do not think of her from one month to the next. She is an orphan, they say, and her only companion is the bear. If Harry finds pleasure in her, it takes nothing from me.'

'You are a good woman, Alys,' her aunt said lovingly.

'Only by training,' Alys said with a little flash of humour. 'When she first came I wanted to scratch her eyes, to burn the Dower Cottage over her head. I felt — threatened, aunt, but I trained myself to be silent, to ask no questions. And nothing changed in my life. My house is as it was. I even have more of Harry's company these days for he never goes to London now. And all this long while I have prayed so hard, and my prayers are answered.'

'You don't — ?' Mistress Aston broke off in astonishment.

'I think so,' Alys breathed, 'but I've said nothing yet, lest it be a mistake. But it will be born in the spring; in April I think. And this one will live. I felt so sick and listless the other times, but I am so well these days, so filled with energy. I think it will be a boy too. Harry always craved a boy.'

'He can wed my Nell!' Mistress Aston said. 'The two estates can be joined together. She is only a little older than he will be. Oh, Alys, our families will be joined, for that was always my wish. Sir Harry and Lady Eleanor Falcon!'

'Robert,' Alys said. 'This business of naming sons after fathers only leads to confusion. Robert is a strong, plain name. It was always a favourite of mine.'

'Of mine too,' her aunt said promptly. Then her face grew troubled again. 'If this is certain,' she said with a new fear in her voice, 'then you must make Harry get rid of the wench with all speed.'

'She will cease to matter to him when our son is born,' Alys said.

'But he must be born safely. Alys, dear, there is something I didn't say.' She leaned forward, her voice dropping. 'The girl has — a mark on her; a purple mark like a crescent moon. When I was a child there was a woman in the next village with a mark like that; on her neck. Some boys mocked at her one day and threw stones, and a month later the plague came to our village and two of the boys died of it.'

'I haven't harmed the girl,' Alys said instantly.

'But she would have no cause to love any child of yours,' Mistress Aston said. 'She might overlook it, or wish harm to your womb. Marks like that are signs of the devil. The devil's kiss, my mother used to say.'

'It's nonsense,' Alys said robustly. 'It's nonsense, aunt. Why, I have a mole myself, on my shoulder, and I don't go around overlooking people.'

'You don't strip naked and expose yourself to strange men either!'

'Oh, Aunt Eleanor!'

Alys rose impatiently, her skirts rustling as she crossed to the window. The lattice was open and the elusive scent of honeysuckle drifted to her nostrils. Beyond the window the walled courtyard drowsed in the sunshine. It was safe and warm and beautiful, with no place in it for the darkness of ancient belief. Yet she felt chilled suddenly, as if an animal had stepped lightly on her grave.

With her back to the room, she said, 'I think this is a great to-do about nothing, but I'll speak to Harry. Not tonight, else he'll guess we've been discussing it, but I will speak to him. If a husband could be found — but I'll think of something, and

131

you are not to mention the babe to anyone yet. I wish to tell Harry myself when I'm certain.'

'Not one word,' Mistress Aston said promptly. Then she said again, 'You're a good woman, Alys.'

'I try to be,' Alys replied, and her face was placid as if she had schooled it to conceal uneasiness and fear.

They heard Harry returning soon afterwards and then William arrived, and Mistress Aston was persuaded to risk the drive home in the dark and sit down to enjoy the goose, borne in triumphantly under its covering of flaky pastry.

If there was a certain constraint between the two men, it mellowed perceptibly under the influence of good food and spiced malmsey. Alys talked a little more than usual, teasing her cousin to name his wedding day, seeing that her aunt was well provided with the sweetmeats she loved, listening eagerly as Harry described for the tenth time the merits of a young bull he had just acquired.

As darkness stole over the house and the candles were lit, Alys looked down the length of the trestle table to where the maids were sucking the goodness out of the last of the goose bones. At her side Harry sank his excellent teeth into a crisp apple. Mistress

Aston had wiped the sugar from her fingers and moved away, to strum gently on the lute that resisted her niece's ungifted touch. The music stole through the great hall, soft as the candlelight.

She bowed her head, moving her lips silently.

Dear Lord, let it all remain like this, safe and warm and sweet. Let my son be born safely and the wench leave in peace. Help me to hold what I have.

A spatter of rain blew against the casement and was followed by a jagged white flash.

'God's death!' Mistress Aston dropped the lute and shrieked. 'What was that?'

'The beginning of a summer storm,' William said calmly.

'A storm! We must leave at once! Harry, where did I put my cloak?'

'You had better wait until it passes or bed down here for the night,' Harry suggested.

'We cannot. Nell is terrified of thunder, and Maggie will not be able to quieten her. Surely we can get home before it's fully begun.'

'If I get your horses hitched now. John!'

Harry went through into the kitchen, the steward at his heels.

'Alys, it was a beautiful supper and you must tell me how the goose was done. Do bid your maids to fasten the shutters and cover the mirror. And that other matter — you will take heed of what I said. Oh dear, I cannot find anything.'

'Your cloak is here, aunt,' Alys said, amused. 'And here is your spectacle case, and your handkerchief, and do you want a pair of overshoes? I can lend you some.'

'No, no; Harry can lift me up to the seat. Can you spare John to lead us with a lantern?'

'No need, mother,' William said with a touch of impatience. 'The horses know the road blindfold and there is still plenty of light, but we will have to hurry if we are not to be stranded!'

Lightning flashed again as they hastened into the courtyard. From her seat in the cart, Mistress Aston peered through the increasing rain to call, 'Now go inside, Alys. You have to take particular care of yourself!'

The horses, restless under the approaching thunder, leapt forward at a light touch of William's whip, their hooves slipping over the damp cobbles.

'We ought to have made them stay,' Alys fretted as they stepped back within the shelter of the screened porch.

'They would have spent the entire night worrying about Nell,' Harry grinned. 'I never met a woman who fusses and chatters as much as your aunt does.'

Mistress Aston was still chattering as they bowled down the main road towards the bridge.

' — must take the greatest care of herself, for though I promised not to breathe a word of it I think we can all hope for a very happy event in the spring. If it is a boy then Nell may become mistress of *Kingsmead* one day, and of course if you and Mistress Stone — '

She screamed as a flash of lightning forked down, and the horses, panicked by the blinding light, and loosed for an instant from the tightness of the reins as William half turned his head to answer his mother, broke into a frantic gallop.

'William! We shall be overturned!' Mistress Aston screeched and lurched against him, clutching at his wet cloak.

The bridge loomed up through the driving rain and something black and squat moved in the road. Somewhere in the wind a girl's voice rang out.

'Mott! Mott!'

The bear, paralysed with fear, shambled towards the well-known voice just as William Aston tried desperately to swerve and another sheet of lightning cracked open the sky. Cart and horses were torn apart as they crashed into muscle and bone and black fur, and above the screams of the dying bear came Mistress Aston's last, terrified cry as she was flung over the low parapet into the river below.

An hour later, Harry and Alys sat, numb with shock, in the parlour and made a pretence of drinking the hot tisane, a weeping servant had prepared. The two bodies, carried back to *Kingsmead*, lay on pallets in the solar — William's face crushed to a bloody pulp between wheels and hooves, Mistress Aston's neck as limp as the embroidery silks in her niece's unfinished tapestry.

The wheelwright, who stood before them nervously gulping his drink, seemed unable to stop talking.

'Only this afternoon did I see them, driving along pretty as you please. 'We're off to *Kingsmead* to see my niece,' calls Mistress Aston. Such a friendly soul she was! Always ready with a kind word and a smile! And her waving her hand as they went past. And then the storm blew up so sudden like, and I ran out to see my brood mare for fear the noise frighted her, and there be the cart and one horse going hell-for-leather across the field, and Master Aston under the cart and that great bear lying across him. And no trace of the poor lady until we brought flares and found her below, half in, half out of the water. Parson said we'd best bring them here.'

'You did right,' Harry said heavily. 'Has somebody gone up to Aston Manor?'

'Parson went, sir, and my good wife went with him, to see if there was anything needed to be done.'

'You'd best get home yourself then. Your clothes are wringing. I'll be over to the manor myself in the morning. There'll have to be an inquest, but it's obvious what's happened.'

'I never did think,' the man said, putting down his tankard, 'that such a thing could ever happen. 'We're going over to *Kingsmead* to see my niece,' she said, and her never guessing, poor lady, that God was waiting to strike them down before they ever got home again.

'I'll have to ride to Maidstone to see Mistress Stone,' Harry said miserably. 'And Roger will have to be told. You write a fairer hand than I do. Best for you to break the news. Alys?'

He had risen to close the door after the departing wheelwright and frowned anxiously, for his wife sat, tearless and pale, only her eyes moving in her heavy face.

'It was not God,' she said.

'What? What did you say?'

'God. It was not God who struck them down. It was the bear. They ran into the bear.'

'My Lord, I forgot Mott!' He struck his forehead with a clenched fist. 'She will be frantic when she hears, if she doesn't know already! She dotes on that animal.'

'She?'

'Margred,' he said, discretion lost in a burst of nervous reaction. 'I must go to her at once; at once!'

'You must make her go,' Alys said in the same tight voice. 'You must make her go away.'

'Go?' Harry looked at her in surprise. 'Go where?'

'Anywhere, back to her own country, back to the devil from whom she sprang! She's the devil's child, Harry. I wouldn't listen to Aunt Eleanor when she warned me — '

'Warned you of what? In God's name, what are you babbling about?'

'The wench you set in the Dower Cottage, Aunt Eleanor warned me that she bore the devil's kiss and would do us harm. I wouldn't heed, and now my aunt and my cousin are dead.'

'And so is Mott! Would she wish harm to a creature she loved?' he asked impatiently.

'She used the bear as an instrument,' Alys said stubbornly.

'Mott probably slipped his chain and was confused by the storm,' Harry said, pulling on his cloak.

'You're not going to her now? Not with blood on her hands?'

'I'll be less than an hour,' he said. 'Just make certain she's safe indoors and then be back.'

'I'll not have her here any longer,' Alys said loudly. 'I've kept silent for too long, but I'll speak out now. I want her gone from my land.'

'My land!' Harry said sharply, his temper beginning to rise. 'My land and my father's before me. You may do as you please in the house, for that is a wife's province, but I'll choose my own tenants and you'll not meddle!'

'The wench is evil! My aunt and cousin — '

'Are dead! I know. And you have seized upon their deaths as an excuse to vent your own jealousy. I had not thought you to be so spiteful.'

'You're blind,' Alys cried, her voice high and harsh, patches of colour staining her white cheeks. 'The wench has enchanted you, drawn you into her net. Harry, listen to me! Before God, it is not jealousy or

139

spite. I fear for us; I fear for us all if you let her stay. She may overlook the child.'

'Nell?'

'Not Nell. *Our* child!' Her voice broke and she faced him trembling. 'I had not meant to tell you until it was certain, but in my own mind I am certain now. I am with child again, Harry, and I want this one to live.'

So that was it! His anger which had sprung partly from guilt drained into what he imagined was understanding. Women were notoriously hysterical when they had quickened. He could not recall seeing Alys in such a state during her previous pregnancies. She had even accepted the deaths of the babes with resignation. But she was past thirty and this was probably her last chance to be a mother. And then she had been fond of Mistress Aston and of William.

'A child?' The full import of her words sank into him. 'After all these years, can you be sure?'

'He will be born in the spring,' she said. 'I don't want any harm to come to him. It will be a son, Harry. I've prayed so long and so hard and never really lost hope.'

'Then you must take care of yourself,' he said, awkwardly patting her shoulder.

Her eyes, swollen with fatigue, were colourless, her body already thick. In a month or two it would be heavy and clumsy and she would retch at the smell of meat. No doubt she would feed the child herself for as long as she possibly could, and by the most modest calculation it would be at least two years before he could seek her bed again.

There was always London, of course, but a man past thirty lost the relish for dashing up and down. He needed a mistress who was always there, waiting for him alone.

'We'll talk later,' he said. 'The storm is dying away now, I'll be no more than an hour or two.'

'Promise me you'll get rid of her. Promise!'

'Alys, be reasonable,' he said wearily. 'We pride ourselves on being good Christians. Now is it good Christian practice to turn a poor orphan out of doors on the very night she loses her pet? You would speak scornfully of anyone who attempted such a deed.'

'It is a Christian's duty to resist evil,' she interrupted. 'You must drive her away!'

'I'll not take orders from a woman,' he said, flushing. 'You're overwrought now, and don't know what you're saying. Let me alone to do what I think best.'

'You'll let her stay,' she said flatly, and her face was hard.

'I'll not pander to your whims,' he retorted. 'Go to bed, Alys, and don't wait up for me. Matters will seem different in the morning.'

'Aunt Eleanor and Cousin William will still be dead,' Alys said.

Her words echoed uncomfortably in his mind as he rode down the drive. The rain had eased and only an occasional murmur of thunder reminded him of the abating storm; but the trees dripped moisture and the road gleamed under an emerging moon.

William had seen Margred naked and frightened her with his threats, and now William was dead. Those were two facts, and Alys obviously thought they were related. And that meant that somehow or other Mistress Aston had found out about the unfortunate episode and told her niece. And Mistress Aston was dead too.

I grow womanish, he told himself, and jerked the reins as he guided the horse to the narrow bridle path which led to the Dower Cottage. He averted his eyes from the bridge though he could hear the river, swollen since the downpour, rushing beneath it.

Margred was standing under a tree, a spade in her hand, Her kirtle was plastered to her shape, her slippers thick with mud, her hair twining in black snakes around her face.

'Mott is dead,' she told him, her hand reaching up to the bridle. 'Mott is dead, Harry. I dug his grave myself and dragged him into it. He slipped his chain just before the rain began, and I didn't fret at first for he never strays far. But then the thunder and lightning came, and I called and called. He was on the bridge, Harry, and he must have heard my voice, because he started to cross, just as the horses came. I couldn't move. I couldn't make my legs move to go to him. Some men came running and took the others away, and pushed Mott into the ditch. I waited till they'd all gone and I buried him.'

'I came as soon as I could.'

He looked down at her, framing in his mind the words that would send her away.

'The rain came down the chimney,' she said, 'and the fire won't light again.'

The words jumbled, separated and were discarded. He reached down and lifted her before him on the saddle, cradling her as she wept quietly against his shoulder.

'I'll mend the fire,' he said, and clicked his tongue, signalling the horse to proceed.

In the greyness of dawn Alys sat sleepless by the window. John was downstairs keeping vigil for the dead, but she kept a vigil for the living, and for the unborn. Harry had not yet returned, but she had known in her heart that he would not. He loved the girl, or was bewitched by her, and not even knowledge of the coming child would cause him to give her up.

He won't listen to me, she thought. He thinks me full of fancies, but I am not a fanciful woman, nor a jealous one. I fear for the child, for my son.

If Roger were there — but she had no right to involve him. He was Harry's friend too, and he would have troubles enough of his own, with the manor to keep up and small Nell to rear.

There was only one thing to be done, but it meant bribing one of the Aston servants to go to London with two letters, instead of the one she must write to Roger. Never in her life had she been treacherous or underhanded, but now she would have to hope that God could see into her heart and understand.

Quickly, before she could change her mind, she went to the writing desk where quills, ink, sand, paper and seals were kept. Seating herself, she began to write, the letters a trifle larger than usual.

> 'Kingsmead,','
> Marie Regina,
> Kent.
> August, 1593.

Most Gracious Majesty,

Knowing my own unworthiness and Your Grace's state, it is with great fear that I take my pen in my hand, but knowing too of Your Majesty's great love for her people, I do beg and entreat Your Grace to persuade my husband and bedfellow to put from our estate the woman whom he keeps here, and to return to his wife who, at this time of writing, awaits the birth of a child.'

Steadily, as the first fingers of sunshine reddened the pale sky, Alys's quill moved over the paper.

8

'But why should the Queen wish to see you?' Margred had asked.

'How can I tell?' Harry shrugged his shoulders in bewilderment. 'Perhaps she recalled my face and wonders why I have ceased to attend at court.'

'Perhaps she will make you an Earl,' Margred breathed.

'I doubt it. Her Grace is not in the habit of advancing knights to earls,' Harry said dryly. 'But she chooses a bad time to send for me. With the babe due at any day — '

He paused, aware that mention of the birth annoyed her. When he had first told her about it her face had gone cold and still.

'I never realised that you still went to her bed,' she said quietly. Then she had given him a wry little smile and said, 'So you will have an heir. I wish you joy of him.'

She was always making odd, double-edged little remarks like that, he thought uncomfortably. She had grown thinner and sharper since Mott had been killed, but her fascination was as great as ever for him. Twice and sometimes thrice weekly he rode over to the Dower Cottage and she was always waiting for him, waiting for her hair to be unbound and her kirtle unlaced, and the subtle excitements of her body to be revealed.

Compared with her, Alys was gross, clay instead of silver, unleavened bread instead of honey wine. Thank the Lord she had got over her fit of hysteria and ceased to nag that he should send Margred away. The girl was never mentioned between them, and the deaths of Mistress Aston and William Aston were fading into an old grief. Roger had come back and settled down to administer his niece's estate, in which task he was succeeding better than anybody had expected. He frequently brought Nell over to spend the day at *Kingsmead*, and Alys had begun to teach the little girl her letters.

Life, Harry thought, had a way of sorting itself out. The winter had been rainy rather than snowbound and the spring was glorious. Part of him was pleased at the summons to Court, for there had been a time when he had waited long hours in the draughty corridors hoping to be noticed. Perhaps he had become a trifle dull, he thought, tied to *Kingsmead* and the farmland. It would do him good to travel to the city again.

Alys had seemed downcast and subdued

when he showed her the crested parchment. 'I am directed by Her Majesty to bid you, Sir Harry Falcon Esquire of *Kingsmead* in Marie Regina in the county of Kent to attend Her Grace at the Palace of Whitehall — '

'I cannot imagine why you are summoned,' she had said indifferently, and gone back to the hemming of baby clothes.

It had been infinitely more satisfying to show Margred the letter, to watch her vivid little face light up.

'Depend upon it! Essex is out of favour and she will raise you to his honours!'

She was only teasing him, he knew, but Alys never teased or pouted or sang in a sweet, husky voice as she arranged branches in a tall jar. Alys moved slowly, her keys jangling at her side, her hands clasped over her bulging stomach or sat for hours trimming shawls with lace.

Well, he had left them both, and was riding towards London, with John a few paces behind him, and a pouch of gold sewn within his doublet. Overhead the sky was a clear blue, fleeced with white clouds, and primroses starred the hedgerows.

He took lodgings near the Palace and spent a day in strolling about the waterfront, watching the sleek, black swans, keeping an eye open for acquaintances. He saw nobody he knew, but it amused him to observe the fashions. He must remember to tell Alys that farthingales were bigger and more unwieldy than ever, and that many ladies were wearing tiny hats, clamped to the sides of their heads in some mysterious manner, and ornamented with long, curling plumes.

Harry himself had dressed very carefully for the audience, changing his russet travelling suit for purple doublet and breeches with bronze hose and shoes and a short purple cloak faced with dull gold. He had recently grown a small, pointed beard which he considered, rightly, was flattering.

As he made his way up the stairs, past the Shield Gallery, however, he was conscious that his ruff was a small one, his tall purple hat a year or two out of fashion, and the earring in his right ear quartz and not diamond.

'You must take a gift to the Queen,' Margred had said. 'I've heard she is very fond of presents.'

He had been at a loss until, passing a silversmith's he had noticed a set of spoons, their handles carved into swans' heads. They had been much more expensive than he had expected, but now reposed in a small, flat case within his pouch.

The corridor was packed as usual, the

double doors at its further end closed and guarded. Several gentlemen were attempting to present petitions and letters of introduction to a harassed clerk who stood at a high desk, taking names and trying to explain that they must wait their turn.

There was a brief lull as heads turned to watch an old gentleman clad soberly in black limp the length of the corridor and be admitted without question through the high, gilded doors. Cecil, Lord Burleigh, High Treasurer of England, Premier Counsellor to the Queen's Majesty, gazed neither to right nor left as he went, but his heavy-lidded eyes had taken in faces to which his retentive brain was now putting names.

Within the doors he stopped for an instant, wriggling his toe cautiously inside its padded slipper. His gout was troubling him again, but it was of no use to ask for leave of absence from Court. Even had it been granted it would have been unwise to go, with reports every day of fresh landings by the Jesuits and a plot to poison her Grace nipped in the bud scarcely three months since. And that young fool, Essex, swaggering like a peacock and openly quarrelling with Raleigh. Sometimes he was heartily sick of the lot of them and longed for the peace and quiet of his country estate. but the Queen would not hear of his retirement.

Her Grace was seated in a small room beyond the Audience Chamber, with two women of the bedchamber and four maids of honour seated around her on low stools. The two older ladies wore black, the girls white, and in their centre the figure of the Queen rose like the vivid calyx of an unknown flower.

Her dress was of pale fawn, its pointed bodice and long, puffed sleeves sewn with narrow bands of peach ribbon in a lattice pattern. In each pane of material was set a crystal eye, lidded in gold, and the narrow pleats of the gigantic skirt were held down by rows of similar eyes.

A ruff of golden gauze spread its fan behind the high-curled wig of dark auburn, matching the hanging oversleeves which fell from the round puffs of pink velvet at each shoulder. Ornaments of topaz and pearl set in gold decorated the wig and filled in the shallow square of the neckline.

It is incredible, Burleigh thought. She is close on sixty and yet she eclipses us all.

The Queen, hearing his step, looked up from the pink feather fan in her shapely hands and gave her chief minister a warm smile tinged with disappointment. She had hoped Essex might have arrived.

'Have you good tidings for me?' she enquired, raising her voice out of consideration for Burleigh's deafness and flapping away her attendants.

'A request for monopolies,' he answered wryly.

'Let them wait! Every fool claims a monopoly these days. And sit down, do! It irritates me to have you hovering there.'

Not for worlds would she have acknowledged his stiff joints and aching back. To do that would have been to remember that he was past seventy, and she scarcely twelve years his junior.

'Are your grandchildren well?' She envied him those high-spirited youngsters.

'I see little of them Your Grace,' he hinted.

'Tush, tush! they will do better without your constant fussing. Have you word from Cadiz? Essex went off in a sulk because I would not give him leave to go there. He would venture all for me, foolish boy!'

'Your Grace shows wisdom in keeping him at Court.'

'Why, where else should the jester be but where the Queen is?' she asked, her mood swinging downwards, faint lines of discontent etching themselves on the thickly painted surface of her skin.

'Your Grace needs distraction,' Burleigh said frankly.

'I have too much of it,' she answered gloomily. 'If it is not Bacon angling for the Solicitor Generalship, it is Essex begging me to renew the lease on his monopoly of sweet wines; or Anne Russell asking me to allow her to marry her sweetheart! And so many papers to read, letters to write — I carry this kingdom upon my back.'

'The world marvels at Your Grace's energies.'

'And never stops making demands upon me. That passage yonder is choked with them! Men who consider they have been swindled out of an inheritance, women who swear husbands — that reminds me!'

She snapped shut her fan and turned to a litter of papers on a small table by her side. Extracting one, she held it out to her minister.

'Some woman in Kent,' she told him, 'begs me to anchor her husband closer to her! The man apparently keeps his mistress upon his estate, and divides his time between the two of them. The letter has lain for months, pending reply, but I sent for the husband to come to Court.'

'Sir Harry Falcon? I think I passed him as I came in.' Burleigh gave back the letter.

'He has not been in the city for some time, but I noticed him today.'

'Is he of interest?'

'None at all, Your Grace. A country squire, if my memory serves me right. Tall, well-set.'

'Handsome?'

'Aye, madam. At all events it is obvious from the letter that two ladies consider him so.'

'And he is from Kent?' Her eyes began to dance. 'Watch me how I mend a marriage and set Essex down a notch,' she said mischievously. 'Go and bid the clerk tell Sir Harry Falcon to enter.'

Harry, having presented his letter, had taken his place on a carved bench and was preparing for a long wait. The summons in itself was no guarantee that he would receive audience that day, that week, or even that month. His name, called loudly, sounded odd as if it belonged to somebody else.

Only when it was called a second time, with a distinct note of impatience, did he spring up, conscious of heads and eyes turning towards him as he hurried up towards the doors. They were open now and a gentleman with a gold-topped stick stood there, beckoning him forward.

An expanse of mosaic floor, walls hung

with a bewilderment of tapestries, a chair cushioned in purple and there, enthroned like some goddess out of an ancient tale, a lady who was covered with sparkling eyes, each crystal orb seeming to fix itself upon him.

'Sir Harry Falcon, Your Grace.'

The man banged his staff upon the floor and backed away.

The glittering figure stared down at the kneeling man. In one swift glance she had summed up his outward qualities and made a shrewd guess as to his inner ones. Handsome and healthy, if slightly stupid. His suit was obviously new and not in the latest fashion.

'Do rise, Sir Harry,' she said, her voice louder than he had expected. 'It is some time since you came to our Court.'

'I did not know Your Grace had heard of me,' Harry stammered.

'Oh, we know all who visit here,' she said lightly.

'Your Grace, I have a small gift, if you would be so gracious — '

The Queen's eyes brightened as he drew out a flat package.

'For me? How very kind of you, sir.'

Her long fingers reached out to take the package, tearing eagerly at the wrappings like a child deprived of birthday presents.

'Silver spoons! And beautifully chased!

You have excellent taste.'

Her smile displayed rotting teeth, but it was wide and unforced. Elizabeth Tudor was always genuinely delighted to receive a gift.

'Look, my lord, are they not splendid?'

'Very elegant indeed.' Burleigh, who had stood unnoticed, came forward to take the velvet lined box. 'Sir Harry is to be congratulated on his choice.'

'And now tell me, Sir Harry,' The Queen leaned forward slightly. 'Is your good wife delivered of her child yet?'

'Not — not for a few days.' ' Harry gazed at her in stupefaction.

The Queen laughed lightly. 'You are surprised that I know of it?' she asked. 'Why do you think I wear eyes upon my gown unless it be to make clear that nothing happens in my realm of which I am ignorant? And I take great pleasure in hearing about the birth of children. Perhaps I may be induced to stand gossip to yours.'

'My wife would — we both would consider it a tremendous honour,' Harry said.

'Make a note of it, Burleigh.' Her Grace nodded affably and turned again to Harry. 'Your land is in Kent, is it not? Is it grazing pasture or orchard?'

'Both, Your Grace. I think it wiser not to put all my profits into one crop.'

'My own policy exactly! Do you sell your produce?'

'Some wheat, some cattle, some crab apples — we send those over to Maidstone. We pay full customs dues,' he added hastily.

'Do you brew cider?'

'Only for our own use, madam. The Earl of Essex holds the monopolies on sweet wines.'

'Cider is not a sweet wine.'

'Your Grace, I believe it is classed as such for the purpose of customs dues,' Burleigh interposed.

'Is it so? I'll not have it so!' She banged her fist on the arm of her chair. 'Burleigh, take note that I am granting a monopoly on all the cider brewed in — where was the place? — Marie Regina; am granting it to Sir Harry Falcon for the duration of my reign.'

'Your Grace, ought you not to consider?' Burleigh asked in a low voice. 'The question of monopolies is a delicate one at this moment.'

'I cannot imagine the granting of a limited monopoly within a specified area will upset the balance of the economy,' the Queen said dryly. 'It may, of course, upset the Earl of Essex, but he shall learn it is not wise to sulk for too long.'

'It will set a precedent.'

'We Tudors are accustomed to set precedents,' she answered. 'What report tells me of Sir Harry is good, save in one respect and that can be remedied, shall be remedied before I set my hand to the patent.'

'Your Grace?'

He stared at her uneasily for her smile, her affable tone had vanished, and her eyes and lips were tight and pale.

'It has come to our ears,' she said, 'that you have a mistress, Sir Harry; that you keep a strumpet upon your estate. Adultery is a grave sin, my friend. I would not have it upon my conscience that I granted a favour to a man who would deceive his wife, bring shame upon his heirs with light and wanton conduct.'

So it was true what they said of her. The Queen had her spies in every corner of the kingdom. Cold sweat broke out at the back of his neck and every eye on Her Grace's dress accused him.

'The woman shall go,' he said hoarsely.

'And you must plant more cider apples,' she said. 'There is no reason why the men of Somerset should have all the trade. You are excused, Sir Harry. Send word to me when the child is born and I will see the patent reaches you. As to the other matter, we shall hear no more ill reports, I trust?'

'You have my word, madam,'

She was extending a shapely hand for him to kiss, and he was bowing and moving backwards towards the corridor again, where one or two of those who had previously ignored him now waited to shake his hand and invite him to dice or a cock-fight.

He heard them only vaguely, his mind in a whirl. He had been received in audience by the Queen who, for some mysterious reason, known only to herself, had evidently set her spies to enquire into his circumstances. And she had granted him the monopoly on the local cider and promised to be godmother to his child! Alys would be pleased in that.

The monopoly would bring little revenue, and Elizabeth Tudor had no doubt stood gossip to hundreds of infants, but the honour would give him a new standing in the neighbourhood. Yes, Alys would be pleased. It was strange how, without loving her, the thought of her delight should pleasure him. He could dig up the west meadow and plant more trees there, invest in a decent press.

Margred would have to leave. The thought dropped like a stone into the pool of his contentment and spread ripples in his mind. Margred would have to leave, for now she stood in the way of his advancement. Her pointed face, framed in black hair, her slender shape and husky laughter, passed before him like a dream.

It was, he thought, a sweet, wild dream that had enriched his life, but the day had come for him to awake. It would hurt him cruelly to make her leave. From now on there would always be something missing from his existence, and yet a part of him acknowledged a kind of shamed relief. Matters had never been exactly the same between them since William had caught her naked on Aston land.

Even as he thought that the old desire caught in his throat. No other wench had held his heart for so long, and, though he could plan sensibly when he was away from her, he knew his own nature well enough to be sure that once he was in her company all his good resolutions would fly out of the window. He resolved not to see her again, not to ride out on his estate until she was gone. And he would not, could not, tell her personally that she must leave. He would never be able to bring himself to do it.

Hailing a boat, he decided he would spend an hour or two in Cheapside. Alys would be pleased if he took her a present. From now onwards Sir Harry Falcon intended to be a model husband.

Within her apartment at Whitehall the Queen faced her chief minister with a triumphant gleam in her eye.

'Am I not wise?' she demanded.

'A veritable Solomon, Your Grace,' Burleigh agreed.

'Essex will be furious when he hears some of his profits are being whittled away,' she said with satisfaction. 'Oh, not so many, I agree, but it is the principle of the matter. He will realise that what I can grant I can also take away, nibble away like a mouse.'

'Your Grace is hardly that,' Burleigh objected.

'What am I then?' she asked, avid for flattery. 'A lioness, a wise snake, a peacock? What am I?'

'An exasperating, fascinating woman,' he said slowly.

'And you are the only man from whom I would permit such impudence!' she exclaimed. 'But then you are the only man I know who was never in love with me. Leicester, Hatton, Raleigh, Blount, Heneage, not to mention every monarch in Christendom! They all desired me. But you never did, and yet perhaps you serve me more faithfully than any.'

'I have spent my life in your service.'

'And been well rewarded for it,' she flashed. 'They say you are one of the richest men in the land. Does it never trouble you that with one snap of my fingers I could take it all away from you?'

'No, Your Grace.'

'How so? Do you fancy yourself so high that you cannot be cast down?'

'Your Grace is too high to stoop so low!'

'God love you for that!' she cried in delight. 'You know I think you must be a little in love with me, eh?'

'Not a whit, madam,' he answered calmly.

'Ah well!' She shrugged a jewelled shoulder. 'All the others are. Essex worships the ground I walk upon, and yet he is — somewhat younger than I am.'

More than thirty years, Burleigh calculated. Aloud he said, 'Love is not something that can be weighed and measured, Your Grace.'

'And Essex does love me.' For an instant she mused and then swung round in her chair. 'He loves me, but he must learn that I rule here. He demanded that I make Bacon Attorney-General, and sulks because I advanced Coke to that place. Now he demands that Bacon be given Coke's vacant position as if we were at a supper party and the Lord of Misrule ordered us to change seats!'

'Bacon is my sister's son,' Burleigh said cautiously, 'but I hesitate to press his claims on that account.'

'Hypocrite! you fear lest his ambition should cast your own boy into the shadow! Well, you need not fear, my friend. Your son's abilities have been noted and will be recognised. As for your nephew — let him wait a while. Essex may be his patron, but he cannot promise what is only mine to give. As for me, I am sick of wrangling! I shall move to Hampton Court for a few weeks; or perhaps to Windsor. I cannot decide which will amuse me more.'

'If Your Grace goes to one you will wish yourself at the other.'

'You know me very well! Oh, to have only one small estate! What bliss that would be!' she cried. 'Do you think that Kentish gentleman appreciates his good fortune? He was comely, was he not, but not over-burdened with intelligence? Did you note how he gaped at me?'

'He was dazzled, as you intended him to be,' Burleigh smiled.

'For the rest of his life he will remember that a Queen smiled upon him,' she said happily. 'And he will never be certain who is watching him to see if he is keeping a mistress on the premises!'

'He will be the most faithful husband in the world, Your Grace.'

'And I have a feeling that his wife is a lumpish, virtuous woman. Certainly she writes with a very miserable hand.'

'Compared to Your Grace most women are lumpish.'

'Essex would have said 'all' where you say 'most'. But it's true. Even if I were not a monarch, men would still have desired me?'

Her voice lifted into a question and for a fraction of time her eyes were old and pleading.

'Your Grace, had you been set down in that Kentish village, Sir Harry Falcon would have left wife and mistress long ago.'

'Ah, yes, the mistress. I had forgotten her. You know, Burleigh, I could find it in me to pity the wench,' the Queen said thoughtfully. 'Perhaps she believes the knight loves her truly and would never send her from him. But he was quick to promise to make her go, and he is too honest not to keep that promise. Poor wench! to put her trust in a feeble man!'

'She will survive. Women of that class usually do,' Burleigh said easily. 'And there is nothing she can do about it, is there?'

'I suppose not.' Elizabeth cast him an oblique, fey look. 'So many little lives,' she said slowly, 'and I speak a sentence and they are all changed. But I never hear the end of the story, never learn what happens to those little people whose destinies I touch. Is it not strange, Burleigh?

9

'But this is a task you should perform yourself!'

Roger Aston set down his tankard and frowned across at his friend.

'I know, but I cannot. I still have a deep fondness for the wench. If I were to see her again the words would stick in my throat.'

She has great charm,' Roger agreed.

Unlike his brother, he had also recognised his own response — the half terrified lust that the girl's presence called up from the deepest recesses of his nature. It was an emotion that had nothing to do with the quiet, warm faithfulness of his love for Alys.

Thinking of her now he moved restlessly in his host's chair, saying, 'God's death, Harry, but this is a coil of your own making! You were mad to bring the girl here in the first place, and Alys is a saint to have endured it these three years. And now, with your wife in full labour above us, you still hesitate to do what will advance your family and clear your own conscience!'

'Margred will be hurt!'

'She is bound to be hurt, however the news

is given,' Roger said.

Worry over Alys was making him short-tempered, but then he had risen early, at John's summons, and ridden over to find *Kingsmead* full of women and Harry, newly returned from London, with an astonishing request.

'She would receive it better from you,' Harry insisted. 'It must be a clean break, Roger — no splinters of affection left to fester. And it must be done quickly, else I stand to lose the monopoly. How could I possibly ride out today, with Alys giving birth to my child? And if I rode out tomorrow, the words would never come. But if you were to go — '

'And say what?'

'That she must go. But put it kindly. Tell her — that after long reflection I have decided to put duty before inclination. Thank her for the happiness she has given me and — oh, Lord! you know the kind of thing that has to be said!'

'And will you turn her off with nothing?'

'Do you think me completely ungenerous?' Harry demanded indignantly. 'I shall give her a purse of fifty guineas and send her Coral — '

'She's your most valuable filly!'

'And therefore worthy for Margred to ride.

167

Tell her too she may keep the dresses she altered for herself.'

'What of the Dower Cottage? Will you put another tenant in there?'

'Later, perhaps,' A twinge of pain distorted his countenance. 'It would be better if it were locked and left for a while.'

'And the girl is to go back to her own land, I suppose?'

Roger was unable to prevent a certain dryness from creeping into his voice.

'She told me once that her grandfather had a little farm somewhere in the north. With that and fifty guineas — she may make a good marriage,' Harry said.

Roger gave a small, uncomprehending shake of the head. Himself more subtle than his friend, he could not understand Harry's apparently casual attitude. Against his will a feeling of sympathy for the girl welled up in him. He had seen her once or twice since his return, but she had merely bowed her head modestly and hurried past.

It was difficult to imagine her, passionate and sensual, lying in Harry's arms. She kept herself to herself, they said in the village, but she went to church every Sunday, and when folk were sick she sometimes offered them remedies of her own devising.

'If I see her again,' Harry said, with a note

of desperation belying his calm. 'I will never be able to send her away. Do this for me, Roger.'

'Very well.'

But it was for Alys he would do it, to bring her peace of mind. He had seen her moving slowly about the house, carrying the burden of her pregnancy before her, pressing her lips together if by any chance the Dower Cottage was mentioned.

In his eyes she would always be the eager, clumsy young girl who had wept so bitterly when their marriage had been forbidden. That Harry should have brought his mistress to *Kingsmead* was an insult to Alys that Roger resented on her behalf.

'What takes them so long upstairs?' Harry muttered. 'It's close on four hours since her first pang.'

'Births take time,' Roger said.

'And Alys is no longer young.' Harry took a purse from his pouch and tossed it to his friend. 'When the child is born, take the purse and the mare and tell the wench to go,' he said, and Roger's sympathy veered again as he perceived that Harry was more moved by the decision he had made than his pride could allow him to admit.

A sudden flurry of rustling skirts crossed the hall, and Cook appeared, breathless, a ladle in one hand and her coif askew.

'It's here and the mistress is well and it's a boy, sir, a fine boy fat as a pudding and Maggie's gone all of a tremble, sir!'

'A boy? Roger, I have a son!' Harry's face flushed with excitement.

'And my cousin is well?' Roger addressed himself to Cook.

'Sitting up when I peeped round the door and Mistress Agatha says she's borne it very well, and can I tell John to open the malmsey?'

'Tell him to open the best we have and to send word to the village that every man, woman and child is to have a drink at my expense. Can I go up?'

He was already out of the door taking the stairs two at a time. From above floated the wails of a very young infant.

'Give Alys my love and tell that I'll bring Nell over to see the babe in a few days,' Roger called.

Cook had departed kitchenwards, presumably to tell John to open the malmsey, and Roger was alone.

'A healthy boy,' he said aloud in satisfaction.

Alys had said they would name the child Robert and Harry had said that the Queen herself had promised to stand gossip at his baptism. It might have been his own child who wailed upstairs if he and Alys had been allowed to follow their hearts. Well, at least he had Nell, who was a sweet, biddable little girl. And Alys had her son, and a husband who had been frightened into faithfulness.

And I will see that she has peace of mind, Roger thought, taking the purse out for a brief glance before he went through to the stables.

It was obvious from the excited chatter in the yard that nobody was going to do any work that day, but John did emerge from the dairy as Roger led out the mare.

'Sir Harry said I was to take her,' he began, and the steward nodded.

'The master told me about the wench deciding to go back to her own people,' he said. 'Better all round if she goes, Master Aston. Kinder to her in the long run to be with her own folk.'

'I'm sure you're right.' He wondered how much the steward knew or guessed.

'This is a proud day for us,' John said, helping him to his own mount. 'The old master would have been over the moon to have a grandson. You'll be wetting the baby's head with us?'

'More than once, when my business is done. I'll bring Nell over too.'

'To take a peek at her future bridegroom,' John said shrewdly.

'As to that, we must wait and see.'

But Roger was smiling as he rode off. Only four years between them and a mere river dividing the two estates. Worse things might happen than the marriage of Robert Falcon to Eleanor Aston.

Smoke was rising from the chimney of the Dower Cottage and a pile of freshly cut reeds lay at the front door. He paused in the clearing, feeling again the odd reluctance to enter which had assailed him on that first meeting, but the girl must have seen him from a window, for the door opened abruptly and she appeared on the threshold.

His first reaction was one of pleasure. He had forgotten how dainty she was and how enchanting her smile. Her gown was a simple one of grey wool over a small farthingale, its pleated yellow ruff crossing into a modest fichu that matched her wide cuffs. Her black hair was drawn back into a chignon of yellow silk, and her voice was sweetly polite.

'Master Aston, is it not? Please to come in, sir.'

As before the cottage sparkled, a fire burned on the hearth.

'It grows chilly here,' she said, following his gaze. 'Will you take some wine, sir?'

'Nothing, thank you.'

'Then, a chair at least.' She indicated the larger of the two.

'For a moment only.'

He sat down, absently rubbing the calf of his leg. Ever since he had given up the cloth trade and come back to Marie Regina his leg had ached intolerably. He hoped vaguely that it wasn't rheumatism.

'I come from *Kingsmead*,' he said abruptly.

Alarm rippled across her small face.

'Harry is back safe from London, isn't he?' she asked.

'Yes. Quite safe.'

'He took John with him this time anyway. He was summoned by the Queen herself,' she said proudly. 'I'm expecting him to ride over tonight and tell me all about it. I made jugged hare. It's one of his favourite dishes and only needs to be heated up. I've cooked it every day this week and had to finish it up myself.'

'You said you were expecting him.'

'I expect him every night of my life,' she said simply. 'But now he's back from London he's sure to be here tonight.'

He wished she would stop chattering so innocently; wished she were dressed as a loose woman should be dressed; wished she were not so small and young. Now he appreciated why Harry had shirked the task.

'I wish you would try some of my elder wine. It's very good,' she said, with the half proud, half anxious air of a child playing hostess.

'Lady Alys has borne a son,' he said flatly.

Something that was not childlike at all gleamed in her eyes, and it was gone so swiftly he thought he must have fancied it.

'Are they both well?' she asked politely.

'The boy is fine and lusty, and my cousin's ordeal was so short that I heard she was already sitting up when I left.'

'Then I will drink their healths by myself, if you won't join me.'

She crossed, swift and graceful, to the dresser and poured liquid from a tall, green jar into a tankard. Sipping it, her eyes went big and watchful above the rim.

'Is that why you came, Master Aston? To tell me about the child?'

He shook his head, hating his task, conscious all through his body of his throbbing leg.

'Harry has asked me to tell you that he — won't be coming,' he said.

'You mean he's delayed.'

'No. He won't be coming at all; and

he — he bids you begone, back to your own people.'

He had said it! At the last moment he had blurted it out crudely and cruelly. He had not meant to be cruel.

'You mistook the message,' she said gently. 'Harry would never send me away.'

'Mistress, you have already stayed three years too long,' Roger told her.

Margred set down her tankard carefully and folded her arms about herself as if she feared she might break.

'Harry and I are bound together for the rest of our lives,' she said.

'Alys is his wife, mother of his child.'

'I never harmed her, never tried to take her place.'

'He wants you to leave.'

'Then why doesn't he come here himself?' she demanded. 'Do you think me such a fool that I would leave on your word alone?'

'He sent his mare, Coral, to bear you on your journey,' Roger said. 'I did not steal the animal from his stable.'

'It couldn't be so! He loves me as I love him. He would never treat me thus!'

'He bade me tell you that you may take what dresses you wish, and this purse as well. There are fifty sovereigns in it.'

As he held out the purse he felt suddenly

shamed. Only whores were paid off in money, and this girl was no whore.

She took the purse in silence and laid it on the table without looking inside it. Her face was so colourless that it seemed to reflect the green leaves of a tree moving outside the window. Only her eyes blazed like topazes.

'He loves me,' she said, in a hard, cold, clear little voice. 'I vowed myself to him through all the days of my existence.'

'You're very young,' he said.

'And very true. Faithful to death and beyond,' she answered.

Her childish dignity ought to have been touching, but despite the fire he began to shiver.

'I didn't seek this errand,' he said swiftly, as if she had accused him.

'Why?' she asked. 'It is not because of the child, else he would have dismissed me months ago.'

'It was the Queen's wish.'

'The Queen? What has Her Grace to do with me?' Margred asked in astonishment.

'She evidently made enquiries into Harry's circumstances. At all events she has granted him the monopoly of all cider brewed in this district and has promised to stand gossip to the babe on condition — '

'That he puts me away? Is Tudor Bessie so moral then?'

'She offered him a choice,' Roger said unhappily.

'So I am sold, for a keg of cider,' she said quietly. 'And he did not even have the courage to tell me himself.'

Something was wrenching her apart inside, until she felt like screaming with the pain. But she stood motionless, schooling her face to indifference.

'Is there anything I can do?' Roger said. 'I offered you friendship once.'

'I need nothing.' She looked at him with bleak humour. 'I have a horse and a purse of fifty guineas and the dresses of a dead woman. Are those not riches enough?'

'Likely you'll wed,' he said encouragingly.

'No!' Her voice was sharp. 'No, I'll not wed!'

'That is your choice.'

He wished she would weep or lose her temper again and not stand, like a frozen creature, staring at him.

After a moment she said, in a dry, almost indifferent tone, 'When does he wish me to leave? Today, I suppose?'

'Would you like me to send one of my servants, to bear you company.'

'I found my own way out of Wales. I can

177

find my own way back,' she said.

'If you're sure — ' He stood up, his face filled with a mixture of embarrassed sympathy and a desire to be out of the place.

'Quite sure. I thank you.'

She had moved to the door and held it open, her bearing one of great dignity. Outside the horses stood patiently, their heads lowered to the sweet grass.

At that moment there was nothing he could think of to say or do which would help her. He was not even certain that she would welcome any offer of help or sympathy. It seemed to him that her hurt went too deep for that.

As he rode away he glanced back and saw her still standing at the door, her eyes wide and blank as if she were in some waking nightmare.

Margred stood there for a long time. She had the curious sensation of being somehow apart from herself, looking down from an immense height at the small figure in the grey dress. A fit of shuddering seized her, and the trees at which she was staring tilted and wavered.

A long, or a short time later, she became aware of her surroundings again. The mare was still cropping the grass, the sun made a pool of brightness in the green glade, a slight breeze had leapt up to ruffle the long trails of ivy that twined about the roots of the apple tree. Margred was cold, so cold that her fingers had a blue tinge as if she had died and begun to rot. It would have been easier to have died, she thought, and tensed herself against the returning anguish.

It was like nothing she had ever known, worse than the worst pain she had ever suffered. It was like the corrupting within her of all kindness, all hope, all love. She was sitting on the step, her head in her hands, a terrible sickness in her throat. After a while she leaned over and tried to vomit, but nothing came. The sickness was become a part of her, turning her heart to stone, her blood to ice.

She rose, as wearily as an old woman, and went indoors again. The fire had burned low, but sunlight gilded the rushes and the threads of gold in the tapestries shimmered as if the embroidered figures stirred at her coming.

She had mended the hangings herself and beaten the dust out of them. She had kept the house warm and dry, lovingly polishing the furniture, the cups and plates of pewter and silver-gilt. She had gathered herbs and roots from the surrounding woods, dried leaves and flowers for the remedies which she sometimes offered.

For three years the cottage had been her home and Harry her only visitor, and now it was ended with a few awkward, stumbling sentences from an embarrassed neighbour.

She began to pack the two saddlebags that lay in the corner, her hands moving briskly as if they were not part of her gigantic pain. Her few clothes — for she had not altered all the dresses — were rolled up in one bag, into the other went bags of dried herbs and spices.

Her hands, delving into the spice chest, touched the silk wrapped bundle of tallow figures. For an instant she hesitated. Should a miniature Harry and a miniature Alys join the four? But that had been a foolish, childish spite, which had not even worked very well. Mistress Aston and her son had died by accident; Roger Aston and his niece were still hale and hearty. As well make an image of Elizabeth Tudor and stick pins in that!

She tumbled the remaining spices back into the chest and banged down the lid. There was the remaining fire to be damped down, the windows to close, the door to lock. Everything would be left perfect, as an extra reproach to Harry if he came. She would have liked to leave the fifty guineas behind, but she had no money and a long journey lay ahead.

As she mounted the horse she cast a swift look into the undergrowth where Mott's grave was protected by a cairn of stones, and for an instant her eyes were misty and she longed to bury her head in the bear's warm, rough fur and sob out her heartache.

Then she struck Coral sharply on the flank and moved through the darkness of the wood into the fields and orchards beyond.

She had never been so close to the manor house before, though from the upper windows she could glimpse its tall chimneys. The land sloped imperceptibly down to the river and rose into Aston property on the other bank.

She rode without pleasure through the flower-starred meadows and bridal orchards, her heart settling like a stone into its cage of ice. Under the grey hood, her face was proud and sombre as if she were setting out on some savage crusade.

The gates of the courtyard were open and thick straw had been laid over the cobbles so that the newly-delivered mother could sleep in peace. The door of the big house was closed and there was no sign of life. Presumably the servants were all in the kitchen, drinking the health of the babe.

If Harry only knew how eagerly she had

waited for his return, how closely she had hugged her own news to herself. If she had told him before he left, everything might have been different. Harry was not cruel. He would not knowingly have turned her away.

Dismounting slowly she approached the door. If she could only speak to him, make him understand that she wanted nothing more than she had already asked . . .

'The master bids me tell you to begone!'

The voice broke into her fruitless dreaming, jerking her back into the reality of hatred. The man who stood with his hands on his hips wore a steward's livery. She had seen him often, engaged on business in the village. Harry had told her once that John knew more about the running of the estate than he did, but she had never exchanged a word with him till now.

'You may stand there all day, mistress, and the rest of the night too,' John said, 'But you'll not see him. Now be a sensible wench and mount up again, do!'

But she went on standing there, her head tilted towards the upper window. John, twisting his own neck, saw Harry at the lattice, a bundle held tightly and tenderly against his shoulder.

'Mistress, don't make trouble,' John said urgently. 'The master did wrong to bring you here, but he's mended the wrong now. He has a son and his wife is the best wife a man could have. Don't spoil it, mistress.'

Her eyes, blank and blazing in her white face, were fixed upon the window. On her wide mouth was a small, sweet, terrible smile. For a moment John faltered. He had never seen anyone smile quite in that manner before.

A low murmuring lilted from her lips. It was in no language that he knew, but it sounded like a prayer. He watched in baffled compassion as the liquid sounds flowed from that gently smiling mouth.

Margred herself had not known that she was so well-versed in the obscenities of her native tongue. Every lewd and loathsome epithet she had ever heard sprang from her, and the shaping of each word gave her a fierce and bitter delight.

She turned at last and led the mare across the courtyard again. John would have followed to close the gate, but a wind swept about the corners of the house, sending straw flying into his face and he was anxious suddenly to get back to the warmth of the kitchen and the comfort of the malmsey.

Beyond the gate Margred stopped and drew from her neck the leather pouch in which the dried and crumpled leaves she had picked from her mother's grave were stored. A few wrinkled brown seeds fell into her palm, and she looked down at them, remembering the queer brownish-red leaves veined with purple. She had seen nothing like them in any other place.

Kneeling at the base of the wall she scooped at the earth, dribbled the seeds into the hollow, and smoothed it over with the flat of her hand.

The words she whispered came into her head as if someone were dictating them.

'Grow, little vinegar tree! Grow tall and strong and overshadow the house of Falcon. Let them taste the bitterness of your leaves, in season and out of season, by night and by day, in sun and rain, in wind and snow. Let them bleed from your branches and tangle their hearts in your roots, until Margred comes as a bride to Harry Falcon of *Kingsmead*.'

The wind had dropped as if the world held its breath. In the stillness she mounted the horse and rode away without looking back.

1616

1916

10

It was high summer and Nell Aston had a new dress. It was, her Uncle Roger told her, the very latest fashion from London. He had been on one of his rare visits to the city the previous month and brought it back for her.

'Wear it to dazzle Robert,' he had urged, and she had smiled a little sadly, for Robert never noticed what she wore and seldom told her she was pretty, so that she constantly found her self looking in the mirror as if for reassurance.

What she saw was pleasing enough, for Nell had a fresh complexion, blue eyes and yellow hair that curled of its own accord. Her uncle told her she was a beauty, but she knew that wasn't true. Her ankles and waist were thick, her features ordinary, her lashes and brows so fair as to be almost invisible, her hands badly shaped.

But the dress, spread out across her bed, was certainly charming. Its orange silk was banded with cream ribbon at the high waist and low neck and brown oversleeves hung from the shoulder frills. That the colour was too bright with the yellow hair and that the ribbons drew attention to an over-ample bosom were facts of which she was happily unaware. Nell loved gay colours and shiny materials, and never related them to herself.

From her window she could look out across the fields towards the river threading its way under the bridge. On the other side of the river the acres of *Kingsmead* sloped up towards the manor house. In a month's time she would leave her uncle's house for the last time as a maid, and drive over the bridge and down the winding left hand street to the parish church to be married to Sir Robert Falcon.

When Nell thought of Robert, her heart bumped in her chest and she felt quivers of anticipation thrill along her nerves. In her mind he was all the knights in all the story books, all the heroes in all the poems she had ever read. The fact that he treated her with no more than a teasing affection made no difference to the picture she had in her head.

Robert was tall and broad-shouldered, his hair the colour of a hazel nut, his eyes a deep, warm blue. He took it completely for granted that she should worship him, for he had been surrounded by adulation since his birth. The old Queen herself had stood gossip at his baptism, not coming in person, of course, but sending a lady-in waiting as proxy and a handsome stirrup cup engraved with the baby's name and the date of his birth. The cup had pride of place on the huge dresser in the great hall at *Kingsmead*.

Nell knew *Kingsmead* as well as she knew her own home. The Lady Alys had practically reared her, teaching her to read and write and sew, patiently listening to her childish woes, sitting with her in the parlour while a fire sang on the hearth and her uncle and Robert's father stood in the yard, arguing the merits and demerits of a horse or a cow.

She had loved Lady Alys, loved the older woman's placidity and gentleness, her calm way of speaking, the tinkling of the keys at her waist. Alys had been so kind to her, so pleased when Robert wandered in to join them.

'We waited so many years before a son was granted to us,' she had confided. 'It was always our wish that the two families should be joined, and it will be the happiest day of my life when you and Robert are wed.'

Only once had Nell ever seen Alys less than her usual gentle self. The girl had ridden on her pony to the river one afternoon and wandered into the belt of trees that grew thickly down to the water's edge. In the midst of bramble-dark paths she had emerged into a small clearing and seen there a house, its panes encrusted with dust, its walls smothered in ivy. The door had been locked and she had seen nothing through the grimy windows save the outlines of a few pieces of furniture. She had been late for supper, but when she told Lady Alys of her discovery the other had flushed an ugly red and seized her by the arm.

'You must never go there again! Never! Never! The cottage is a bad place, Nell. You must never go there!'

Frightened, she had promised, and kept her promise, not ever mentioning the incident to Uncle Roger. Indeed she had pushed the matter deep down in her memory, so deeply that she had forgotten all about it, until the day of Lady Alys's funeral.

Alys had died in winter, of a chill caught while she was visiting the sick in Marie Regina, and she had been buried on a cold morning with ice so thick along the road that the horses had had cloths tied under their feet.

After the service Sir Harry Falcon had turned away from the grave and ridden slowly into the icicle hung wood, with a lost, bewildered look on his face. She had remembered the cottage then and wondered if he had gone there, and why.

After that she had divided her time between the two houses, trying to do what she believed Lady Alys would have wished in order to make the two men comfortable. It meant a great deal of hard work and sometimes she was so tired at the end of the day that she could hardly drag herself upstairs. Uncle Roger protested that he could perfectly well manage alone, but his rheumatism was so bad that there were days when he couldn't bear to put his foot to the ground.

And Sir Harry never seemed to have recovered from his wife's death. He had grown morose and silent, not noticing what he ate or when his linen was soiled. Recently he had lost an alarming amount of weight and begun to cough, not loudly, but steadily and quietly, on and on.

'Go and dazzle Robert,' her uncle had said, patting her hand fondly.

Now, looking at the orange dress, she wished suddenly that she could. Their marriage had been delayed for too long, but Robert had declared that no man was fit to be a husband until he came of age, and in the past year he had been away in London for much of the time, receiving his knighthood from King James, going to bear-baiting and cock-fighting and the theatre.

'Every young man needs to sow his wild oats,' Sir Harry had said indulgently. 'He will be all the more faithful as a husband if he is not held on too tight a rein now.'

The truth was that neither Sir Harry nor Uncle Roger could bear to curb Robert at all, and nobody seemed to notice that Nell was almost twenty-six years old and still unwed. She had adored Robert ever since she had been lifted up to peep into his cradle, and having spent so much time with Lady Alys she had grown up seeing him through his mother's eyes, with a golden glow about him.

Suddenly she had a great longing to ride out and meet him. He was coming over that day to take his leave before he went to London again. It would be his last visit alone. Indeed it worried her that he should ride alone at all, but he brushed aside her fears exclaiming that his father had often made the same solitary journey in his youth and never once been attacked or robbed.

'Maggie!' She called over the stairs for her old wet-nurse who came panting and puffing up to the landing, holding her sides as she gasped.

'Lord help us, but are you having a turn again?'

Nell's 'turns', as the servants designated the blinding headaches which prostrated her for days at a time, came with no more warning than a few minutes' distortion of vision. Then a black curtain descended in which brilliant, jagged lights whirled and flashed. After that it was a nightmare of pain and vomiting, and then the slow emerging into a grey, fuzzy world where it was hard to gather one's thoughts into a coherent sentence.

The attacks had begun when Nell was little, and neither purging nor bleeding had ever helped. Sometimes several months would pass without any sign, and then she would have two or three turns in the space of a week, and lie on her bed, vomiting weakly into a basin and long only to die and be freed from the pain beating at her temple.

'No pain at all,' she said gaily. 'I've decided to ride over and meet Robert. Tell James to saddle Duchess and help me to change my dress.'

The gown, she had decided, was beautiful, though Maggie declared it was too low in the neck for daytime wear. To placate her, Nell tucked a muslin scarf beneath her ruff and tied on the steeple-crowned brown hat which had completed her uncle's gift.

Maggie had the privilege of sleeping in the

kitchen, for she and Nell did the cooking and housework between them with the aid of two little girls from the village. Uncle Roger occasionally spoke of adding an extra couple of rooms to the building, but nothing had ever been done and with the wedding so near it was unlikely that anything would be.

He was in the parlour when Nell came downstairs and she paused in the hall to call through the half-open door.

'I'm riding to meet Robert, Uncle!'

'And wearing your new gown,' He limped out and stood, leaning on his stick, to survey it.

'Do you like it?'

'It's most becoming, my darling.'

Vaguely he wondered why he had chosen orange. Although he believed implicitly that his niece was the loveliest girl in Kent, he was aware that the colour didn't suit her. Yet he had wanted her to look nice for Robert. She was a good girl to have waited so long, Roger thought, unconscious of the fact that he had encouraged the delay. It was not that he didn't want the marriage, or that he was too selfish to dispense with her company. It was not even that he wasn't fond of Robert. It was simply that in some part of his nature he doubted if the handsome, high spirited

194

young man would make Nell as happy as she deserved.

'I won't be long,' she promised, kissing him.

Sometimes, remembering that he had never married, she felt a little guilty, hoping that it wasn't on her account. Certainly he had devoted his life to her, for she could barely remember her father or her grandmother. She knew they had been killed in an accident when their cart smashed against the bridge during a thunderstorm. Maggie had once started to say something about a bear, but Roger had told her curtly to hold her peace.

In the yard, James Fleet held Duchess at the mounting block. His face as he glanced at Nell was slyly adoring. An orphan, he had been taken on as groom ten years before, and was now virtually steward of the modest establishment. Of Nell's own age and not ill-favoured, save for a cast in one eye which gave him an undeservedly sinister appearance, he was setting out to render himself indispensable to Roger Aston.

James, under his quiet, respectful exterior, thought himself as good a man as his master, and took pride in the trust reposed in him. His passion for Nell Aston was an emotion he held strictly in check, for she was promised and, apart from that, even the easy-going Roger would not have countenanced her wedding to a servant.

Yet James could not resist the indulgence of waking dreams in which Sir Robert Falcon broke his neck out hunting and Nell turned, gratefully weeping, to the faithful servant.

'The stirrup was a mite loose last time you rode her, mistress,' he said, touching his forelock. 'I took the liberty of tightening it.'

'Thank you, James,' She smiled her thanks as she mounted and gathered up the reins. Her teeth were white between her pink lips. She was wearing a new gown too, he noticed, admiring its brilliant colour. It was not his place to pass comment on her appearance however, so he lowered his eyes and stood back as she trotted down the drive.

At the gateway she paused to nod to the man approaching her. The pedlar was an occasional visitor to Marie Regina, coming once or twice very couple of years since she was about fourteen years old. She had never heard his name nor where he lived, though he gave the impression of having come a long distance. Certainly he never stayed more than a day or two, and then wandered off again. He never seemed particularly interested in selling his wares though they were cheap and of good quality, but he evidently managed to make a living for his garments, though of old-fashioned cut, were decent, and his accents were those of an educated man. Once she had seen him chanting loudly as he walked along and his eyes had stared vacantly, but at all the other times he had been quiet and sensible, with none of the jokes and puns that were a pedlar's stock-in-trade.

'Good-day, Mistress Aston.' He stopped his cart and took of his hat.

'Good-day. Are you going up to the house?'

'I have fine lace today.'

'Show it to my uncle. He knows good quality.'

'I thought it might be fit for a wedding?' He made the statement into a question.

'Not for another month, and then I'll wear my mother's veil,' Nell said.

'A month to go, eh?' The man tilted his head and squinted up at her. He was old, she thought, with a pang of pity, too old to wander the roads trying to sell his goods.

'You ought to rest a while,' she said on impulse. 'Tell Maggie you're to have a meal.'

'You've a kind heart, mistress,' the pedlar said. 'I've often thought of you, wished you well at the end of it.'

'The end of what?'

'Life and death, lady. The one's short and the other's long, and they both have a bitter taste in the mouth.'

'You're very gloomy today!'

'I'm gloomy every day,' he corrected. 'But there! I've seen sights that would tear the young eyes from your head. I've seen honest Christians burned in bloody Mary's time, and Papists quartered under Merry Bess, and more Papists hanged and 'headed under our present sainted King. They're emptying the world, mistress, and still it fills up again.'

'With my own children one day, I hope,' Nell said cheerfully.

'Don't hope for too much,' the pedlar said, so earnestly that she stared at him. 'Don't hold your heart in your hand for a stranger to bruise. Keep close and silent. You're one of the weak ones of the earth, mistress, and the weak never overcome the strong.'

'You speak in riddles,' she said crossly.

'Aye, it's one of the few pleasures left to the old,' he agreed. 'And if you want to catch Sir Robert you'd best ride like the wind. He's away to the city today.'

'Tomorrow! He's to travel tomorrow.'

'I met him in the village. He said he was going today,' the pedlar said.

'I'll see him myself.' She jerked the reins, trouble in her face.

'I think he found good cheer in that inn I recommended a year ago,' the pedlar said.

'Yes. It was very kind of you. Excuse me now.'

She flicked Duchess lightly with her crop and the animal bounded down the road.

The way led straight over the wooden bridge, past the lane leading to the village and thence at right angles between the stone gateposts and up the curving drive to *Kingsmead*. Robert would have gone home first to bid his father farewell, and surely he would ride over to see her too. Perhaps he had already set out and she would meet him on the way.

She met nobody, however, but Robert's horse stood saddled in the yard, and Robert himself was on the threshold, drinking the stirrup cup. He was dressed for travelling and she felt a pang of bitter disappointment.

As she dismounted he turned and a faint guilt showed on his face. It was vanished in an instant and he strode forward.

'Nell! Now you have spared me a ride to the manor! Come indoors out of the heat. You look quite cooked.'

'You were coming over for supper,' she reminded him.

'Sweetheart, I cannot! I am called to London a day early.'

'Called? For what reason?'

'Business. Nothing for you to bother your head over.'

'But wouldn't the business keep for one day?'

'Not for one hour,' he said gaily. 'Father, you have not greeted your daughter-in-law!'

'Not for a month yet,' Nell said smiling, and went to kiss Sir Harry.

Despite the warmth of the day he wore a heavy robe over his doublet, and his cheekbones were sharp under the hollow blue eyes and iron grey hair. He greeted her cordially, coughing a little, his voice a pale echo of his son's.

'To me you are a dear daughter, Nell, and more dutiful than my son! The rogue goes down into the village and rushes home, swearing he must leave at once, and not wait until tomorrow. Shall we scold him heartily, you and I?'

'I have no liking for a long journey on such a dusty day,' Robert told them. 'But this concerns a friend, and I must offer help where I can. You would not have me turn my back on an affair of honour?'

'Not a duel! Sir Harry, forbid him — '

'Not a duel! I never fought in my life, and am not likely to begin now,' Robert said impatiently. 'This is a matter of a gaming debt, and a friend who is in danger until I can offer my surety.'

'Then we will not harass you,' Sir Harry said.

'Will you be away long?' Nell asked wistfully.

'A week or two, no more. I must buy the ring.'

'And engage the portrait painter,' his father reminded.

They were to be painted in their wedding clothes.

'Alys and I waited until Robert was born before we had our likenesses made,' Sir Harry said, 'but I'd not want you to delay.'

Unspoken were the words, 'Lest I die before the pictures are completed, and so lose the pleasure of them.'

In his own picture he looked strong and healthy. Alys, too, looked as hardy as if she might have borne a dozen children. And now Alys was dead and Sir Harry was a shell of a man, coughing his life away.

'The portrait painter too,' Robert promised.

'And you will ride carefully?' The older man looked up anxiously.

'As if I were treading ice,' Robert said gravely. 'Nell, you'll explain to your uncle, won't you?'

'Yes, of course,'

201

She was not certain what had been explained, but as always when she was with Robert she either fell clumsily silent or babbled like a fool.

'I met the pedlar,' she said now. 'He said he had seen you in the village.'

'Aye, we passed a sentence or two,' Roger said. 'He's out of his wits half the time, if you ask me. Look after yourselves now. John! John, have you secured that pack properly? It was swinging loose the last time.'

He was gone, long booted legs clattering down the steps, his face alive with anticipation of — what? Nell didn't know. She knew only that all the light and colour had fled from the hall, even though sunshine still flooded through the open door.

Despite her efforts, *Kingsmead* was not as well kept as it had been in Lady Alys's day. There was a fine film of dust in the corners and some of the silver plate was tarnished. Only the cup presented by the Queen was kept shining. Elizabeth Tudor had granted Sir Harry a monopoly on local cider too, but it had lapsed after her death, and King James only gave monopolies to his boy favourites.

'Will you come for supper tonight, Sir Harry?' she asked.

The other shook his head. 'I'll bide at home,' he said. 'The night air wearies me.

You'll give my regards to your uncle?'

'Most surely. He would come himself but his London visit brought the rheumatism back into his leg.'

She thought sadly that it had been a wasted trip. Robert had never even noticed her new dress. He had not even kissed her goodbye.

As if divining her thoughts Sir Harry said, 'The lad is young and heedless, girl. He'll settle once you're wed.'

'Surely he will.' She gave him a bright smile and said, 'Before I ride home I'll check that you've a supper fit to eat.'

'You're a good wench,' he said, and fell to coughing again, slowly and patiently.

Robert, riding away from *Kingsmead*, was also thinking of Nell's goodness. He had never known her do anything mean or unkind and, reared by Lady Alys, she had absorbed many of his mother's habits and mannerisms. That was partly the trouble. She was so much like his mother that marrying her would hold no surprises at all. He already knew exactly what meals she would prepare and how the keys would jangle at her waist as she moved about her household tasks. Marrying her would be like crawling back into childhood and closing the door.

For that reason he had postponed the

wedding for as long as possible. Robert was tired of childhood, sick of the over-protected life he led in Marie Regina where there was nothing to do but ride round the estate and drink ale down in the village.

As a boy he had been given the services of a tutor when he would have preferred to seek service with some great lord, and his mother's death had ended his hopes of going to the University for Sir Harry could not endure to have his son so far from home.

Even his visits to London lost their savour when his father said indulgently that younglings needed to stretch their wings a little, and given him an increased allowance.

Had it not been for the pedlar Robert could not imagine how he would have endured so much loving tolerance. The man had been coming once or twice a year to the village since before Alys's death. It seemed to Robert sometimes that he came by not to sell his wares, but to find out what had been happening since his last visit.

It was the pedlar who had remarked the previous summer, 'If you ever go to London, sir, you could do worse than stay at the *Three Bells*, hard by the Tower.'

Robert had exclaimed that he was riding

to the city within the month and would take the advice. He shuddered now, thinking how easily he might have forgotten the hint, how easily he might have missed stepping into a land of enchantment.

Four times since then he had ridden to the city and stayed at the timbered inn, with the three golden bells jangling over the door. Each time he had returned to *Kingsmead* with accounts for his father of bull-baiting and visits to the theatre, and never mentioned his companion at these affairs, never spoke of the long evenings in the firelight, the morning strolls through Chelsea Village with the dew still thick on mushrooms and strawberries.

'Pick me a ripe strawberry, Robert,' she had begged, and her mouth opened to receive the fruit, was pale and secret, her dark red hair which she wore smooth and straight lay across his arm like a silken scarf. Her voice was sweet and lilting and she was small. Like a doll, he thought, and indeed there was something doll-like in her gentle passivity. He had the impression that if he ever shouted at her she would cease to breathe and sag limply down, the sleepy lids half closing over the amber eyes.

'If we had never met — ' he had said once.

'You would have missed me all your life,' she answered.

It was true, Robert thought. She filled a need in him for mystery and charm, both qualities sadly lacking in poor, clumsy Nell. Even had she not made him promise he would never have mentioned her to anybody else. What made her mysterious and more charming was that she was not yet even his mistress, though he was certain that she loved him.

And now the urgent little message had come, muttered by the pedlar.

'She bids you go to her with all speed, sir. It is most important, the lady says.'

It was the first time she had sent for him, and Robert held his head higher as he urged his mount onwards, and forgot Nell whom he was going to marry, and thought only of Catrin whom he loved.

11

Catrin had risen early and now sat opposite her mother in the panelled dining room of the inn. She had tried to eat some breakfast but had given up the attempt and now sat, crumbling bread on her plate, and wondering how long it would be before Robert came. She kept her eyes lowered to avoid meeting the cold yellow gaze of the woman whom she loved and feared more than anybody else in the world.

'Your dress suits you,' her mother said, now.

She spoke approvingly, having chosen it herself, as she had chosen all the clothes in her daughter's wardrobe.

All her life, Catrin had dwelt under those cold bright eyes, had listened to that clear, sweet voice telling her what to do and what to think. Her earliest memory had been of her mother's hands stretched out to catch her as she took her first unsteady steps. Sometimes it seemed to her that those hands had never let her go, that they would always be there, guiding and supporting her, and limiting her freedom.

It was, she knew, very wrong to think like that. Her mother had had a difficult life, her young husband having died of the plague before Catrin was born. She had never told Catrin where he was buried or of what family he came, though she had hinted once that he had been a nobleman who had jousted before Queen Elizabeth. But most of the time she kept silent about him, so that Catrin was left to wonder if he had ever existed at all.

The only other person she might have asked was the Englishman. He, like her mother, had always been part of her childhood, not at the centre of her existence but on the fringe of it. He had looked after the little farm when Catrin was a baby, and by the time she was old enough to be aware of her surroundings he had become a familiar figure. He slept out in the barn and once or twice a year he would hitch up the cart and drive away.

'He's gone into England and we must not question him,' her mother had said.

But after his return Catrin had often lain on her pallet in the back room and listened to the low murmuring of their voices far into the night. Only an occasional fragment reached her ears.

' — well-grown, you say? And is he a healthy lad?'

' — and nobody will live there again until I return!'

And after he had gone to the barn she had heard her mother walking up and down, up and down, pacing out the hours between darkness and dawn.

Her childhood had been a lonely one, for her mother had no friends and did not encourage her daughter to make any. Yet she was not unhappy, for her days were filled with a multitude of tasks. She learned to speak both English and Welsh from her earliest years, and the Englishman taught her to read and write a little. Her mother expected help in the house and with the cattle and sheep, but on market days Catrin was left at home.

'When you are a woman and I have saved enough money I will take you to London,' her mother had told her.

The saving of money had been the most important factor in their lives. The Englishman worked for no wages except his food, and they hired no other help. The farmhouse was bare of everything save necessities, and her mother boasted that when it came to the selling of cattle she could drive a harder bargain than anybody else in the market place.

Once, Catrin had overheard the Englishman

say, 'You'll not do it, Margred. At the last moment your heart will fail you.'

And her mother had answered, 'I have no heart. And I will not fail.'

And a year ago, when Catrin was twenty, they had come into England. The Englishman came too, stayed long enough to see them settled at the inn, and wandered away again. She had seen him once or twice since, talking to her mother, but by then she had met Robert and nobody else in the world was of any interest to her.

'Do you truly think he will come?' she asked now.

Margred's eyes dwelt on the pale, delicate featured girl, red hair drawn back from a centre parting and tied with a slate-blue ribbon which matched the overdress of her gown. Beneath the overdress with its tight sleeves could be seen the kirtle of pale green worn over a small farthingale. The stomacher reached to the neck where a narrow lace ruff made a frame for Catrin's pointed chin and high cheekbones.

The girl, she thought, was very lovely, her lack of animation investing her with a strange, airy quality as if she sprang from some realm of dreams. Margred herself carried her years lightly, her black hair unpowdered with grey, her skin still smooth and brown, her wide mouth touched lightly with carmine.

'He will come,' she said in answer, 'and when he does, you know what to say?'

Catrin folded her hands obediently and rehearsed the words in her mind. She wished it could have been arranged more openly, but her mother had explained that this was impossible.

'The young man is to be wed to a neighbour's daughter, though he has no love for her. If you went to his father together and pleaded your love, the family would find means to separate you both. Once you are wed the knot cannot be untied.'

Now, Catrin said, 'If he does not wed me, you would not truly force me into marriage with anyone else, would you?'

'With the first stranger who comes along,' Margred said, and her eyes were cold. Then she laughed, wrinkling her small nose at her daughter, and said, 'But you need not fret. Sir Robert is mad for you and you have been clever to hold him off.'

It was not cleverness, Catrin thought, but fear. She had been so strictly reared that the thought of Margred's anger if she allowed any man to possess her without a marriage licence outweighed her own dawning desire. Margred had high standards of conduct and did not expect her daughter to fall short of them.

'Wouldn't it have been dreadful,' Catrin mused, 'if we had lodged at some other inn? I might never have met Robert then.'

'It was certainly a fortunate chance,' Margred agreed dryly.

'And you were so good not to forbid me his company,' Catrin said, with a glance of real affection.

'I could wish you had chosen a man who was not already betrothed,' Margred said, 'but it is not in me to deny your heart's desire.'

The girl, she thought half loving, half contemptuous, is a fool. Has she never wondered at the coincidence? Has she never connected the Englishman's absences from home with the long conversations he and I have when he comes back?

She sighed briefly, her chin in her hand. They had been a twelvemonth in the city now and her money was running out. There had been months of constant anxiety, lest Robert blurt out his friendship to Catrin and Sir Harry come rushing to London to forbid it.

'Will the Englishman have given the message?' Catrin asked.

'Aye, he knows the district,' Margred said briefly.

Robert had evidently not mentioned the pedlar who gleaned gossip once or twice a year from Marie Regina. It would be as well, she decided, if the Englishman returned with her into Wales when the business was concluded. He would be glad enough to cease his visits to England.

Sometimes she wondered why he agreed to help her. She had told him the whole story for it was necessary not to have to bear the whole burden of guilt alone, and then she gave herself a mental shake for she had resolved never to feel guilty again, never to feel anything again.

It was a pity that she would have to go home after they were safely wed. She could not risk meeting Harry again, could not relish her revenge except in secret. He would probably never guess the truth, for she used the name Margaret here in London and even if Catrin let her real name slip out he would be able to prove nothing.

'Robert is here! He just went past the window!' Catrin cried.

She had risen from her seat and was staring imploringly at her mother.

'Then go to him,' Margred said, amused. 'Say what I told you to say, and keep in mind that I meant it.'

Catrin was on the stairs when Robert,

standing in conversation with the landlord, looked up and saw her descending. Her face in the dim light had a greenish cast as if she reflected water, and her hands were held out to him.

'Oh, sir, I am so happy you are here, for I am in such trouble!'

'What ails you, love?' Dismissing the landlord with a nod he hurried to her. 'I rode as hard as I could.'

'Come into the back room. Mam is in our room.'

She clutched at him as if she were drowning, pulling him into the little room at the back of the bar.

'What is it?' he repeated. 'I was due to come anyway.'

'It is Mam,' Catrin said. 'She says I must not see you again, that I must be married to some other gentleman.'

'What other man?' Robert demanded.

'She says she will choose him herself and wed me to him whether I will or no,' Catrin said.

She recited the words glibly as she had learnt them but to Robert her tone had the blankness of shock.

'She cannot do it,' he said. 'You are mine, Catrin. You have been mine since the moment I picked up the glove you dropped as you were going through the door.'

'And you ran after me right down the street and Mam was cross because people turned round and stared at us.'

'And I loved you from that moment and no other man will claim you,' Robert said vehemently.

'Mam will not have it so,' Catrin said.

'*Mam* will listen to me!' Robert exclaimed in a rare burst of anger.

'And what did you wish to say to me?' Margred enquired sweetly from the doorway.

'Madam, is it true that you've forbidden Catrin to see me?'

'Quite true, but we need not tell everybody in the street of the fact.'

She closed the door softly and stood looking at them both for a moment. When she spoke her voice was gentle.

'Sir Robert, the blame is partly mine, but you must excuse it in me that I am indulgent with my daughter. Her wishes count for a great deal and she took such pleasure in your company that I could not deny her.'

'And I in hers!'

'So you say, and perhaps that is true, or you believe it to be so. But we are not rich or important people, and Catrin must marry. I did not bring her to London to become a man's leman.'

215

'Before God, Madam, I never touched her!'

'And will it always be like that?' Margred asked sadly. 'Is it not true that you are to be married soon?'

'I will love Catrin all my life,' he said earnestly.

'So the old Queen said of Essex, but he was beheaded in the end. Love that is not fixed within marriage cannot endure, and it is better for you to part now, unless — ' She hesitated, and then said demurely with eyes cast down, 'Unless you are ever in a position to offer her marriage, and your affection is not strong enough for that.'

'I told you that I love her best of all creatures,' he said.

'And yet you are betrothed to another? Oh, I credit your honesty in telling us of it at the start. The woman you are going to marry will be most fortunate in her husband for I know you to be kind and unskilled in double dealing. Indeed, if matters were only different, there is nobody in the world to whom I would rather entrust my Catrin, but you have chosen otherwise.'

'It was my family!' he cried. 'I had no choosing to do. It was all arranged by my family.'

'But you are of age,' Margred said. 'Surely

you may do as you please.'

'Yes. Yes, of course.' He stared at her uncertainly.

'And you choose to wed this neighbour's daughter. She is somewhat older than you, you said?'

'Four years.'

'As much as that!' Margred clicked her tongue. 'Well, there are advantages in that. She will be past the age of frivolity and she will always be grateful to you.'

It was odd, but her words conjured up for him a vivid picture of an ever grateful, perpetually solemn Nell.

'My father would not have me wed a girl without dowry,' he said awkwardly. 'And you are Welsh, Catrin. He dislikes the Welsh. He told me once they are a nation of barbarians. Oh, I do not share his opinion, and I believe he would alter it if he met you.'

'Catrin is not a horse to be inspected at the fair,' Margred said sharply. 'It is your opinion that should concern you — or perhaps you fear lest he should cast you off.'

'He would never do that.'

'Then it is of your choosing after all, this marriage. I cannot blame you. The woman sounds sensible and suitable. She brings land with her, you told us? You will settle down and raise a family upon it, and your neighbours will respect you. Catrin too will learn to forget.'

'I will not! I will never forget!'

The girl spoke for the first time, her eyes moving fearfully between them. She was not certain how many of her mother's words were sincere, or how far the comedy was to be played out, but she was afraid, seeing with every sentence her lover moving further from her.

'I fear she will not,' Margred said. 'Her affections run deep. But that is her misfortune, not her fault. Come Catrin, Say goodbye to Sir Robert quickly.'

Catrin was weeping in earnest now, the tears sliding down her pale face and wetting her hands as she put them up in a pathetic attempt to hide her distress. Robert stared at her in anguish.

'Come, Catrin,' Margred said again.

She had turned towards the door, her fingers on its handle, her face masklike. Beneath her frozen calm emotions bubbled within her. Pity for the girl, contempt for the young man, both fear and elation lest her scheme had succeeded — all mingled together.

And then Robert said chokingly, 'Catrin, I'll not let you go! I'll marry you. I'll forget Nell and marry you!'

'Your father would not permit it,' Margred said.

'I'll not ask him,' Robert said. 'I'll marry her and tell him afterwards. I'm of age — you told me that yourself, I'll marry her and take her back to *Kingsmead* with me.'

'I would not have you take her out of pity,' Margred said.

'Out of love,' Robert said. 'I love her, madam. Catrin don't weep so, sweetheart. I can get a licence and marry you within the week. I'll tie the knot between us so tightly that not even God can loose it!'

'Your father doesn't like Welsh people,' Catrin sobbed.

'Then we'll tell him you're Cornish,' Robert said promptly. 'They're all Celts after all.'

An ignorant fool, Margred thought, and looked at him almost with love.

The conflict of emotion within her was cooling into a hard triumph. It was working as she had planned, and so many things might have gone wrong in the years since she had slowly and painfully conceived her scheme.

'It is not in me to encourage disobedience,' she said aloud, 'but from what you have told me of your father, it seems you need to be reminded that you are of an age to please yourself. And above that it seems — ' Her yellow gaze flickered between them and she allowed a small smile to touch the corners of her mouth. 'It seems that you love each other truly.'

'So truly,' Catrin said, rubbing her cheeks with one hand and holding out the other to Robert. 'So truly.'

'And I love Catrin,' Robert said. 'I will always love you, as long as I live.'

They believe it, Margred thought, and sadness laced her triumph.

'How is it to be contrived?' Catrin asked. 'Will it take very long for us to wed?'

'I will apply for a licence at once,' Robert said eagerly 'We can be wed in three days' time.'

' 'Tis a short betrothal,' Catrin said.

'I will bring you a ring this very day,' Robert said. 'I will buy you a golden ring set with a green stone.'

'And I will wear it always,' Catrin said, but when he would have put his arms about her Margred moved between them.

'It is not fitting,' she said primly, 'to allow a man and a maid too much licence before vows are exchanged. We will have your company at supper, sir?'

It was a victory, she told herself later that night, when Catrin lay sleeping and Margred sat by the darkened window, her chin on her hand, and watched stars powder the sky. For more than twenty years she had watched and waited, and now the sweetness of revenge filled her mouth. A pity that Harry would never know, but she could share it with the Englishman.

'Why do you help me?' she had asked him once.

He had looked at her for a long moment and then said, 'I remember you as a barefoot girl setting out to conquer the world with eyes full of dreams and a dancing bear at your side. It amuses me now to see you flourish like a green bay tree.'

But it was the wicked who did that, Margred thought, with a little clutch of fear. And the wicked died and went to hellfire. Prys had told her that, but he had told her too that the love of a man for a maid lasted for ever. That wasn't true, so probably the other wasn't true either. In any event it was too late to draw back now.

Three days later at St. Saviour's in Southwark, Sir Robert Falcon, bachelor, of Marie Regina, in the country of Kent, was married to Catrin Prys, spinster, of the *Three Bells* tavern in the city of London. Both parties were of full age and signed their names in the register as did the two witnesses whom the minister called in from the street.

The minister thought them a charming, well-spoken couple and being himself newly wed, sympathised with the young bridegroom when he confided that the match was a love match, misliked by the bridegroom's family because the girl lacked a sufficient dowry.

The girl herself was all pale loveliness, in a white gown with a veil like snowflakes over her red hair. She made her response in a frightened whisper, continually glancing at her mother who knelt, clad in widow's weeds, near to the couple.

She too, the minister decided, remembering the five guineas she had pressed into his hand, was a charming lady, with more animation in her face than her daughter. It was a pity she had never chosen to marry again.

'I wish you would come with us back to Kent,' Catrin said, as they toasted the occasion over supper at the inn.

They were to sleep there for one night and ride east together the next day.

'Lord help us, but what would I do in Kent?' Margred enquired, amused. 'You must live with your husband, now, and no man wants his bride's mother to clutter the house.'

'You would be most welcome.' Robert said.

He spoke sincerely, but a small part of him felt relief. Catrin's mother was small and sweet-spoken, and yet he was not sure if he really liked her. She had an odd, mocking air about her sometimes that disconcerted him.

'I will visit you one day,' she said. 'But you must make a new happiness for yourselves.'

'My father's anger will not last long when he has seen you,' he told Catrin.

She answered, a troubled pucker between her brows, 'I was thinking of the other poor lady who thinks you are going to marry her.'

'Nell?'

In the excitement of the last few days he had entirely forgotten her. Now, the idea that he had once been prepared to wed her was as fanciful as a dream.

'She will be hurt,' Catrin said.

'For a little while, yes,' He reflected for a moment and then said cheerfully, 'But she's not one to bear grudges. This betrothal we had was not of her making either, and she's too good-hearted to wish to hold me to it.'

He was good-hearted himself and disliked causing pain, but he was also a young man caught in the toils of a headlong love, and in this mood it was easy to convince himself that Nell cared as little for him as he did for her.

As they rose to go to the room Robert had hired for the night, he took Margred's hand.

'I will always be most true and loving to your daughter, madam. I will not let the wind blow upon her if it is within my power to prevent it.'

He was so like Harry, though more vivid in colouring, that for a moment she was again shielded within his cloak on the night Mott died. Her yellow eyes were misty as she looked up at him, and then he was leading Catrin from the room and all her youth and the last of her tenderness were going out of the door.

She sat down by the table with the remains of the supper upon it and gritted her teeth, forcing her mind back into its accustomed channel.

They are legally wed and by the morning their marriage will be consummated. Even if Harry ever guessed whose daughter she was he could never be certain, and there is little chance after all this time that he would even remember me. As for the Englishman — if those two young fools ever get to realising that the man who helps on our farm is the pedlar who has been going for years to glean gossip from Marie Regina, why they will dismiss it as an incredible coincidence.

She had already said casually to Robert, 'Catrin was very disobedient to send for you as she did, but she chanced to see the pedlar who goes sometimes to your part of the world, and begged him to take a message.'

And the fool had answered innocently, 'It was he who first recommended me to this inn.'

Margred tilted her goblet to drink the last of the wine, but it was flat and sour on her tongue. Behind the closed door of the bedroom Robert would be uncovering the beauty of his bride.

'I kept her for you,' Margred whispered savagely. 'All these years I kept her innocent and unspotted for your pleasure and my own revenge. She will take the place I should have had, and nobody will ever throw her love back in her face for the sake of a keg of cider.'

A low whistle below the window attracted her attention. She leaned over, pushing the casement wider, and saw the Englishman below in the yard. In the darkness he was like some gaunt ghost risen from nightmare to haunt her waking hours.

'What now, Margred?' he hissed. 'Now

that the knot is tied, how will you spend the rest of your life?'

'In wishing them well,' she answered. 'Now get you gone back to the north. I'll join you as soon as I can. I've the land to restock and the house to be cleaned.'

'Like a green bay tree,' he said. 'And when the wood is no longer green, why they'll lop its branches and make a stake of it. Can you hear the flames crackling?'

'I can hear two cats fighting and you babbling nonsense,' she said coldly, and slammed the window shut.

She was past forty, but her skin was still honey-brown over small, high breasts and narrow hips. She was past forty, but her black hair still hung, thickly shining to her hips. She would never love another man as long as she lived and no man would desire her. In sudden desolation of spirit she heard herself whisper. 'What am I going to do with the rest of my life?'

12

Sir Harry Falcon sat in the carved chair by the fire and stared helplessly at the two who stood before him. Here was a situation he had never envisaged, for though Robert had been indulged from childhood it had never occurred to his father that he might take his future in his own hands and marry a woman of his own choosing. Yet the girl was a pretty little thing, though Harry was no admirer of red hair. She stood, clinging to Robert's hand, her eyes downcast, her whole attitude one of terrified submission.

Catrin was, in truth, more frightened than she had ever been in her life. At home on the farm, even in the crowded city, there had always been her mother close at hand. Now there was Robert but as they had travelled nearer to her bridegroom's home she had sensed a subtle change in him. He was as loving as ever but he began to talk about people she didn't know, about places she had never seen.

'The ruins of the old monastery are on that high hill. The land hereabouts all belonged to the Papists once. You can just see the spire of our parish church down there in the village. Parson Grimshaw used to be minister when I was little, but now we have Josiah Bewling and he's a miserable man with a face as long as his sermons. He'll be over to read us a lecture on the follies of wedding for love. This is where our land begins. The gates are further along, and past the bridge is the Aston place.'

They had ridden up the curving drive between tall young oaks through which she glimpsed orchard and pasture, and then they rode through another open gate set in an ivied wall and were in a cobbled yard with the house opposite them.

It was bigger than Catrin had imagined and there hung about it a neglected air, for though it was passably clean the rushes were dank underfoot and in the hall there were none of the bright and graceful touches a woman would have added. And Robert's father matched the house in some indefinable way she couldn't understand. She had prepared herself to meet the blusterings of an angry father, but this grey-haired man with stooped shoulders frightened her so much that her knees shook pitifully.

He was evidently aware of this for he said, quite kindly, 'Where are you from, child?'

'Cornwall, sir,' Robert answered for her.

'But I have lived in London for some time,' she ventured.

'I thought you had no accent.' He stroked his short beard thoughtfully and went on staring at her.

'Her father is dead, sir, and her mother is widowed,' Robert said.

'And she approved this marriage?'

'She did not wish, that is, she wanted her daughter to live in honour,' Robert said awkwardly.

So the wench who was probably a bastard had been dangled before his unsuspecting son as marriage bait. It was not worth enquiring if she had a dowry. He was certain that all she possessed were the pretty clothes her mother would have fitted her out in.

She spoke suddenly in a breathless little rush, 'Sir, please don't turn Robert away. I know it was wrong of us to wed secretly, but we were afraid something would happen to stop it! And I will be a most loving and obedient wife.'

She spoke like a lady, he conceded, and there was no doubt of her sincerity.

'What of Nell?' he asked sternly. 'She is as dear to me as my own daughter and you are troth-plighted.'

'Nell would not hold me to my word,' Robert said.

'Her uncle might. Roger Aston thinks the sun rises and sets on his niece.'

'I cannot marry to please Uncle Roger,' Robert said sulkily.

'I will send word to him privately,' Harry said. 'He will find some way of breaking it gently to her.'

His tone was defeated. He could have turned them both out, he supposed, but the thought of *Kingsmead* without Robert was not to be endured. The only good thing left in his life was his son, and if that son was spoiled he had only himself, and Alys, to blame.

'I will send John over with an urgent message to the manor,' he said. 'You must be prepared for him to be very angry, very angry indeed. You have behaved dishonourably and offered a grave insult to poor Nell. She has every right to take you to court and claim damages for breach of promise.'

He broke off and began coughing painfully. Catrin, her terror subsiding now that the worst was over, hastened to pour wine into the pitcher at his elbow. As she handed it to him something in her face made him gasp.

'You must not think I despise love, child. The happiest marriages are founded upon it. You are welcome here for your own sake, even if it is difficult for me to accept you as my son's bride.'

He was only a sick, elderly man after all. Catrin's fear was melting and an almost maternal affection was growing in her.

'If you please, sir,' she said breathlessly, 'I can make you a hot posset that is marvellous comforting to the throat.'

It might be pleasant, after all, to be the mistress of *Kingsmead*. She would have fresh rushes laid on the floors and new tapestries hung, and bake saffron cakes for the two men. She was suddenly quite certain she could be happy here.

Later that same afternoon at Aston Manor, Nell, glancing out of her window, was astonished to see her uncle hoist himself painfully to the saddle and ride out, with a look on his face that told her something was wrong. She dropped her sewing and ran downstairs into the hall, almost cannoning into Maggie at the foot of the stairs.

'Where is my uncle going?' she demanded.

'Over to *Kingsmead*, mistress,' the servant said.

'Was that John with him?'

'He just brought the message,' Maggie began.

'What message? What's amiss?'

'Nothing as far as I know. Lord, what a

231

pother!' Maggie exclaimed. 'John said the master was needed urgently.'

'Urgently? Sir Harry must be worse!'

'If he was worse they'd send for you or me. The master'd be no use in a sickroom.'

'Then it's Robert. Something must have happened to Robert. James! James, saddle my horse!'

'Now there's no need to be making a fuss,' Maggie began but her erstwhile nursling had gone.

James Fleet was standing with bent head at the stable door when Nell hurried up. He had been deep in thought for several minutes and the appearance of the object of his thoughts threw him off balance so that he gaped at her foolishly.

'James, please saddle Duchess for me. I'm going over to *Kingsmead*,' she said briskly.

'It's late,' he said.

'Late?' She looked at him in surprise. 'It won't be dark for a couple of hours yet, and my uncle will ride back with me.'

To her astonishment he remained where he was, gazing at her, and said, 'Mistress, it's best you stay at home until the master returns.'

'Something *is* wrong.' Her face taut with apprehension, she stared back at him. 'Something *is* wrong! I knew it when I saw my uncle riding away. Is it Sir Robert? Is he hurt?'

'No mistress. He's in good health and higher spirits,' James Fleet said.

'You've seen him? Is he back then?'

'Yes, mistress. With a — a lady.' He gave her his odd squinting look.

'What lady?' she asked blankly.

'A young lady,' the steward said. 'They rode past me as I was coming up the village road. They didn't see me, but I heard — '

'Heard what?'

'Mistress, I'm sorry to have to tell you this,' he said, 'but I heard Sir Robert say, 'He'll be over to read us a lecture on the follies of wedding for love'.'

'Wedding?' She said the word slowly as if it had no meaning. 'But the wedding is not until next month.'

'It was the way they were looking at each other,' James Fleet said.

There was reluctance and an unwilling excitement in his face. He would have liked to run Sir Robert Falcon through with a sword for daring to hurt Mistress Nell. On the other hand it was an ill wind that blew nobody any good.

'Mistress, I'd not have brought you bad news for anything in the world,' he said earnestly, 'and perhaps I'm wrong — '

'No, you're not wrong,' Nell said.

It was so obvious now, his rushing off to London to see a friend about a gaming debt. That had been the excuse to leave early, to ride away and claim his bride. She would be young, of course, and pretty.

'Mistress, may I get you something?' James asked, alarmed by her grey pallor and her silence.

She focused her eyes upon him with difficulty, but answered in her usual placid tone.

'I'll ride over anyway, so saddle the horse. I'd best change my dress.'

Her feet mounted the stairs out of habit for the world was a blur. She took out the orange dress and, for the first time in her life, garbed herself without help. It didn't occur to her to cry or to call Maggie. Her fingers moved automatically, lacing ribbons, setting the tall hat on her fair hair.

Robert didn't love her. Deep down she had known it all along, but marriage for love alone was rare except among peasants. Affection grew after marriage, and was cemented by the rearing of children. But she had always loved Robert and she had thought he was at least fond of her. That he was spoiled and selfish had been facts she could endure, but that he could shame her before the whole neighbourhood was something she had never imagined.

Nobody would want to marry a jilted woman of twenty-six, even for Aston Manor. And she could never dream of any other suitor. Her whole life had been bound up with Robert and the hope of *Kingsmead*. There was nothing left to her now but her pride. Some rag of pride must be salvaged if she were to be able to endure to go on living.

When she came down into the yard again she looked so calm that James Fleet was filled with fresh admiration. She had courage, he told himself, and again the odd, triumphant little feeling moved in the depths of his pity for her.

'Would you like me to ride with you, mistress?' he asked hopefully.

'No. Thank you, but no.' She shook her head as she mounted Duchess.

'Perhaps it's not true. Perhaps I mistook the meaning of the words,' he said.

'No, you did not mistake. I felt it to be true, here.' She touched the orange silk bodice of her gown and winced as if her finger probed into the soreness of her heart. Then she rode beneath the arch into the long drive.

It seemed unfair that the sun should still

be shining and that the land looked as fair as she had ever seen it. Aston acres sloped down to meet *Kingsmead* acres with only the river winding between. The land might have been joined as she and Robert would have been joined and everything would have bloomed and blossomed in a new fertility. Now the two estates would remain separate and she and Robert — she closed the door of her thoughts and rode on, along the main road, over the bridge, and through the stone pillars that marked the entrance to Kingsmead.

Part of her wanted to spur Duchess on; and the rest of her longed to turn round and gallop away, back in time to the days when she had planned her wedding with a happy heart.

She rode forward steadily, willing calmness into her face, her hands careful on the reins. In the cobbled yard John came forward to help her down, his face creased with worry and concern.

'Mistress Nell! Before you go in — ' he began uncertainly.

She interrupted him. 'I know what has happened. Keep Duchess saddled, for I don't intend to stay very long.'

And then she was walking up the steps into the high-raftered hall with its dusty corners and tarnished pewter and silver. They were gathered round the fireplace at the left of the wide staircase; grouped as if they were posed for an artist. Her uncle leaned on the back of one chair and his face was twisted with anger as she had never seen it. Sir Harry sat opposite to him and had evidently reached the end of a bout of coughing for Robert bent towards him with a goblet of wine in his hand. But Nell's eyes were drawn irresistibly to the figure who stood a little apart from them with one hand resting lightly on the stone balustrade. The girl was young as she had guessed, but she was far prettier than imagination had painted.

Nell had never seen such palely perfect features set off by dark red hair rolled back into a chignon in which tiny gold feathers were placed. And it was surely the most cruel of coincidences that this girl too wore an orange dress, not vivid as Nell's was, but pale and subtle, its stiff bodice outlined in pearls, its skirts held out over a wheel farthingale, its oversleeves slit to display narrow sleeves of gold lace matching the wide ruff that spread its fan behind her head.

For a moment the two stared at each other across the width of the hall. Then Nell moved forward swiftly, her hands outstretched, her voice light.

'You must be Robert's bride! I rode over

as soon as I heard, to meet you and — bid you welcome!'

'Nell, who told you?' her uncle demanded.

'Rumours travel like the wind,' Nell said gaily. 'If you wished to keep your wife a secret you should not have ridden with her in daylight. The very hedges hereabouts have ears and eyes.'

'There will be some better explanation of this before I am satisfied,' Roger Aston said grimly. 'My niece has been insulted beyond bearing.'

'Surely that is for me to decide,' Nell said, smiling. 'You did not think me pining for love of a boy whom I have always thought of as a brother, did you? I am truly sorry that you and Sir Harry should be disappointed over the joining of the land, but for myself I wish them both happiness with all my heart!'

Even as she spoke some wild, irrational hope that it was a jest or a mistake leapt up in her, and died as Robert came forward, relief in his face and voice.

'Dear Nell! I told them you would understand. Catrin and I are so deep in love that we could not endure to wait.'

'Catrin? That's a very pretty name.' She turned from Robert to where the girl still stood and held out her hand.

Catrin's own hand felt tiny and boneless as Nell's fingers enclosed it. She had to resist the urge to press it too tightly.

'I am glad you are not angry,' Catrin said nervously.

'I am a little hurt that Robert kept you such a secret,' Nell said. 'I thought we were better friends than that.'

'I am disturbed by the whole business,' Roger Aston said heavily. 'I blame you for this, Harry. You always spoilt and indulged the boy, brought him up with the idea that he had only to wish a thing for it to become instantly available. It will cause a scandal in the neighbourhood.'

'Uncle, since when did we heed the babblings of lesser folk?' Nell cried. 'Come, you would not be so severe if I was the one who had wed secretly for love!'

'You would not do such a thing,' Roger said curtly. 'But there has always been a wild, undisciplined streak in the Falcons.'

'Then you should be glad for me that Robert has married elsewhere,' Nell said. 'Come, let us be done with scolding. Poor Catrin — may I call you so? — will think we do nothing but quarrel in Kent! You are not from these parts?'

'I have lived in London this past while,' Catrin said shyly.

'She was born in Cornwall,' Robert said.

He had moved closer to his bride and put his arms about her shoulders. Nothing, Nell thought with anguish, would separate them now.'

Roger Aston stared at them gloomily. In his opinion the young fool wanted a horsewhipping for hurting Nell. That she was deeply hurt and shocked he knew only too well, despite the brave face she was putting on. Mingled with his anger was a small and shameful relief that there would be no wedding and Nell could continue to minister to his comfort as she had done for years.

'I am ready to pay compensation,' Harry said.

Roger looked at his old friend almost with dislike. There was something essentially vulgar about the man for all his knighthood and his five hundred acres. He wondered how Alys had stood him for all those years.

But in the end Alys had borne her son and loved him, and for the sake of her memory he would not quarrel with the lad.

He held out his hand, saying gruffly. 'Since Nell is satisfied, I'll say no more on the matter, though my opinion of you is lower than it was. But we'll let it rest there and wish you and your bride well.'

'And you'll stay for supper?' Sir Harry asked.

There was a pathetic eagerness in his tone, as if he dreaded the severance of an old friendship.

'I'll stay for supper,' Roger agreed.

'And Nell too? I want you and Catrin to be friends,' Robert said.

He was so stupid, Nell thought, looking at him and loving him so desperately that she dare not move closer lest she fling herself into his unwilling arms. Did he really believe there could ever be friendship between her and the girl in the amber dress?

'I promised faithfully that I'd be back,' she said. 'Maggie's going to set my hair in the new style, and you know how she grumbles if her plans are overset.'

'I'll send John with you,' Sir Harry began, but she shook her head, laughing.

'The shadows are scarce lengthening,' she said. 'Stay and enjoy your supper, uncle. I'll have a hot cordial ready for your return. Sir Harry, though, I am not to be your daughter-in-law, I know you will think of me as a daughter of your heart. Catrin, if you need help with the management of the house, you must not fail to call upon me. Robert.'

But she had nothing she could say to

Robert. He stood, his arm about his wife, the firelight striking gold from his brown hair, and there was nothing she could say.

'You've been very generous,' he said, and then, unforgivably, as if he claimed absolution from all guilt, he said, 'After all, it was not as if you loved me deeply, was it?'

'No, Robert,' she said, smiling still, 'it is not as if I ever loved you deeply.'

She left them gathered about the fire, walked to the door, even turned and sketched a wave. The tableau had shifted and regrouped, her uncle now sitting in the chair with one hand massaging his aching leg as he listened to some remark his friend made, and apart from them, as if they drew an invisible circle about themselves, Robert and Catrin stood private and beautiful.

'It's not my place to say so,' John said, bringing Duchess up, 'but it's my opinion the young master's behaved shamefully, mistress. Even Sir Harry never acted in such a fashion as to jilt a young lady when she's almost at the church door. And who is she? That's what we'd like to know. A foreigner out of Cornwall or some such wild place, for all her fine dresses and soft speech! And not a groat to bless herself with, I'll be bound.'

'Nobody asked you for an opinion,' Nell

said sharply. 'You're not paid to gossip about the doings of your betters.'

'No, mistress.' The elderly steward touched his forelock, sympathy all over his face.

Halfway down the drive the blinding zigzags of light began to trouble her vision. She blinked, trying to dispel them, to hold off the dreaded moment when the unrelenting pain would stab at her temple.

At the open gateway, through the bright pyramids and cones that whirled in the dark tunnel to which her world had been reduced, she saw James Fleet, mounted on his cob.

'It looks like rain, mistress,' he said, 'so I took the liberty of bringing an extra cloak. 'Twould be a pity to spoil such a pretty dress.'

He was lying because there wasn't a cloud in the sky, but the lie was kindly meant and comforted her.

'I have a headache beginning,' she said, speaking with difficulty through the confusion and pain.

'Then we'll ride easy,' the steward said. 'I'll take the rein, mistress, and guide us both.'

'Do you really think my dress is pretty?' she asked, wistfully.

'Aye, mistress, I do,' he said, 'but then you grace anything you wear. Like a spring morning. That's what comes into my mind, if you'll pardon me. Like a spring morning.'

'It will be winter soon,' she said bitterly.

'And after that the spring,' said James Fleet. 'Year in, year out and never failing to astonish folk.'

In the hall at *Kingsmead*, Sir Harry, shifting in his chair in an attempt to ease his breathing, said, 'Nell had gallantry, Roger. She would have made my son a fine helpmate.'

'The boy has chosen for himself,' Roger said grudgingly. 'And she is sweetly pretty, I grant you.'

'Must I stay down for supper?' Catrin was whispering to Robert.

She was bone weary after the long day, and though she had changed into her loveliest dress to keep up her courage, it had not been easy to face first an angry father and then an indignant neighbour.

'Catrin is tired and begs to be excused,' Robert said.

'Then you may retire, my dear.'

Sir Harry nodded at her kindly. Damn it, but she was a sweet little thing! Everything about her called up his protective instincts.

'Master Aston, I am truly sorry if we caused hurt to your niece,' she said timidly. 'The blame is mine as much as Robert's, for

I never thought of dishonour or insult when I wed him, only that I loved him so!'

Roger peered at her, wishing he had remembered to bring his spectacles. He could see well enough to know that she was very lovely, but it was hard to read expressions without the magnifying lenses. There was something about the wench, something in the way she moved and held her head, that teased his memory like the fragrance of some vanished perfume.

'What's done is done,' he said aloud, 'and I'll not hold it against you.'

In the room upstairs where her bags had been carried Catrin looked round, noting the wide, curtained bed, the carved chests, the thick tapestries. Robert had slept in this room all his life, and in the apartment which led out of it and faced the front of the house he had learned his lessons, first with his mother and then with tutors. It was very different from the bleak little farmhouse ringed round by marshes which stretched to the sea and beyond to the distant mountains.

Tears came into her eyes and she blinked them resolutely away. This was her home now and she must accustom herself to its ways. This was a green and pleasant country, yellow with corn, heavy with apples. They had ridden past fields thick with tall, green plants.

'Hops,' Robert had said. 'People put them in the ale, to make it stronger. I have a fancy to turn some of the pasture over to hops.'

She could help him with his plans, she told herself. And there was the house to be cleaned and brightened. The servants must be made to mind her orders, for it was evident they had grown slack in their duties.

At the thought of giving orders she began to tremble, for she had never given an order to anybody in her life. Nell Aston would have been able to do it so much better.

To Robert, when he came upstairs at last, she said dolefully, 'You should have wed Mistress Aston. She looks much cleverer than I am!'

'Goose, I don't choose a wife for the quality of her brains,' Robert said, putting his arm about her. 'I choose her for her looks.'

'But I will try to help you,' she said earnestly.

'And you'll do it beautifully,' Robert told her, beginning to pull the feathers out of her hair.

13

'Lord knows I've no right to think of you in such a way,' James Fleet said earnestly, 'but a man cannot help his heart, mistress, and mine has been fixed on you these ten years or more.'

In a moment, Nell thought, I will wake up and find out that I'm dreaming. It simply isn't possible that I should be standing here listening to my uncle's steward propose marriage to me!

Her uncle had gone over to Maidstone to consult yet another doctor about his rheumatism. She was only too relieved that he wasn't here to listen to such an extraordinary proposal. She had imagined that James wished to request permission to go into the village for something, but that he should be standing before her, twisting his cap in his hands, and pouring out a tale of lifelong devotion struck her as beyond the realms of all reality.

'There have been no sweethearts in my life at all,' he was saying, 'for ever since your uncle took me on as groom I've had it only in mind to better myself. I can read and write as well as the next man, and I've saved most of the money I've earned, so I'd be no charge on your generosity.'

'You do me a great honour,' she began formally, but he interrupted her.

'No, mistress, if we were to wed the honour would be all mine, for you're as far above me as the stars. But I do respect and admire you most truly, and I'd be a faithful husband and a good father too if the Lord sent us any younglings.'

He really did love her, Nell thought in confusion. This stocky peasant with eyes that looked in different directions, though that wasn't his fault, poor soul, actually loved her sufficiently to want to wed her. Perhaps the manor house and its fertile estate had something to do with it too, but the way he spoke of love convinced her that he knew something of its pain.

Gently, because she pitied him and because his words had warmed her cold heart, she said. 'If I had it in mind to wed I can think of none who would take better care of me. But I am occupied with the care of my uncle.'

'I will ask you again, mistress,' James said stolidly. 'I don't expect an answer now, but you are your own mistress and may please yourself in the bestowing of your hand.'

Except that nobody has asked for me, she thought with dismal humour.

Neither she nor Robert had ever been encouraged to mix much with other children, partly because nobody had envisaged any future for them apart from marriage with each other, and partly because in the tiny parish of Marie Regina only the Falcons and the Astons could lay claim to any gentility.

'You may go now,' she said, and wasn't sure whether to laugh or cry when he touched his forelock and went out obediently, as if he had not thought of wishing to marry her at all.

She ought, she supposed, to tell her uncle but he would feel bound to dismiss the man, or at the least, to be angry at his presumption. And James worked very hard and was moreover pleasantly spoken. She herself had come to rely on him to a greater extent than she was willing to admit. He was always quietly and unobstrusively there, grooming the horses, going over the stock accounts, settling an argument in the kitchen, running errands for her at inconvenient times.

Anyway, Uncle Roger had enough upon his mind. He was in constant, crippling discomfort that nothing seemed to ease, and he was sending daily to *Kingsmead* for reports on Sir Harry's health. As winter drew on Robert's father had grown weaker. Climbing the stairs brought on such an anguish of coughing that his bed had been moved into the solar where he now spent all but the mildest days.

Nell seldom went over. It was too upsetting, not only to see him declined from his former vigour, but to see Catrin installed as mistress in the place she had always thought of as her second home. Sweet-voiced and lovely, wearing a succession of pretty dresses with the innocent pride of a child, Catrin was friendly and eager to please. She seemed, Nell thought, to have no opinions of her own at all, for she was constantly quoting Robert. Neither had she done much towards keeping the house in decent order. It was dustier than ever, and John confided that the young mistress never took heed of what the maids were up to, or worked in the stillroom.

'She does nought but wander about, waiting for the young master to come in so she can sit on his knee and whisper nothings in his ear,' John said in disgust. 'She won't come near the stables, for fear of the rats, she says; and she winces if one of the horses gets too close. She's a poor seat too, no style or elegance. Yet would you believe it but she came prancing into the kitchen last week with a little grass-snake over her arm! She made me line a box with straw so that it would sleep away the winter, she said. Beds for snakes if you please, and not a single jar of currant preserve left on the shelves!'

'I'll bring some over,' Nell had promised.

Now, mindful of that promise, she donned her cloak, packed a bag with currant and rhubarb preserve and called to James Fleet to saddle Duchess.

She had a moment's embarrassment when he appeared, but he behaved with the usual mixture of respect and friendliness.

Only as he bent to tighten the stirrup for her did he look up to say, quietly but with deep sincerity, 'Please think over what I said to you, mistress, for my heart is set upon you and there'll be none other.'

She should have refused him at once, but she had lived without hope for so long that she was reluctant to quench it in another, so she nodded, murmuring politely and rode away.

It was a cold, crisp afternoon with December frost riming the hedgerows and the trees tracing patterns against the sky. In less than a month it would be Yuletide. She had hoped to celebrate it as Robert's wife. Now it would be a quiet season with few mummings and only sad little thoughts of might-have-beens.

As she crossed the bridge and glanced towards the path that wound through the trees at the edge of the river she glimpsed a small figure wending its way between the trunks. Nell reined in Duchess and frowned thoughtfully. Nobody ever went to the little house she had once found among the trees, but she remembered suddenly the anger in Lady Alys's face, when she had told her about it, and how Sir Harry had walked there on the day they buried Lady Alys.

Dismounting she began to lead the horse down the steep path.

Oblivious to her follower, Catrin walked slowly with bent head. When she was out here by herself, she could admit that in many ways she was very unhappy. She loved Robert desperately, of course, and he loved her, but he was beginning to take a great interest in the running of the estate and was usually out all day, or closeted with his father, adding up accounts and discussing the pride of crops.

Catrin avoided the sickroom as much as she could. Sir Harry spoke to her with a remote courtesy that was very far from being unkind, but she hated the sound of his coughing and the way blood flecked the pillow when he had finished.

She had tried to carry out her good intentions with regard to the house, but the servants either ignored her or did her bidding so slowly that the task was never completed. Sir Harry and Robert didn't seem to notice what they ate as long as there was plenty of it, and her efforts to mend the tapestries went unnoticed.

She had gone down into the village once or twice, but the people had treated her with such frostiness that she knew they resented her. They would have preferred Nell Aston to be Robert's wife, she guessed, and looked upon her as an intruder, the foreign girl who had snared Sir Harry's boy.

She would have liked to explore the countryside but the sleek beasts in the Falcon stables were very different from the sturdy, gentle little ponies she had ridden at home. Instead she went for long, solitary walks, bringing home bunches of flowers and grasses, and once a little snake, and once a hare injured in a trap.

She had found the little house more than a month previously,, stumbling on it by chance when she had walked further than she intended one day. It was quite invisible from the road, being thickly surrounded by trees and creepers. Its window panes were all cracked and grimed and its door swollen with damp, but she had taken a stone and broken one of the windows and reached inside to unfasten the rusted bolt and then she had scrambled inside, choking as dust rose in clouds from the floor.

Obviously nobody had lived here for a very long time. Her small feet made prints in the dust, and cobwebs spread silvery tendrils as if some friendly ghost fingered her face. The rushes on the floor were mouldered; in each hearth were bird droppings and bits of twig; dishes on the table were green with age. She walked quietly as if fearing to disturb some invisible resident and heard only the rushing of water from the river some yards distant and the soft plop-plop of leaves as they fell yellowing from the surrounding creepers.

In the little room, at the side of what had evidently been the living room, were jars and bottles, some filled with dust and dried roots, others with seeds which had split to send out new sprays that writhed and twisted as if they sought release from their containers. Other bowls held pot-pourri, the fragrance gone; and oranges stuck with cloves hung, mould-coloured, from a frayed line of rope. It must, Catrin thought, have been a magician's house. The thought was half fearful, half exciting.

She lifted the lid of a chest and the scent

of lavender drifted out vague as a dream. Sachets, brown and spilt with age, were piled here. Catrin plunged her hands among them, imagining rather than inhaling the scent. Her fingers touched silk, closed over a lumpy bundle. She drew it out and sat back on her heels to examine her find.

The silk unrolled and there in her lap lay four stiff little objects, roughly representing human figures. She picked one up and gave a cry of pain as a sharp point drew blood from her finger. Each little figure had, she saw, a pin embedded in it.

She frowned down at the little doll-like creatures, wondering who had made them and why. Such things were used in magic, she vaguely knew, but of their purpose she was ignorant.

After a few minutes she wrapped them up again in the silk and pushed the bundle into the drawstring bag that hung from the pointed waist of her stomacher.

She had meant to ask Sir Harry about the little house and show him what she had found, but when she reached *Kingsmead* again the physician was there attending to her father-in-law, and later on Robert came in from hunting and was too busy describing the chase to be interested in how Catrin had spent her day.

Later, when she lay with Robert in the big curtained bed she did say, 'That house down by the river — does nobody live there?'

'The old Dower Cottage? Lord, no! it's been empty ever since I can remember. My grandmother lived there for a time, I believe, after my grandfather died. Why?'

'Nothing,' she said.

If his grandmother had lived there then presumably she had put the seeds and roots into the bottles, and stuck the pins into the stiff little images. It wouldn't be very polite to ask too many questions.

But after that she had been drawn back to the cottage more than once, attracted by its seclusion and by some indefinable charm that soothed her loneliness. There were even times when she admitted to herself that it would have been pleasant to live there with Robert, rather than in the big house where Sir Harry coughed all day and the servants ignored the orders she tried to give.

But on this day she was not unhappy. She had come, in a way, to bid farewell to her haven. Soon she would not be able to take such long, tiring walks, especially in the winter. At the thought of what was to be she wanted to dance and sing, but even when Catrin was alone the quietness of her nature overcame her impulses, and she walked on demurely, mittened hands beneath her cloak.

A twig snapped behind her and she spun around, expecting to catch a fleeting glimpse of a rabbit or a stoat. Instead she saw Nell Aston, leading her horse carefully along the winding path.

As always she felt tongue-tied and nervous in the other's presence. Nell Aston was a part of Marie Regina as Catrin could never be, and on the rare occasions she visited *Kingsmead* she moved about the house with an air of authority as if she really lived there and Catrin was only visiting.

Now, she spoke first, her voice stiffly formal, 'Good-day to you, Catrin.'

'Good-day, Nell.' She used the Christian name awkwardly.

'You're far from home,' Nell said. Her tone seemed to imply a reproof.

Catrin flushed, saying quickly and defensively, 'There was nothing to be done at home.'

'You're fortunate,' Nell said dryly. 'I seem to be occupied with household tasks from morning till night. How is Sir Harry?'

'He is not well,' Catrin said, trouble coming into her face.

'Then ought you not to be sitting with him?'

Nell wished she could sound more friendly, but she could never look at the other girl without imagining her in Robert's arms.

'Robert is there. I came — came for a walk,' Catrin stammered.

She had no wish to talk about the little house or the four strange pin-spiked objects now hidden beneath her dresses in the kirtle chest.

'If you wish to see Robert,' she said, eagerly friendly, 'he is not going out today.'

Nell's fair skin reddened. The remark, she thought, was intended to humiliate her. The wench was letting her know she was aware of her passion for the man who had jilted her.

'I had some preserves for Sir Harry,' she said coldly. 'If you could take them for me it would save me a great deal of trouble.'

'Yes. Of course.' Catrin sighed inwardly. Evidently she had said the wrong thing again.

'They are in the saddle-bags,' Nell said in the same frosty tone. 'Will they be too heavy for you to carry?'

'Lord, but I'm stronger than I look!' Catrin exclaimed. 'I've never been sick in my life!'

She was probably telling the truth, Nell reflected. There was a resilience in her step and a sparkle in her eyes. It was impossible to picture her groaning under a sick headache.

'You spend a lot of your time wandering about,' she said, and the remark emerged carping and critical.

'Very soon I'll have to stay closer to home,' Catrin said, and her quiet joy brimmed over suddenly as if it could no longer be contained within her. 'I am with child,' she said, and her tone exulted. 'In June he will be born if I've counted aright.'

Never in her life, not even when she had heard of Robert's marriage, had Nell experienced such bitter pain. All her days she had loved children and dreamed of bearing them to Robert, and now this wench with the glowing face stood before her and told her she was with child. In some hidden corner of herself she had hoped that Catrin was barren.

'I wish you a safe delivery,' she said dry-mouthed, and thrust the preserves into Catrin's arms so abruptly that the younger girl almost fell.

That this hasty marriage should bear fruit so speedily was unbearable. It conjured up scenes that lay like a dark stain across the fabric of her days. Catrin and Robert turning and twisting together in the act of love; Robert and Catrin mouth to mouth in the intimacy of their shrouded bed.

'Perhaps you would stand gossip?' Catrin said.

Nell mumbled something in reply, mounted Duchess and rode down the path, dipping her head to avoid the spiteful briars.

Roger Aston, returned from Maidstone with nothing but soothing words and a jar of evil-smelling ointment from the new physician, was resting by the fire in the parlour when his niece came in. She had evidently returned from riding for the cold wind had stung bright colour into her cheeks. Above the fiery red, her eyes were hard, pale as water when the sun has gone in.

'I am going to be married,' she said, in a low, fierce voice he had never heard from her before. 'I am going to be married to James Fleet, uncle. I won't ask for your permission because I know you would refuse, and it would grieve me to disobey you. But I'm twenty-six years old and I want a husband and babes of my own.'

'My dear, James is — '

'An orphan of no family who began in your service as a groom. He's also a steady, respectable man who will run Aston Manor very efficiently. And he will be a true and faithful husband to me and be grateful that I accepted him.'

There was a set to her round jaw he had never seen before, and her fists were clenched. Ringless hands, he thought, and felt a surge of dislike for the red-haired girl who had trapped poor Robert into a secret wedding.

'I have never tried to prevent your happiness,' he said mildly, 'but have you thought about this?'

'Until my brain is fit to burst,' she said. There was an ominous quiver in her voice, but she steadied herself and went on, calmly, as if she were talking about somebody else. 'James Fleet has loved me for a long time, uncle, and spoke of it because he could not keep silent any longer. It is flattering to be loved so tenderly, and I would be a fool to let such a chance slip by.'

'You're not a fool, Nell,' he said gently, and could have wept, remembering her soft and gay and full of hope in the days when she had expected to marry Robert.

'I will tell James then,' she said in the new, brisk voice that grated along his nerves. 'I think a quiet wedding after Yuletide will be best. You will find we will go on very comfortably just as we did before.'

It was not true. Nothing would ever be the same, but he nodded and smiled, and she went out of the room, holding herself very carefully as if she might break.

Catrin was tired when she reached *Kingsmead*. It had been stupid, she thought ruefully, to walk so far. Her elation had gone, to be replaced by the nagging thought that she ought not to have blurted out her news to Nell Aston. Perhaps Nell was fonder of Robert than she had admitted.

'But Robert loves me,' she said aloud on the doorstep, and hurried into the hall, calling his name into the emptiness.

John, crossing to the kitchen, informed her sourly that the young master had gone down to the village to watch a cockfight.

'Poor birds. It's a cruel sport!' she exclaimed.

John gave her a disgusted look. Cockfighting was a man's business and no soft-hearted wench had the right to pass comment.

'Sir Harry's not well,' he said chidingly. 'I've been sitting with him this past hour, but I've my other duties to attend.'

'I'll sit with him,' she said quickly. 'Oh, and put these in the stillroom. Mistress Aston met me while I was walking and sent them for Sir Harry.'

'Ah! Mistress Nell was always thoughtful,' John said provokingly. 'A kind, thoughtful lady like the mistress was, God rest her!'

And I will never match up to either of them, Catrin thought. Even the servants know it.

But Robert had chosen her and loved her

and she was going to bear his child. Her feeling of optimism returned as she untied her cloak and went through into the solar where Sir Harry lay, wrapped in a dressing gown and propped on the day bed.

He glanced at her with scant interest as she came in. Like many invalids his illness had become of great concern to him, and others moved in and out of the sickroom without causing more than a ripple on the surface of his self-absorption.

He was glad that Robert had gone to the cockfight. The lad was too healthy, too handsome, too full of energy. He himself had once been like that, riding solitary to London to visit the theatres and stand in the corridor at Whitehall hoping for a smile from the Queen.

Those days were gone. The glittering monarch was dead and Essex slept headless. King James and his mincing catamites occupied the royal apartments now, and the heir to the throne was a shy, stiff young man who stammered and collected paintings.

And I, thought Sir Harry, am limping towards sixty with little prospect of ever reaching it.

'My wife,' he said aloud, following some obscure train of thought of his own, 'was a very virtuous woman. We were betrothed by our families, you know.'

'It must have been a great grief when you lost her,' Catrin said politely.

'Aye, it was.' He sounded faintly surprised as if he had not thought himself capable of so much feeling.

'And you never married again,' she ventured.

'I might have done, if she had come back.'

'She?'

'A wench I knew,' he said dreamily. 'I sent her away, you see. When my wife died I promised myself that I would seek her out and wed her. She was a good girl and wanted marriage. But I never did — pride, I suppose. And I always had it in mind that one day she would come back, but she never did. Nothing turned out as I hoped.'

'I'm truly sorry, sir.' Wondering what he was rambling about, she made her tone cheerfully solicitous. 'Shall I put more wood on the fire? Or would you like some mulled ale?'

'Nothing. Sit down instead and bear me company.'

Her hair glowed redly in the firelight as she obediently lowered herself to a stool. He wondered what she found to do with herself all day.

'Are you ever homesick for Cornwall?'

'No, sir,' she said in surprise. 'Why should I be?'

'Your home is there, isn't it?'

'Oh, yes,' She had forgotten for a moment that he disliked Welsh people and so she was supposed to be Cornish.

'And your mother has gone back there?'

'Yes, sir.'

The room was darkening but his perceptions were growing sharper. From where he lay he could see her, outlined in firelight, her eyes as yellow as the flames. Yellow eyes, a small head set on a narrow neck, a certain way of moving her hands.

'Did you,' he asked, panting in the stuffiness of the room, 'ever have a dancing bear?'

'No, sir, I'm feared of bears and all big animals,' she admitted.

'But you must have heard of one.'

His hand reached out, fastening upon her wrist, shaking her feebly.

'Your mother's name? What is your mother's name?'

'Mar — Margaret, she is called, sir. Margaret Prys.'

She was alarmed by the veins that bulged

in his forehead and the thickness of his slurred voice.

'Margaret Prys. Margred Prys. How old are you, child?'

'I am twenty-two this month, sir.'

And Margred had left in the spring, after Robert's birth. She had ridden away silently and he had stood at the window and watched her leave.

This girl was not like Margred save in subtle ways, and in the colour of her eyes. He had not bothered to look closely at her eyes before, nor to make enquiries into her parentage.

My child. Robert's half-sister. Robert's wife.

The words screamed in his mind. He opened his mouth to speak them but could only grimace helplessly at his face twisted and a thousand lights exploded in his brain. His hand, steel like, was still fastened upon her wrist as he sought desperately to rise.

'Please, sir, I beg of you!'

Her voice was Margred's voice, her eyes were Margred's eyes.

'Please, sir, you will hurt the child!'

But the child was his, his and Margred's. And Margred was riding away without telling him.

He tried to say, 'I meant to marry you.

After Alys's death I meant to come after you, but time passed and I never did.'

Only unintelligible sounds issued from his lips as unintelligible as his whole life had become, for where was the meaning in a marriage without love, a love that was flung away at the demand of an ageing queen, a family built upon a secret so monstrous that his soul shivered to contemplate it?

John, coming to enquire if candles were wanted, found Catrin huddled mutely on the stool, and Sir Harry lying half on, half off the bed, his breathing laboured, one side of his face twisted into an appalling grimace.

14

Sir Harry died three days later without regaining consciousness and was buried next to Lady Alys in the churchyard of Marie Regina. It began to snow on the day of the funeral, white flakes drifting down into the hollows of the valley, settling on the branches of the trees, icing the banks of the river.

Within its black hood Catrin's face looked small and pinched. For the first time, she had experienced a death, and though she felt little real sorrow, the event cast a shadow over her own news.

She had told Robert and he had kissed her and said that he was pleased, but when she would have talked of the coming child he said that there was much to be arranged concerning the funeral. With a little pang she realised that the baby meant no more to him than a vague hope for the future. He was more interested in the fact that a man was coming to paint their portraits.

'My father arranged it as a New Year gift,' he said with a tinge of sadness.

It was hard for him to realise that the good-natured parent who had always indulged his smallest whim was dead. There had been a very real and deep affection between them. It was not even as if Sir Harry had died of his lung disease. The physician who had been hastily summoned from Maidstone pulled doubtfully at his beard and said it looked as if the gentleman had had a bad shock. Catrin when questioned could only shake her head dumbly. But then she was with child and not likely to be in any sensible condition.

Robert knew she had expected him to be more excited about his coming heir, but babes were a woman's province, He was sure he would be very fond of it when it was born, but meanwhile she was putting on a large amount of weight very rapidly. It dismayed him to see her tiny waist thickening, her hips spreading, her voice growing querulous as she complained that in the mornings she felt sick.

Early in January Nell Aston married James Fleet, her uncle's steward. On the whole the village took the wedding calmly. Mistress Nell was a good, kind soul who deserved a steady husband, and James Fleet, for all that he came from nothing, had worked hard and deserved to better his position. If Master Roger was disappointed he wasn't showing it, for he gave his niece away with a smile on his face though anyone could see that it pained him to hobble into church.

Nell wore a dress of white brocade with the lace veil that had been her mother's. She looked cool and self-possessed, her cheeks a delicate pink, the gold locket that had been her husband's gift resting in the hollow between her full breasts. At her side James Fleet looked proud and loving. It irritated Robert to see the steward with that expression on his face, just as it had irritated him when he had learned of the betrothal.

It was time that Nell married, of course, but he thought her choice demeaning. The fellow was not only lowborn but had a squinting eye.

As they rode home after cutting the bride cake, Catrin said, 'I think they make a pleasant pair.'

He said, more sharply than he had ever spoken to her before, 'If she had waited she could have done better for herself.'

Catrin flushed and bit her lip, her eyes filling with tears. Tears came easily to her eyes these days, and once or twice she had woken up sobbing. It was not sorrow for Sir Harry that made her weep. Nor was it lack of love, for she and Robert were very happy together. She wondered if it were her condition and if, with the birth of her child,

270

she would grow strong and wise.

'Do you think we could ask Mam to come and stay for a few months?' she asked wistfully.

'I thought she had gone back into Wales,' Robert said.

'She comes to London again at Eastertime,' Catrin remembered. 'We could send John to the inn to ask her to come.'

Robert frowned, thinking of the tiny, elegant, black-haired woman with the quick lilting voice. He had never been certain whether he liked Mistress Margaret or not.

'She has a farm to run,' he said.

'It is only a little place,' Catrin pleaded, 'and she would come here if she thought I needed her.'

A girl, he supposed, needed her mother with her when she had her first babe.

'Nell would be happy to come over,' he said.

'She is new married,' Catrin said, 'and will want to stay in her own home.'

The idea of Nell Aston handling her child, preparing food for Robert, moving about the big, dim rooms of *Kingsmead*, made her uneasy.

'I would like my Mam to come,' she repeated obstinately, blinking back tears.

Robert suppressed a sigh, and spoke with careful gentleness.

'If you wish it, we'll send John to London at Eastertime to see if your mother is there and will come back with him.'

But there were three months to be lived through before then, and the icy roads and snow-packed lanes would confine her to the house. She shivered, thinking of the long hours when Robert would be out, of the slow, insolent servants, and the memory of that terrible afternoon when her father-in-law had seized upon her wrist and died, with his face twisted up and gutteral sounds issuing from his lips.

Some distraction was provided by the artist who came to paint their portraits. He was a shy, withdrawn young man who had failed to find a rich patron in London, and had cheerfully settled for the painting of small squires and their wives. He was neither talented, nor clever enough to make people believe he was talented, and the finished portraits were stiff and lifeless.

Robert stood like a jointed doll, his face a mask, holding a fowling piece as if he had never used one in his life. Catrin he had painted head and shoulders only, and she stared out of the canvas with an odd, fey look that disturbed people when they looked at it, though they couldn't have told why.

The artist was duly paid and rode away through the melting snow to fulfil another commission. The portraits were hung in the solar and Catrin sometimes went in the room to look at herself. She had seen her face in mirrors and Robert had told her that she was lovely, but she had the odd feeling that the picture on the wall was more herself than she was; as if the artist had caught the essence of her nature and hung it up for other folk to see.

'It makes you look a mite stupid,' Robert said critically.

'Perhaps I am stupid,' Catrin said.

She waited for him to contradict her, but he only gave her an embarrassed little smile.

In truth she was beginning to bore him a trifle, though he did not yet realise it. He had been mad for her in London, entranced by her hair and gentle face, and he loved her still, of course. It was not her fault that her slender grace had become unwieldy, or that her eyes were sometimes reddened as if she had been weeping. Woman, so he understood, had frequent moods when they were with child.

Yet he could not refrain from snapping irritably, 'Isn't it possible for me to be able

273

to sit down in one chair that doesn't need dusting?'

'I'm sorry. I'll wipe it for you,' she said quickly.

'Not you. Call one of the maids. It's not your place to be cleaning!'

'They might be doing something else,' she faltered.

'Then bid them cease! My love, you must learn to make the servants mind you.'

Robert flung out into the hall and shouted for John, who appeared so quickly that one might almost have suspected him of listening for the summons.

'Yes, Sir Robert.' He was all eager, respectful attention.

'There's a layer of dust on every piece of furniture in the house,' Robert said coldly.

'I'll see to it myself, sir.'

'Where are the maids?' Robert demanded.

'Helping Cook to salt the meat, sir.'

'Helping Cook to — that should have been done weeks ago.'

'We had no orders about it from the mistress, sir,' John said humbly.

'I forgot,' Catrin said miserably.

At home, her mother had always seen to the salting of the meat and the making of preserves. Catrin had helped, but under Margred's direction, and she could not have told at which season these things needed to be done.

'Leave the chairs. My doublet is filthy anyway,' Robert said. 'It was for you to remind the mistress of these things. She has not been well since my father died and I rely on you to spare her trouble.'

'Yes, sir.'

John touched his grizzled forelock and withdrew, but before the door had closed behind him, Robert's pent up irritation broke out.

'Catrin, you're not a child! John manages the land and oversees. It's no part of his job to do women's work. Surely your mother trained you in such things!'

But Mam had said, 'One day you'll be a lady and live in a fine house!'

'I'm sorry,' she said helplessly.

'And don't begin to cry again,' Robert said. 'Upon my soul, I never saw such a wench for weeping.'

'The maids don't do as I bid them,' she sobbed. 'I do try, Robert. Truly I do! But the servants despise me and ignore my orders or do everything slowly to make mock of me.'

'You imagine it,' he said. 'You spend too much time fancying insult where none is meant. What was that?'

'That's was a loud crash, followed by a

shout of pain. Robert, running through to the kitchen, found John spread-eagled on the step with one foot at an awkward angle. A patch of melting ice told its own story.

'One minute I was standing up and the next I was flat on my back,' John said. 'I was thinking of the mistress at the time. She gave me such a cold, queer look when the master was scolding me about the dusting. And the next thing down I fell!'

He was not, of course, speaking to Robert or Catrin, but sat with his broken ankle splinted on a stool before him while Cook sat with open mouth and ears.

'You're not usually unsteady on your legs,' Cook allowed.

'Just thinking of the mistress,' he mused, 'and down I went.'

'She was with the master when he died,' Cook said. 'I wonder if she gave him a queer look too.'

'He didn't perish of his lung fever, that's for sure,' John said. 'Shock, that was the word the physician used. Shock! And what shocked him? That's what I'd like to know.'

'We'd all like to know that,' Cook agreed.

It was comfortable by the big fire in the kitchen, and Sir Robert had gone over to Aston Manor. Shaking her head a little, Cook pulled her stool closer to the blaze and turned back her skirts over her knees.

'She's from Cornwall seemingly,' she said, lowering her voice. 'They do say that folk from the West Country have odd ways.'

'It's always a risk, to marry a foreigner,' John agreed.

At that precise moment Robert, sitting by the fire in the parlour of Aston Manor, was saying, 'She feels strange and lonely here, for all I try to do. The servants won't do as she bids, and she's too gentle to scold them. I wish I could be with her more, but I've my own duties to attend and a man cannot be expected to sit indoors all day.'

'It will be better when the child is born,' Nell said placidly.

She was entertaining Robert alone, her uncle enduring the agonies of a mustard plaster in the privacy of his room, James Fleet having gone down to the village.

Nell looked contented, Robert thought with a twinge of annoyance. It was hard to imagine that she could be content with a man like James Fleet; even harder to imagine her in bed with him. Yet she looked, if not happy, at least tranquil, and the blue kirtle she was wearing enhanced her fair colouring.

'I wish you and Catrin could be friends,' he said.

The line of her lips thinned a trifle, but

she answered calmly.

'She is, I think, one of those women who prefer to be solitary. I fancy she thinks me very dull too. I have never been to London in my life, but then I spent most of my life waiting for you to marry me.'

'I was very selfish,' he said, blushing deeply, 'I can only be grateful that you were not in love with me.'

'My pride was hurt,' she said, her eyes lowered to the piece of embroidery in her hands. 'But James suits me very well. He's a good man, very careful of my happiness, and my uncle thinks highly of him. One could look further and find worse.'

'That splendid!' he said heartily, but the shadow remained over his spirits.

'James will be home soon,' she said. 'You will wish to see him, now that you are neighbours, so to speak.'

So he was expected to treat the steward as an equal.

'I needed a favour,' he said unwillingly. 'I promised Catrin that I would send to London for her mother to visit us. John's ankle will keep him confined for months yet. Though he'll not admit it he's past sixty and bones don't mend so speedily at that age. I'd go myself, but I don't like leaving Catrin too much alone.'

'And you want James to send one of our own men?'

Robert had thought more in terms of the steward's going himself.

Nell went on, pleasantly, 'I'm sure we could spare Gideon. He's a very sensible and trustworthy man, and would take a message for you.'

'In a week or two then, when the roads are completely clear,' He hesitated and said, 'I'm very grateful to you, Nell.'

'I must ask James first, but I'm certain that he'll agree,' Nell said demurely. 'You'll stay for supper? My uncle may be down then and he enjoys company.'

'Is he any better?'

She shook her head and her face was clouded. 'He is like your John,' she said. 'He won't admit that the years have passed. But he's in pain for much of the time, though he won't admit that either. My marriage was, in many ways, a comfort to him.'

'And to you?' He was suddenly anxious to find out what lay behind her tranquility.

'I am with child,' she said, and her glance was half triumphant, half sad. 'It will be born in October, four months after your own.'

'I'm happy for you,' he said in a low voice.

'So your child and mine may be playmates,'

she told him. 'Both my uncle and James are happy with the news.'

'And you?'

'I always hoped I would have a child one day,' Nell said. 'I hear James! Excuse me, please.'

She rose and left the room, her blue kirtle whispering over the rushes. Marriage had given her a certain dignity that suited her ample frame and stolid features. She would never be beautiful, but there was a comfort in her presence.

It was reflected in the parlour with its well-polished furniture, its bowls of lavender mingling with the fragrance of apple logs burning on the wide hearth. A dish of freshly made sweetmeats shared the table with a crystal goblet filled with Nell's sugared pears and a tall jug of sack.

Robert knew, without looking, that the kitchen would be scoured, the meat hung and salted, the preserve jars filled. Now that Nell no longer had to divide her time between the two houses, she had made of the manor a charming and comfortable home. He could not help thinking of *Kingsmead* with its bigger apartments, but how dismal they seemed in comparison to where he sat now.

'Sir Robert, it's good of you to call.'

James Fleet, his attitude a nice blend of friendliness and respect, came in with outstretched hand.

Marriage evidently suited him too. The glow of health was in his broad face, his manner had a quiet authority.

'Robert is staying to supper,' Nell said, smiling.

'It will be our pleasure,' he said at once. 'But it's a pity your lady-wife did not come. Nell misses woman-chatter.'

'Catrin is not well,' Nell said, as if she feared that her husband might be hurt by an apparent slight. 'Her mother will be coming over soon to care for her, but it will be necessary to send a message to her. We can spare Gideon, can we not?'

'Certainly. I heard of your steward's accident, and was sorry for it. But Gideon would be able to take a letter.'

'It would be a verbal invitation,' Robert said. 'My wife's mother — she is not well-versed in reading.'

For an instant surprise flashed in his host's face. It said quite clearly, 'So Lady Catrin is not so high-born as you would have us believe.'

Aloud, James said smoothly, 'Well, Gideon will do as you wish. But shall we have supper now? Nell has a trout baked in almond cream that dare not be kept waiting.'

'And some potatoes,' Nell said. 'They are proving such a useful vegetable that I am minded to plant some in my garden.'

'Nell boils them in milk and mashes them with nutmeg,' James said. 'How does your lady-wife deal with them?'

'We have not tried them in any form,' Robert said stiffly.

'Then if you enjoy them I will give you the recipe for her,' Nell said. 'Will you sit here? I will send for more candles.'

It was an intimate, friendly little threesome. Despite himself, Robert began to relax, to enjoy the good food, the trivialities of local gossip. The parson was becoming more puritanical in his observances. He spent more time preaching about sin than praying for the King, and he had publicly scolded Dame Fiske for wearing so wide a farthingale that she had to tilt her skirt sideways in order to get through the door.

'They say he will take a wife even though the bishops have spoken out against married clergy,' James said.

'I think parsons should stay unwed,' Nell said thoughtfully. 'A man should serve God alone if he has a religious vocation. In that respect, at least, the Papists have the right of it.'

'It is not between bishops and parsons that conflict will come,' James said. 'It is between court and Parliament. The King seeks to silence the voice of the people and raise taxes as he chooses. The old Queen had more sense than to insist on her prerogative too loudly.'

The man was well-spoken and moderate in his views, Robert thought. And there was something touching about the way he deferred to Nell's opinion and praised the various dishes set upon the table.

Roger Aston did not, after all, come down to supper but sent his apologies. Robert suspected that the older man felt ill at ease with his niece's former betrothed. He had spoken kindly to Robert at the funeral and at Nell's wedding, but since then he had stayed within doors and not even ventured to church.

'My father had an audience of Queen Bess,' Robert said.

'Ah, they say she had an eye for a handsome man,' Nell smiled.

'So does King James,' Robert said wryly, and they broke into laughter.

It was good to be with one's neighbours, he reflected, stretching his long legs under the table. The candles cast pools of gold on the pewter dishes and the tankards of spiced wine. For a moment he thought of how it would be if Catrin were with him, her face flawless in the candlelight, her red hair gleaming. But when he tried to picture her eyes he could see only the eyes in her portrait, wide and wild and alien.

When he left Aston Manor the moon had arched itself across the sky. He looked back at the house and waved briefly to Nell, who had come out to the step. In his sleeve was the recipe for almond cream that Catrin would never bother to try out. When the door closed it was as if he had been shut out from something cherished and familiar.

'I ought to visit Catrin if she is always so sick,' Nell said, as she turned from the door.

'Her mother will care for her,' James said.

More sensitive to his wife's feelings than even Nell guessed, he was aware of her shrinking from Robert's wife. It meant, of course, that she still loved him. James didn't resent the fact, nor brood because he was only her second choice. She was a good wife and she would be a splendid mother, and one day she might turn and gaze at him with the same devotion as he regarded her.

'I must go up and see if uncle is settled for the night,' Nell said.

'And I will ride over to see if John is improved tomorrow,' James said.

He would have liked to put his arm about her, but there had been a hint of desolation in her face when Robert rode away, and he was too wise to point the contrast between what she had and what she had lost.

'I won't be very long,' she said and went tranquilly up the stairs, only an almost imperceptible heaviness of step betraying her heart's disappointment.

Catrin had waited until it was certain that Robert would not be coming home for supper, and then she had come down to sit alone at the head of the trestle table. The two girls who helped in the house had gone back to the village before darkness fell, and only John, hopping on a crutch, and Cook bore her company. They took their accustomed seats at the end of the table, their heads leaning together, their voices low as if they whispered about her.

The food was indifferently cooked and cooling rapidly, and the wine produced by Cook was thin and vinegary. They would not have served such fare for Robert, she thought, but she hadn't the courage to complain or to send it back. Instead she sat, pushing her meat listlessly around her plate, aware of the glances cast in her direction.

'Sir Robert,' She raised her voice into the silence. 'Sir Robert will probably be late tonight, so there's no need for you to wait up for him.'

'I've always waited up for the master,' John said snubbingly. 'I used to wait up for Sir Harry when he was alive, and now I wait up for Sir Robert. I hope I know my duty, my lady.'

Catrin bit her lip and stared down at the meat congealing on her plate. As usual she had said the wrong thing and made them despise her a little more. She pushed back her chair and stood up, her voice shaking.

'I'll bid you goodnight then. Will you see there is some ale mulled ready for when the master comes home?'

She was halfway up the stairs when she caught John's muttered complaint.

'First I must not wait up for the master and then I must be reminded to have a hot drink ready when he does come! Does the mistress think that I am so old I am past all my use?'

Catrin closed her eyes briefly, struggling against the misery of nausea and loneliness. She wished that Robert had come home for supper. She wished he had not gone over to Aston Manor at all. It was not as if he had ever loved Nell, or felt any real friendship for her husband.

'Nearly four months to go,' she said aloud to the empty cradle in the corner.

Robert had lain in that cradle and his father before him. Strange to think that the grey-haired man with the twisted face had once been a swaddled babe! And soon her own child would lie there. She wished the time would pass quickly, for she was already so large that it was an effort to shift herself from one room to another.

She grimaced as she unlaced her stomacher, aware of her distended body below her small, wan face. It was no wonder Robert went out for supper and stayed late when she looked so drab and ugly.

She climbed into the big bed and huddled beneath the feather quilt. It was cold, but she had forgotten to order the warming pan to be filled, and by now the fires would be damped down.

As she drifted into sleep a series of visual images processed behind her eyelids. Nell was holding a baby but the face of the child was twisted. John was dancing with Cook and as they danced they twined into a tree with purple veined leaves — there was one such tree growing by the courtyard gate. She had crumpled a leaf between her fingers one day and a sharp, vinegary scent had risen to her nostrils. And then in her mind she was running, running, running towards the little house by the river, and somewhere behind her a great bear crashed through the undergrowth.

She woke shivering and saw that Robert had come home. He stood by the unshuttered window, gazing out at the moon, and she feared to speak lest she say the wrong thing again.

15

Parson Bewling leaned on his spade and wiped his brow with the back of his hand. April was planting time and a season he enjoyed, for it satisfied something in his nature to lay brown pods deep in the earth and wait for the green seedlings to emerge. They were like the souls of people, he considered, unimaginable beauty hidden away ready to be coaxed forth or to be neglected and wither away.

He took his duties in the parish seriously, preaching regularly, visiting every home at least once a month, trying to set an example by keeping his small house sparkling and his garden well weeded. It was a pity that his people were not always eager to listen to what he said. Though they knew he disapproved, they still set up their maypoles and danced about them far into the night, and decorated the well in the ruins of the monastery with flowers and leaves on Lady Day. Pagan superstition! The thought of it made him so angry that he began to sweat all over again.

What he needed was a walk to clear his

head. He dug his spade hard into the rich soil and wiped his hands on the damp rag he kept for that purpose hanging over the wooden fence. The woman who came in every day to clean the house declared that there was scarcely anything for her to do, and that it was a crying pity such a man didn't have a good wife. A good wife might even give him something more to think about than what his parishioners were up to when his back was turned.

Having removed the loose brown smock he wore for gardening, Parson Bewling clapped on the black funnel hat without which he never ventured beyond the gate, and strode up the cobbled street that wound first between houses and then between high banks of meadowsweet until it reached the upper road. The air was sweet and warm, the breeze gentle, the sky a clear, pale blue across which an occasional white cloud was puffed like thistledown.

As he rounded the slope and paused to draw breath, he saw a woman standing further along the road near to the main gates of *Kingsmead*. She had evidently just alighted from her horse and a second mare laden with baggage cropped the grass nearby.

The woman was small and slim, dressed in black and she stood with bent head, tapping her teeth with the handle of her riding crop, obviously deep in thought.

He approached her with his rapid, nervous stride, doffing his hat, and raising his voice in polite greeting.

'Good morrow, mistress! May I be of any service to you?'

She looked up and for a fraction of a second he was chilled by the blankness of eyes yellow as a fox's eyes. Then she smiled warmly and held out her small, gloved hand.

'You're very kind, sir.' Her voice was quick and lilting. 'I am bound for *Kingsmead* to visit my daughter.'

'You must be Lady Catrin's mother. Sir Robert told me that you were expected. But surely you haven't travelled alone from London?'

'No, no, a young man by the name — of Gideon? — was sent to escort me. I told him to go on to Aston Manor. And you — ?'

'The incumbent of Marie Regina. My name is Josiah Bewling.'

'The parson,' She gave him another dazzling smile. 'The man Gideon mentioned you, sir. He tells me you show great diligence in preaching. I enjoy a good sermon myself. One hears too few of them nowadays.'

'I trust we shall see you in church on

Sunday, mistress,' he said.

'Unless my daughter requires my care, but her time is not for two months. I have not seen her since the marriage. It took place very impulsively, I fear, but these young people — '

She raised her hands and let them fall to her sides again.

She was surely not much past forty herself, Parson Bewling thought and she looked younger despite her black garments. He approved the modest farthingale, the partlet of ivory gauze matching the deep cuffs of the tight inner sleeves. What he could see of her hair was parted in the centre and drawn back under an arched hood from which a gauze veil hung gracefully.

Parson Bewling had been as shocked as everybody else when young Sir Robert had jilted Mistress Nell and ridden home with a strange bride. But this was no fortune-hunting mother. This was a lady, decently and charmingly attired, and obviously interested in village affairs.

She gave him now a little, dismissing nod, saying, 'I know you will excuse me if I hurry on. I look forward to your sermon on Sunday, Master Parson.'

He helped her to remount and was rewarded with another wide, slanting smile.

It was, Margred thought, gathering up the reins and tugging the pack horse away from the grass, a blessing that the parson had come upon her when he did, else she might have lost all her courage and galloped back to London again. She had not expected such a reaction from herself, and she was ashamed of her weakness.

She would never have come at all, of course, had not Gideon told her that Sir Harry was dead. It was odd, but in a way she had been expecting to hear the news for a long time and her momentary sadness was not for the ageing knight, but for the man who had carried her on his saddle and warmed her with his cloak on the night Mott had been killed.

She had not realised how hungry she had been for information, and Gideon was a friendly, informative man who, under her subtle questioning, revealed more than his words told.

Sir Harry had died more suddenly than most folk had expected, and Sir Robert was taking over very nicely in the management of the estate. As for Lady Catrin, he couldn't say much on account of she kept herself very close, but then with her child due in June she was likely not feeling sociable.

No, he didn't work at *Kingsmead* himself,

but at Aston Manor. Old Master Aston was very lame now and seldom left his room, but Mistress Nell had wed her uncle's steward and he was proving a good master.

So a brief visit would be safe, for she had no fear of running into Roger Aston, and she doubted if anybody else in the village would connect the veiled and respectable widow with the shy, wild girl who had lived by the river.

She rode slowly up the curving drive until she reached the walls of the inner courtyard and there reined in her mount, and gazed with weary triumph at the slender, rust-leaved tree.

It had survived then, and grown, this symbol of her thwarted love and secret revenge. The words she had whispered over the twisted seedlings were burned into her brain. One day when she was old she would have somebody write them down for her, to serve as memorial for all time.

The main door stood partly open. Margred dismounted and stood still, remembering how she had stood more than twenty years before and watched Harry at the window above with the babe. Then she went quietly up the steps into the hall.

It was big and high with staircase stretching to a gallery and dim silver and pewter dishes ranged on a dresser that towered to the beams. There was a fine layer of dust over everything and motes of dust floated in the shaft of sunlight from the open door. Conspicuous on the dresser was the christening cup with Robert's name engraved upon it. He had mentioned to her that old Queen Bess had stood gossip. She went over and picked up the cup, holding it to the light, her lips parted in a bitter smile.

From the kitchen doorway, a voice said indignantly, 'And who gave you leave, mistress, to come poking and prying into other folks' things?'

John — she had forgotten about John! John would remember her. He had been in the yard on the day she rode away. Cursing her own stupidity, she set the cup down and turned to face him.

'It is John, is it not?' Her face was eager and smiling. 'I hoped I might see you — '

'The master's dead,' he said harshly. 'There's nought here for you now.'

'I heard of it and was sorry.' She went closer to him, her voice softening. 'I think, even if he had ever guessed that my daughter had wed his son, he would have forgiven it.'

'Your — the mistress?' Leaning heavily on his crutch, he peered at her. 'The young

295

mistress is your girl?'

'Her poor father died of the sweating sickness when she was a tiny babe,' Margred said sadly.

'So you wed another man! And you so eaten up with love for Sir Harry.'

'I was very young,' she said in the same gently sad tone. 'I went back to my own land and a neighbour's son wed me. He was very good to me, very kind. Catrin takes after him in looks.'

And, pray God, he doesn't know that Catrin's birthday is in December, and begin counting backwards to the month when I left.

He was still staring at her however, and she fancied he looked a trifle less grim. He said, in a questioning tone, 'And your wench met Sir Robert by chance?'

'If I had only known!' she exclaimed. 'But they had promised marriage marriage to each other before I realised that Robert was the son of the gentleman I had known. And then I had not the heart to tell them. After all, I was here a very long while ago.'

'You've worn well,' he said grudgingly.

There were questions still in his eyes. She went on smoothly.

'It's been a hard life for all that, and I'll confess I was pleased to think my daughter

296

would enjoy some of the happiness I missed. But she's a feckless wench with little in her head save pretty clothes and kisses. I'll reckon you've not found it easy to keep the house in order since Sir Harry went.'

She had struck the right note. The old man positively unbent, his features wrinkling into friendliness.

'It's been hard ever since Lady Alys was taken. The heart went out of the master then, and though Mistress Nell was back and forth between here and her uncle's place, it wasn't easy for those of us who had known *Kingsmead* in the old days. And the new mistress — begging your pardon! — has no more notion than a child how to keep the maids in order.'

'It must have been very difficult,' she sympathised. 'If there is any way in which I can help while I am here?'

'You ought to have trained your wench better,' John said sourly, but his attitude had melted.

There was still some confusion in his mind as to how everything had come about, but it seemed that the girl with the bear had come back as a lady. There was an air of authority about her that she had lacked before.

'Where is my daughter?' she asked.

'In her room, mistress.'

'At this hour? It's scarce midday!'

'She lies abed till dinner time,' John said, with a wealth of disapproval in his voice.

'I will go up and rouse her. Do we have dinner today?'

'There is a goose and some boiled carp,' John said doubtfully.

'Could you make it ready?' she asked. 'And if there is any pie, could you put that out too? Surely the cook is about?'

'She went to the orchard to look for mint.'

'I will come down for dinner very soon,' she said briskly and swept purposefully up the stairs.

Things were happening too quickly for John to take in. Only one thing seemed very clear. After months of disorganised living he had been given a definite order by a woman who seemed to have the habit of authority. He swung about then limped back into the kitchen, calling for Cook.

The gallery at the top of the staircase ended in doors to left and right. Her first guess was the correct one. The door on the right opened into a lofty apartment out of which a bedchamber led.

Catrin was lying on the bed, her long hair spread over the pillow, her kirtle unlaced. Her face as she raised it from the covers

298

was flushed and sullen, but it broke into an incredulous smile.

'Mam! Oh, Mam. I hoped you come! I've been so wretched here, and so sick, and I'm so big I can scarce move, and Robert's gone, and the servants won't do as I bid!'

Her voice broke into sobs.

'Now here's a coil!' Margred spoke cheerfully, loosing her cloak. 'I did not expect to find you still slug-a-bed when it's near dinner time! And why are you not dressed?'

'My gowns are too tight. I'm huge!' Catrin wailed.

'Surely you had the sense to let them out! Never mind, here's a loose robe. This will do very well while you are within doors.' Margred shook out a high-waisted green overdress that had been tossed on the end of the bed. 'And you must sponge your face, child. Have you a comb?'

'On the table,' Catrin heaved herself to the side of the bed.

'I'll braid your hair. You're no maiden to be running about like a hoyden!'

Margred suited action to words, her fingers skilled and soothing.

'I hoped Gideon would find you,' Catrin gulped. 'But I was feared you'd decide to stay home, it being seed time.'

'The Englishman can deal with the farm. I told you I'd be in London round Easter. So you are with child, eh?'

She tweaked her daughter's hair to coax a smile.

'In two months.'

'And the servants are proving troublesome? You must learn to be firmer.'

'They don't like me,' Catrin said. 'John and Cook whisper about me and the maids giggle when I try to tell them what to do.'

Margred stifled a sigh. The girl was a fool as she had always suspected, and in a sense she was not entirely to blame.

I should have given her a harder rearing, Margred chided herself. But I made life easy for her because I wanted her to be a lady and live at *Kingsmead*.

Aloud, she said pleasantly, 'Women near their time often have odd fancies. You will feel much better when the babe is here. I will deal with the servants for you until you are more yourself. I have told the old man, John, to have dinner for us. Now what is all this about Robert being gone?'

'He rode over to Aston Manor,' Catrin said. 'Nell Aston, she's Nell Fleet now, miscarried of a child yesterday.'

'She married her steward, did she not?'

'Aye, James Fleet. A squinting man but

300

well-spoken. They rode here to supper two nights ago. Robert said I must begin to entertain a little because the Astons have been neighbours since his grandfather's time. And I truly tried to give them a good supper. I even made a gooseberry pasty and Nell ate three helpings and asked me for the recipe. And then early this morning one of the manor servants came to tell us she had miscarried, and Robert wanted me to go over there.'

'Why didn't you?'

'I was sick,' Catrin said with weak indignation. 'I cannot sit a horse and the cart jolts me. Robert wouldn't listen and I wouldn't go, and in the end he flung out in a temper.'

'Wasn't this Nell his betrothed before he wed you?' Margred asked.

'Aye, and it's my belief she wants him still,' Catrin said.

'And so you deny her your friendship and drive him straight back to her!'

Margred looked at the younger girl in despair. There was certainly a dangerous weakness in Catrin, something bred in the bone and not entirely due to her rearing.

'I know I behaved foolishly,' Catrin muttered, 'Robert would never look twice at another wench, but he's fond of Nell, and he wanted us to be friends.'

And Robert was a fool too, Margred reflected grimly. Did he really imagine that the wench he had jilted would think kindly of his wife, or that his wife would be at ease in Nell's company? She had gauged him accurately when she had first thrown Catrin in his way. A good-hearted, handsome lad, but spoilt and shallow and bent on his own comfort.

'See to your face,' she ordered, and went out to the gallery again.

In the hall below a maidservant was laying the table in slovenly fashion. Margred crossed the gallery and went into the left-hand room, which matched the one on the other side of the house and had a similar apartment leading out of it. She would use these two rooms while she was at *Kingsmead*. It was at this window that Harry had stood with the child in his arms and looked down with unforgiving face. In the big, curtained bed Alys had lain, weak and triumphant after child-bearing. No doubt she had been relieved to learn that the Dower Cottage was empty again.

Margred's lips moved silently, addressing the empty air.

'But here I am back again, and not at the Dower Cottage either but in *Kingsmead* itself, in the very room where you lay in all your smugness. You're dead now, Alys Falcon, and you too, Harry, sweet Harry, who held me close and lied to me of love. You are no more now than shadows in my mind. But I hope you know that I'm here. I hope you know, sweet Sir Harry, that our daughter is married to your son. Oh, I *hope* you know!'

The room was dusty, the air stale. She opened the casement wide and looked about her frowning. The wall hangings needed to be taken down and beaten, and the rushes swept away. In London many rooms were being panelled now and she had heard that in the grandest houses carpets were being laid on the floors. Even if the Falcons couldn't run to such extravagance there was no excuse for grimed window panes or cobwebs in the corners. Obviously the servants had taken advantage of Catrin to grow slovenly and careless. She would have liked to go down and give John a piece of her mind but she would have to tread warily. The old man knew too much about her.

Margred went downstairs again slowly and into the kitchen. As she expected it was untidy and grease-spattered, the curtain across the corner looped back to show an unmade pallet, ashes piled too

303

high on the hearth. A fat woman looked up as she entered and made a half-hearted bob which might have been a curtsey. Her expression was wary.

'John will have told you that I am Lady Catrin's mother,' Margred said pleasantly. 'I am sorry to find her so sickly and yourself so sorely put on in this fashion. Are the maidservants not here to help you?'

'One of them is, but t'other's not been nigh for over a week,' the woman said. 'John and I do what we can, mistress, but his ankle's still bad after his fall and my task here is cooking.' '

'Then more daily help must be engaged,' Margred said promptly.

'I've been saying that very thing!' the woman declared. 'But Sir Robert is all for horses and crops, and the mistress — '

'Has obviously been sadly remiss.' Slanting a long look at the cook, Margred said persuasively, 'When we have eaten dinner, perhaps you and I could put our heads together and devise some solution.'

'So pleasantly spoken!' the cook would declare later to John. 'A lady from head to foot, and not too proud to ask advice of a servant either! It's my belief she's shamed of her daughter's finicky ways.'

'She seems a good woman.' John, thinking

of what he could tell if he chose, gave Cook a superior smile.

'Not that I set any store by pretty speeches,' Cook said, 'but it's clear to me she's a sensible body. She asked me the recipe for those stuffed pears I made. And she was shocked that I should be washing my own cloths! It's my hope she'll bide a good long time. Why, it's been years since we said a grace before our meat — not since Lady Alys died, and that's a scandal in a Christian household.'

'The praying wasn't to the taste of the mistress though,' John commented.

'I noticed that.' Cook looked thoughtful. 'Green as a frog she went as soon as Mistress Margaret began and never a bite of the goose did she take.'

In the parlour Catrin sat, obediently unstitching a bodice. Wave after wave of nausea had swept over her as the rich smell of the goose wafted to her nostrils. She had forced down a mouthful and then retreated, conscious of the servants' eyes fixed upon her.

At this moment her mother was in the stillroom, checking on what needed to be replaced on the shelves. She seemed to have won the respect of John and Cook with no effort at all. Indeed, John was chatting away

305

as if he had known her mother for years and there was talk of all the linen being washed, the rushes changed, the hangings beaten, and the garden being restocked.

Catrin's eyes rested briefly on the portrait of Lady Alys. Robert had told her once that his mother had been a notable housewife, forever baking and brewing. Perhaps the plain-faced woman in the stiff ruff and her own lively, slender mother were at heart the same.

They belong here, she thought, and I never really belonged anywhere.

It was odd that such a thought should jump into her mind, for her mother had never been into Kent before, but already Margred fitted into the house as if she were its true mistress and Catrin no more than a chance visitor who had lighted for a spell.

'I see your lady-mother has arrived,' Robert said from the doorway.

'She is setting us all to rights,' Catrin said. 'I'm glad you came home early.'

'Nell is weak and not fit for a long visit.' He drew off his gloves and smoothed them absently between his fingers. 'It was a cruel disappointment for her. She has always liked children.'

'But she will have others?'

'Aye. The physician told James Fleet she

would probably rear a large family. This was no more than ill luck, and he could name no cause.'

'I will try to get over to see her,' Catrin said pleadingly.

'Aye,' he said again. 'I'm sorry I shouted at you earlier.'

'It was the shock of the news,' she said excusingly.

The insidious thought that he ought not to have been so shocked at a mishap to another man's wife crept into her brain.

Without meaning to, she said, 'I've been very sick myself today.'

'I'm sorry for it,' he said in the same absent, gentle tone. 'But you'll feel better now that your mother is here. Gideon said he found her without trouble.'

If he had learned of her mother's arrival from Gideon then he should have had the good manners to come home for dinner. But he had been too busy comforting Nell to tear himself away.

Catrin said, trying to keep the sharpness out of her voice, 'Perhaps you had better pay your respects to my lady-mother, unless you have to rush off somewhere again!'

'I'll do it now.'

He glanced at her, not critically but in a puzzled manner as if he wondered where her indolent grace had fled, and went out into the hall. She heard his voice raised in greeting and Margred's voice murmur in reply. Then Robert laughed. It was a long time since he had laughed so heartily — and it was her mother, not herself, who had roused that response.

She laid aside her work and rose heavily, and went close to the picture of Lady Alys. It had a look of Nell, but then Lady Alys and Nell's father had been distaff cousins. They would have wanted Nell to marry Robert. Perhaps Robert himself was beginning to want it too.

If I die in childbed, Catrin thought, Mam will rear the babe and manage the house, and Robert will grieve for a while and then forget, and soon it will be as if I had never existed.

Tears of self-pity beaded her lashes. She blinked rapidly and turned away from the picture. The house was full of women, and under the weight of their disapproval she was shrinking into nothingness.

'Robert looks fit and lusty,' Margred said, coming in with a pile of linen in her arms. 'Marriage agrees with him.'

She sounded, thought Catrin, as if something had amused her very much.

16

'Twin boys and both living!' Nell said bitterly.

'Born ten minutes apart,' her husband nodded. 'The elder is the bigger. He had a tinge of red in his hair. The other is going to be fair.'

'Twin boys!' Nell said again. 'And their mother is well?'

'Already sitting up and declaring she will have a daughter next time.'

Nell turned away sharply. James didn't mean, she knew, to chide her for her own barren state. They had, after all, been married for less than a year and many women miscarried of their first child. The physician had assured her she was capable of bearing many children, and could not explain why her first pregnancy had ended so disastrously. But she had longed for the babe, more than even James could guess. She had sewed a boxful of dainty garments for it. And it had all come to nothing while that frail, red-haired wench had borne healthy twins with apparently little discomfort.

'How are they to be named?' she asked.

'Hal and Robin,' James said. 'After Sir Harry and Sir Robert.' He hesitated briefly and then ventured, 'I said that you would call. Mistress Margaret asked after you most kindly.'

'She's a pleasant woman,' Nell said, fairly.

She had seen Catrin's mother first at church, and after the service Robert had introduced them. The older woman had taken Nell's hand in a confiding clasp.

'I have heard much of you, Mistress Fleet. Robert forever sings your praises.'

She made it sound as if it were quite natural for her son-in-law to praise the woman he had jilted, and her wish to be friendly was so evident that Nell had found herself smiling back.

After that she had seen Mistress Margaret at church every week and once or twice in the village. Catrin's mother had a quick, darting charm that even had James bowing and blushing as if he were still steward and not master of Aston Manor.

'My daughter is not well enough to receive visitors yet,' she had said, 'and I have not the time to go visiting. You must forgive me for my discourtesy, but the house needs better management and one cannot expect Robert to do everything himself.'

She had sounded, Nell thought, as if she

were a little ashamed of her daughter.

'I'll ride over to *Kingsmead*,' Nell said now. 'I would have come with you today, but Uncle Roger felt so bad I was afraid to leave him.'

In truth she was glad that her uncle had craved her company, for it had spared her the necessity of going to *Kingsmead* to enquire after Catrin. She had spent a wretched night ever since one of the maids had come in and said that Gideon had had it from Dame Agatha that Lady Catrin was in labour. Half of her wished the babe would be safely delivered for Robert's sake, and half of her — a half she tried to deny — wished nothing but harm to the girl who had stolen the only man Nell had ever loved. She had sent James over to *Kingsmead* as soon as dawn had broken and then had endured a morning's suspense until James had returned, to tell her that Catrin had been delivered of twin sons.

'I'll go tomorrow,' she said. 'But I'd best tell my uncle now. He'll be anxious for news.'

She gave her husband a bright smile and went upstairs, her feet lagging a little on each step.

Her uncle was in his room, his bandaged leg propped on a stool. He was reading a news-letter from London and looked up as Nell entered.

'My dear, did you know that Prince Charles is said to favour the Infanta of Spain as a bride? A Papist marriage is the one thing that will further alienate the commons from His Majesty!'

'Catrin has had twin boys,' Nell said abruptly.

'Oh?'

Roger Aston settled his spectacles more firmly on his nose and looked at her searchingly.

'Hal and Robin they're to be called,' Nell said. 'Fine healthy babes, James says, and Catrin is very well. She scarcely suffered at all.'

'Your turn will come,' Roger said. 'You will have babes of your own.'

'But they won't be Robert's!' she cried out, and was appalled by her own disclosure.

'James Fleet is a good man,' Roger said gently. 'I was not pleased when you accepted him, but I was wrong. He's a good man and a kind husband.'

'I like him well,' she defended, 'but it's not the same. It never could be the same! Uncle, how can I make you understand? I've loved Robert ever since we were little.'

'As I loved Robert's mother,' he said.

312

'You? You and Lady Alys?'

'Did you think you were the only one who ever felt the fever in the blood?' Roger asked. 'I knew Alys Prescott when we were both children, and as we grew up our love was so strong it blotted out the world. But the world broke in. It always does. We were first cousins and her father would not let us wed. They betrothed her to my best friend instead, to Harry Falcon.'

'You — and Lady Alys.'

'From the day of her marriage until her death, she never spoke to me of love again,' Roger said. 'She was a true and faithful wife, and I respected that.'

'And you never married.' She spoke softly, wonderingly.

'I had the friendship of the woman I loved, and I had my own niece to rear.' He reached out to pat her fondly on the arm. 'You are very like Alys, my dear. You have her strength and quietness. It gave me immense joy to think of your marriage to Robert, but Robert chose his own road. In years to come you will learn to value his friendship, and you will have babes of your own.'

'I miscarried,' she reminded him. 'For no reason at all, I miscarried — just after I supped with Robert's wife. And John — did you know that John broke his ankle just after he'd defended himself against her? He told me of it, and I took no notice at the time. But ever since I have begun to think.'

'Such thinking is foolish,' her uncle said.

'But we don't know anything about her,' Nell argued. 'She said she was Cornish, but she knows nothing of the West Country. She never speaks of any family, save her mother — not that I dislike Mistress Margaret! She's a sweet soul and is setting *Kingsmead* to rights, far better than her daughter ever did.'

'Margaret.' He tested the syllables on his tongue. ' 'Tis a pretty name.'

'And she is a pretty woman,' Nell said. 'Not still and silent like Catrin, but lively and merry spoken.'

'Margaret,' he said again. 'I had hoped she would visit here.'

'She sent apologies for that,' Nell said. 'And soon she will be returning to London, I daresay.'

'Margaret,' Roger said.

'Why do you keep repeating her name?' his niece enquired.

'It — reminds me of something.' He shifted uneasily in his chair. 'No matter. But to come to yourself — you are too good to harbour jealousy against a girl who has done you no harm.'

'Sir Harry died after she was come.'

'Harry had been sick for months. He could not move without coughing.'

' 'Twas not the cough that killed him. He died with his face twisted up, as if he'd seen the devil himself. And Catrin was with him when it happened.'

'Nell, stop this!'

'And my babe died before it was full formed, and John broke his ankle — and she doesn't say her grace,' Nell rushed on. 'I had that from John too. She chokes upon the meat after she has tried to say Amen.'

'You should discourage such idle gossip, not join with it,' Roger said sternly.

'But such things can be. The King himself has spoken out against such doings.'

'King James has spoken out against most things, including the use of tobacco and the practice of tilting,' Roger said wryly. 'Nell, you're a woman of good sense. Don't prate like a peasant. Such talk might do much harm.'

'Aye, maybe so.' She seemed to shake her thoughts into order and when she spoke again she was her usual serene self.

When she had gone downstairs again, however, he sat thinking for a long time. His leg and his memory throbbed alike, and his face was grave.

Three days later Nell brought herself to ride to *Kingsmead*. The fine weather had broken and a heavy downpour had delayed her setting out for more than an hour. Even now the sky threatened more rain and the wind was unseasonably cold.

At the fork in the road that led down into the village she paused to watch two yeomen, sleeves rolled up, shovelling mud from the deep-pitted ruts. They touched their forelocks as she drew rein and clambered up the bank to speak to her.

'The river's running too fast,' one of them said gloomily.

'And too high,' the other chimed in. 'We're ankle deep in water down the street. There's no place for it to drain away.'

'Never had this trouble in summer before. Winter, yes. But not summer.'

'Parson says 'tis the Will of the Lord! But if that be true, 'tis my belief the Lord's a spiteful body!'

'Parsons talk a load of nonsense,' his companion said scornfully.

'It will spoil the crops,' Nell said.

'Aye, mistress, that it will! The fruit cannot come to much harm, but the wheat's not ready for scything, and hops need sunshine.'

'Perhaps it will clear tomorrow,' she suggested.

'Perhaps it'll rain gold and we'll all ride white horses!' the man retorted genially. 'Nay, mistress, this weather's here to set a spell.'

She nodded and moved on, the horse picking its way carefully between the deep puddles. The wind blew gusts of left-over rain into her face and the trees dripped moisture.

Catrin's mother opened the door for her, her expression solicitous.

'Mistress Nell! Such a day to ride out! Come in and warm yourself. John! take the mare into the stable and rub her down.'

'It's bad for the time of year,' She allowed herself to be divested of hood and cloak.

'Bad for any time of year. Will you come upstairs to see the babes? They're beautiful, though I ought not to say it, being their grandmother!'

'You don't look old enough, mistress,' Nell said cordially.

The other looked please. 'Ah, well,' she said. 'I was married young and widowed young. Please to come up.'

The house had been cleared, Nell noticed. There were fresh rushes on the floors and a diamond twinkle in the window panes. Fires crackled in the hearths and the smell of baking drifted from the kitchen.

Nell braced herself mentally and went through into the bedchamber. It was worse than she had expected. This room, like the anteroom, was clean and bright. Catrin, her hair tied back with a ribbon, sat up in the high bed and Robert sat on a stool by her side. In the corner two cradles invited attention.

'Nell! It's good to see you!' Robert came over at once and kissed her.

'It's good to see you.' Conscious of his wife's gaze she disentangled herself gently and forced herself to bend to kiss Catrin's pale cheek. 'You have surprised us all,' she said gaily. 'Two sons at one time!'

'We had to borrow an extra cradle from the village,' Robert said.

'They're fine babes,' She went over and looked down at the sleeping, swaddled bundles.

'Hal is the bigger,' Robert said, joining her. 'He's going to be a redhead.'

'The other is fair, like your mother,' Nell said softly.

She longed to pick one of them up and nurse it. Her arms ached with the wanting.

'You can hold one, if you like,' Catrin said from the bed.

'I'd best not disturb them.'

The desire had fled, but the ache remained.

She put out her finger and touched the fuzz of gingerish hair. The baby twitched his nose and gave a small sneeze.

'I'll send up some wine and comfits,' Catrin's mother said. 'If you'll excuse me, mistress, there's a duckling on the spit that will turn into a crisp if I'm not there to remind Cook to turn it.'

She went out with her brisk, light step, the household keys jangling at her waist. On the stairs she paused, to allow herself a moment's contentment. She had worked hard since her arrival to improve matters and wipe away the bad impression Catrin had made. That she had done so at the expense of seeming to criticise her daughter was regrettable, but necessary.

The house was clean now, the linen washed, the stillroom replenished. John had accepted her, and the barest hint that his lameness and age made him less than useful had been sufficient to close his mouth regarding her earlier history.

She had little fear of discovery from any other quarter. Roger Aston was confined to his room and unlikely to meet her, and nobody in the village recognised her at all. It seemed to her incredibly good fortune, for she was aware that she had altered little.

She was unaware, however, of the more

subtle changes that had taken place. Her step was that of a busy matron now, not a young girl. She chose her words carefully, veiling her yellow gaze, smiling with closed lips when once she would have bubbled with wild laughter.

She went every week to service, gave generously but not too indiscreetly to the poor box, cooked Robert's favourite dishes, and knew that as soon as Catrin was churched it would be wise to leave Kent.

There was nothing here for her now that Harry had gone, and his son's resemblance to him was disconcerting. Once she had almost called him 'Harry' and just stopped herself in time. It was wiser for her to go. Her own small property awaited her, and the Englishman was getting too old and too mad to run it without supervision.

She straightened her narrow shoulders and went into the kitchen, saying, 'Cook! give me your advice on this bird. Do you think a final basting is due or not?'

In the big bed upstairs, Catrin watched her husband and Nell Fleet bend over the cradles. She had caught the yearning on Nell's face and was sorry for her. It must be a terrible disappointment to miscarry. Yet she wished Robert would not stand so close.

'Will you go and bring up the wine?' she asked, more loudly than she had intended.

'Yes, of course.'

It annoyed Nell to see how swiftly he obeyed the request. Kindly as James was, she could not picture him fetching and carrying at the whim of a woman.

'Robert is very good to me,' Catrin said softly.

Leaning back against her pillows she looked, thought Nell, like a self-satisfied and exquisite little fox.

'I'm told you suffered little,' she said abruptly.

'It was bad enough,' Catrin said with a hint of sulkiness. 'It's not easy to deliver two babies and they are both a good size.'

'They're very pretty.'

Nell gave them one final glance of envy, and jumped slightly as rain blew sharply against the window panes.

'Hal is greedy and wants his brother's share as well as his own,' Catrin told her, 'but I've plenty of milk.'

'That's fortunate,' Nell said tranquilly. She wanted to scream, 'Who cares a rap? Who could be interested in your petty concerns?'

'Will you stand gossip to the both of them?' Catrin asked.

'Yes, of course.'

'And if you have a babe, you must ask me to stand gossip to yours.'

She had said 'if', not 'when'. If you have a babe! But I *had* a babe, growing in my womb, until I supped here and then it died and came away from me in pain and blood. You have Robert. Why did you take my baby too?

Aloud she said, 'We will talk of it when the time comes.'

'I feel well enough to get up,' Catrin confided, 'but Mam insists I stay abed for another few days. She and Robert spoil me, I fear, but I was never very good at practical things.'

'You're still young,' Nell said absently. Then thought: Not so very young. Past twenty, and quite clever enough to catch a husband and bear healthy babes and leave the work to your mother.

'I have wine and comfits and some preserve,' Robert said, stepping through the outer room with laden tray. 'Will you stay to dinner, Nell?'

She shook her head. 'I'll ride back before the heavens open. The road's bad already.'

'I like rain,' Catrin said unexpectedly. 'I like to be safe indoors, listening to it patter on the roof.'

'You'd not like it so well if you were out

in the field, trying to save your crop,' Robert told her.

'But I am not likely to be,' she answered, a little hurt at his tone.

'The rain will spoil the harvest unless it holds off,' Nell said with a worried frown.

'I've not been out today.' Robert looked slightly guilty. 'Is it bad?'

'The river is running high,' Nell said briefly. ' 'If it breaks the banks there'll likely be flooding.'

'But *Kingsmead* and Aston Manor are built high,' Catrin said.

'The village isn't,' Nell told her. 'The river runs downhill, under the bridge and around the tor. The main street is below that.'

'But the banks are high,' Robert pointed out.

'The earth is soft after the rain,' Nell said. 'There was a flood years ago when my uncle was a small boy. They spoke then of reinforcing the banks, but nothing was ever done. If you recall, the channel is much narrower there where the river bends. It might spill over.'

'I'd best ride down and see what's to be done,' Robert said,

'The bank should be built higher and backed with stone,' Nell told him.

'Are we not going to drink a toast to the

babes?' Catrin asked.

She was wearied with talk of rivers and floods.

'To Hal and Robin,' Robert said promptly. 'May they grow to be a credit to us. Nell, you've been asked to stand gossip, haven't you?'

'And accepted,' she said.

'And I will stand for Nell's babe,' Catrin said.

'Why, you are — ?' He looked at Nell in quick concern, exclaiming, 'Ought you to have ridden here?'

'I am not yet with child again,' she told him, and her heart lifted because he still cared about her, if only as a friend.

'Tell James I'll ride down to the village tomorrow and have a look at those banks,' he said.

'But we don't own any of the land down there,' Catrin said. 'Why cannot the people look to it themselves?'

'They expect us to give them the lead,' Robert said.

'The monks used to look after the folk,' Nell tried to explain, 'but after they were driven from their monastery the land was divided up. The people of Marie Regina own their own plots now, but they still look to the big houses, to *Kingsmead* and the Manor, to protect them in times of trouble.'

'I see,' Catrin said.

She didn't really see at all! At home they had lived isolated on the hill farm, neither seeking nor offering help. In London there had been a bustle of people, all intent on their own concerns. And she was well aware that nobody in Marie Regina looked at her with friendliness. They disliked her because she had married Robert, and because she didn't ride down into the village as Nell did to enquire about their health and the state of their cottages.

Soon afterwards, warned by the increasing rain, Nell rose to go. Robert brought up her cloak from where it had been drying and fastened it around her. She had lost a little weight since the miscarriage and her pale hair curled damply at her temples. In a very few years the little comeliness she had would have faded, but on this morning she looked at her best.

In the antechamber Robert paused, his hand on her arm, his voice lowered.

'I didn't wish to worry Catrin, but is there real danger of flooding? I meant to ride out, but she fusses if I am long from her side.'

He would not have said such a thing six months before, but his passion had waned. He loved Catrin. He kept on telling himself that he loved her. Granted that she had been difficult during her pregnancy, he had hoped that as soon as the child was born everything would be as it had been before.

He was pleased, very pleased, with the twins. They were fine babies, and he looked forward to them when they were older and would ride with him. But motherhood had raised a barrier between them. She lay, fragile and lovely, in the big bed and talked of the babes, her hand in his was boneless as a kitten's with nothing to remind him of Nell's sturdy and comforting frame.

'The river is very high,' Nell said. 'If you could come tomorrow as soon as possible, it would hearten the village folk. They look up to you, Robert.'

'I'll come.' He hesitated, then asked, lower still. 'And you, Nell? Are you quite recovered now?'

'Yes. Yes, of course.'

'And happy? I'd not want you to be unhappy, Nell.'

'James Fleet is a good man,' she evaded, and Robert, moved by some impulse that transcended his carefree selfishness, put his arms around her and kissed her on the cheek.

As Nell drew away, she glimpsed through the open door Catrin watching them.

'It was good of Nell to come,' Robert said as he returned. 'I'm sorry that she couldn't stay to dinner, but it's likely wiser for her to go home else she'd have been stranded here.'

He sounded, Catrin thought wistfully, truly regretful. No doubt he missed Nell's company.

'How will you build the banks higher?' she asked, stretching out her hand to draw him to her side. 'Will you use big stones, or logs? You would have to fell some trees for that, wouldn't you?'

'It's nothing for you to worry about,' Robert said indulgently.

'I could ask Mam to make soup and send it down to the village,' she suggested.

'If it pleases you.' He kissed her hand and smiled at her.

She was so enchantingly pretty it was a pity she was so stupid.

'I shall get up tomorrow in spite of what Mam says,' Catrin declared. 'I feel perfectly well again and it's time I was on my feet.'

'Your mother will be going home soon, I suppose,' Robert said.

There was a hopeful timbre in his voice. There had always been some quality in Catrin's mother that chilled him without his knowing why. He was grateful for the order she had brought into the house and he knew that she was respected by the servants, but he had never felt at ease in her company.

'I suppose so,' Catrin agreed.

Deep down she dreaded her mother's leaving, for though she treated her like a child, there was no denying that it was pleasant not to have to think for herself, pleasant to sit back and let life lap around her.

Rain was falling steadily past the window panes. She could hear it splashing into the water butts at the corners of the house, cascading from the gutters.

'I'm glad not to have to be out in this!' she exclaimed, and pressed the back of his hand against her check.

But he only answered, 'Nell will be drenched. It was foolish of her to come at all, but she was always the kindest soul in the world!'

17

It rained steadily throughout the afternoon. Margred sent the two maids home early and they squelched together down the curving drive, holding on to their hoods. The babes woke and were fed, and slept again. Robert wandered about in the two upstairs rooms, picking up things and setting them down. At supper time he carried portions of food upstairs for himself and Catrin, and left Margred down at the main table with Cook and old John, and the stable boy at its foot.

Margred liked to sit alone at the head of the table. It was easy to forget the young couple upstairs and to pretend she was true mistress of *Kingsmead*, Harry's rightful widow. But she never allowed herself to forget that it was a pretence.

Soon she would have to go home. A living-in-nurse for the children, and a maid for Catrin would have to be engaged. she would speak to Robert about it, make him understand that a lady should have a personal servant. She must make him see Catrin's helplessness as something that was feminine and appealing, not as something that showed her lack of character.

The windows rattled violently with the force of the rain and the rising wind. Cook waddled over to fasten the heavy shutters, giving a small shriek as the casement was almost pulled from her hand. From the stable echoed the startled whinny of a horse as a slate clattered from the roof.

'Will you listen to that wind!' John exclaimed. 'I never knew anything for the time of year.'

It was a little like that other time, Margred was thinking. But it had been late autumn then and she had been young. One of Robert's two terriers crept under her hand, nosing for a titbit, and she stroked it absently, remembering Mott.

'I'd best see to the horses,' Dickon, the groom, said.

He glanced enquiringly at John as he spoke. He had been taken on at *Kingsmead* after John's accident and regarded the old man with a certain awe.

'Aye. Make sure their stalls are secure, and check the main doors while you're about it.' John scowled into his ale, observing, 'These younglings need keeping up to the mark, else they'll slack off.'

'They'll be having it bad down in the village,.' Cook said with pleasurable gloom.

'The banks'll break for sure, and the poor fools will sit there, wringing their hands, and watch it happen.'

'The banks broke when I was a lad,' John said. 'Two children were drowned, but they were Papists so I reckon it was a judgment.'

'Finish your meal. I'll see to the fire in the parlour.'

Margred took her mug of ale with her into the parlour and nursed it between her hands as she stared down into the glowing flames. All her life she had been fascinated by wild weather. Catrin liked to be snug within, like an oyster in its shell, listening to the wind. Margred liked to feel the rain in her face and the wind in her hair. At such times something strong and fierce and wild rose up in her, cleansing her hatred for a little while.

She went through into the unlit solar and unlatched casement and shutters, leaning over the sill and gasping as water dashed into her face and wind lifted the corners of her veil like wings. As she drew back, the rain parted like curtains and her eyes, dimmed by water, fell upon a blue flame that shimmered above the cobblestones.

'The death candle!' Her lips whispered the words in terror.

Years before she had followed the blue flame over the marshes and found Prys dead in the farmhouse. But this one had come seeking her. She stared at it, her face quivering, all the forgotten fears of childhood crowding into her mind. Then it was gone and Robert called from the other room.

'You'll catch your death if you stand at the open window like that! Come, let me shut it for you.'

He was booted and caped, a hat pulled over his ears.

'Are you going out?' she asked foolishly.

'I feel I must. The river will be flooding before the night's out unless something is done.'

'I'll wait up for you,' she said mechanically.

'Thank you, mistress,' He gave her a swift smile and went out. She heard him arguing with John, and then a door banged, and a moment later, above the rain, she caught the sound of hoofbeats on cobbles.

She went back to the fire and crouched before it, warming her hands. But she was cold to the bone, her whole frame shaking with ague, her face tight as if her skin was being stretched over her skull in preparation of decay.

Above her head the rafters of the house creaked and groaned, the flames in the hearth

332

burned low and died as soot cascaded down the chimney. Her hands were speckled with black as if some inner corruption had forced its way to the surface. She rubbed them down the sides of her kirtle and stood up, gritting her teeth as she coldly and deliberately controlled her shaking.

Somewhere outside in the wind and rain the death candle hovered patiently. She threw back her head and forced a smile to her white lips. Let it come! Let it wait! Her task was done, her revenge complete, and she regretted nothing.

'The master took it into his head to go down to the village,' John said, limping in from the hall.

'I know.'

'The mistress wants you to sit with her a while,' he said.

'I'll go up.'

She went slowly, still rubbing corruption from her hands. John shook his head after her. She was worn out, he thought, and no wonder with that lazy madam sitting about and doing nothing. Well, he'd keep the fires up and the lights burning and wait for the master to return.

Robert, head bent into the wind, rode down the drive, holding his mount on a tight rein for the beast skittered away from the wildly lashing branches of the trees. The main road was a quagmire, the fields at each side flattened to the soil beneath.

Yet he would not have wished to be back in the warm bedroom with the two babes sleeping in their cradles and Catrin's hand in his. Such a small hand, tying him to her side as if with an invisible ribbon — and his soul chafed under the restriction, though his heart still melted into love whenever he looked at her.

The river was almost up to the planks of the bridge, foaming white in the darkness, thundering down the slope towards the village, and then curving away between its banks, behind the row of small cottages that marched along the cobbled street.

Robert could see lights bobbing along the waterline and above the howling wind voices shouted into the darkness. He turned his horse sharply at the fork before the bridge and plunged down the muddy slope, rain streaming from the brim of his hat. At its foot, Josiah Bewling caught at his rein, his face a dim moon of anxiety.

'I've told those whose cottages back on to the river to move their valuables to the upper floors,' he shouted. 'Shall we gather what livestock we can find and drive them into the churchyard, sir?'

'And get the children over to the other side of the street! Is there any way to get the banks barricaded?'

'There are logs cut for the new barn, sir.'

'Tell them to use those!'

Suddenly he was alive and tingling with purpose. These were his own people, men of whose race he was, healthy and sound as the apples that clustered from the trees. Nell would understand how he felt. It was a pity that though his affection for her ran deeper and stronger than he knew she had never held his heart in thrall.

He raised his hand to the parson and swerved the dripping horse around the end of the row of cottages into the wind and darkness.

In the bedroom at *Kingsmead* Margred, lips tight with disapproval, assisted Catrin into a loose robe.

'Rest is what you need,' she scolded. 'I'll stay up for Robert, and I know Cook and John and Dickon won't be abed this night. It would be more sensible for you to go to sleep. You don't want to lose your milk, do you?'

'I'm weary of lying in bed,' Catrin said, an edge of fretfulness to her voice. 'I want to come into the parlour for an hour or two and sit by the fire. It's a wife's duty to welcome her husband home.'

'Very well. I'll help you downstairs.'

Recognising defeat, Margred put her arm around Catrin's waist. Something in its narrow and fragile slenderness touched her in some dormant part of her nature.

She said, quick and soft, 'You do like it here, cariad? Robert is what you wanted?'

'Yes.'

Catrin's clear amber gaze was lifted to the searching yellow of her mother's eyes.

In the kitchen, Dickon slept fitfully on a pallet behind the settle. Cook and John sat by the fire, a mug of ale in John's fist, a long stemmed pipe clenched between his few remaining teeth. Cook, her apron folded about her massive thighs, gave a long and elaborate shiver as the crashing and howling of the elements beat against stone and wood and tile.

'It's not natural,' she said. 'At the height of summer? It's not natural, I tell you.'

'There's a lot happened that's not natural these past months,' John muttered darkly. 'I've stepped on ice a hundred times and never lost my balance. And it wasn't my task to dust the chairs!'

'The crops all spoiled. It'll be a hard winter,' Cook lamented. 'The children are the ones who suffer hardship. Mistress Nell will have her hands full dispensing charity.'

'The poor wench should have a babe of her own,' John said sadly.

'And wouldn't she have one now, right this minute, if it hadn't died before its time?'

'For no reason.'

'Save that the master looks on her with friendship,' Cook said and cast a furtive glance towards the tightly closed door. '*She* doesn't join in the grace, you know. I've watched her, and her lips don't move. Christ and his saints! What was that?'

A dull roar boomed about their ears, seeming for an instant to shake the very foundations of the building. Dickon jerked from sleep, leapt, half sobbing with fright.

'The river!' John cried. 'I heard that noise the other time!'

'The banks? Will the people be safe away?'

Cook lumbered to the door and wrenched it open. Across the candlelight expanse of hall she saw mother and daughter close to each other in the parlour doorway.

'Get me a cloak,' Margred said, seeing the servant blink stupidly at her. 'Tell Dickon to rouse himself and come with me.'

'Is the master — ?'

'Sir Robert is not back yet. Dickon and I will see what's to do.'

Margred's voice was calm and steady, her

expression warning. To Catrin she said, 'Go and sit by the fire again. I'll not be long.'

'Mistress, there are loose slates flying about!' John croaked from the door.

'I've a hard head,' Margred said briefly.

She was gone then, flinging the cloak about herself, pulling open the door that led to the stable, her hood tearing from her head to loose long, black braids.

Catrin stayed where she was, her slight frame outlined in firelight and candlelight, her hair gleaming on her shoulders. Her hand when she raised it against the oak of the door was pearl coloured.

Something has happened, she thought, quietly and calmly. Mam guessed it and didn't want me to know.

Aloud she said, in her sweet, indifferent voice, 'They will bring Robert home on a stretcher.'

And she went on standing at the parlour, listening for the shouts and running feet.

'The bank caved in! He was trapped beneath it.'

'We laboured to pull him out but he was dead when we managed it.'

'Trapped under the mud. God pity him! He hadn't a chance!'

People crowding into the hall. Her mother

338

sobbing with a curious look of relief on her face. Voices.

'Gave his life to save — '

'The Lord's Will be done!'

'Carry him to his own bed.'

'Who would have thought — ?'

He's mine now, Catrin said to herself. *He'll never grow tired of me now, or touch-Nell with gentle hands. He would have stopped loving me in the end. But now be'll always love me, always desire me.*

'You'd best sleep in my room tonight. I've put the babes there.'

Her mother was shaking her arm. The wind was dying away, its fury spent. People were staring at her. She tried to speak to them, to weep, to thank them for their help and their sympathy. But her eyes were dry and the words that issued from her lips were not the words she had meant to say.

'My little snake died, you know. I cried about that.'

Margred said loudly, 'Forgive me for leaving you, but my poor daughter is shocked with grief! Cook and John will bring you wine.'

'You tend your wench,' somebody said with rough kindliness. 'We'll see to ourselves, mistress.'

They had carried Robert upstairs. Catrin

had not moved, had not seen his face. She supposed her mother would wash him and then they would let her go in to sit with him.

'I don't understand it,' Margred was saying in a low voice as they went up the stairs. 'The death candle is for those with Welsh blood.'

Catrin heard vaguely, understood nothing. An immense weariness shackled her limbs. It was an effort to walk up the stairs.

Margred helped her into the room she had chosen for herself and covered her with a quilt. She could hear people moving about downstairs, their voices hushed. There were tears and rain mingled on her cheeks. Her sorrow was genuine. Robert had been comely and young, and it was always sad to see a young and comely thing destroyed.

But his usefulness was over, she thought. He was beginning to recover from his passion for Catrin, to seek again the affections of his boyhood. In the end, he would have betrayed Catrin, as all men betrayed the women who loved them. His dying was a sorrow that would pass.

She drew a deep breath and went slowly downstairs again to ask if any other lives had been lost, any property destroyed. Later people would remember the dignity of that

340

tear-stained little woman who spoke so beautifully of poor Sir Robert's death. Yet, even at that moment, nobody mentioned Catrin's grief or asked how she did.

The rain had ceased by morning save for occasional heavy showers and the wind had faded to a muttering. Parson Bewling had called to express his grief at the accident, and to tell Margred that the damage had been less than they had feared and the village pond was now a lake covering stocks and ducking stool, but only Robert had died.

'The crops are sodden, mistress,' he told her. 'And great havoc has been wrought in the orchards. Half the parish will be on poor relief this winter.'

'Perhaps a fund could be set up?'

'An excellent idea!' He thought again what a sensible woman she was. 'But we must discuss sadder matters — the funeral arrangements.'

'Simple and dignified,' she said. 'With no Papistical frills,' His estimation of her rose higher. 'My daughter and I will not attend. She is quite crushed with grief, and, of course, so soon after her confinement — '

'It would be too much for her. I understand.'

He had spoken to Catrin who sat in the parlour, nursing one of the babes. She had looked sad and remote, but not, he thought, heartbroken.

'As for myself.' She made a little, fluttering gesture with her hands. 'I could not endure to go.'

It would be, she thought, like burying Harry. In death Robert resembled his father even more than he had done in life.

She excused herself briefly and turned to greet Nell and James Fleet who had just arrived. James was grimy and unshaven, having been up all night.

'We were carrying children across the street when we heard the roar of water,' he said, gripping Margred's hand in both his own. 'There was no way of saving him, no way at all. How is his poor wife?'

'Stunned with grief,' Margred said. Her eyes had moved to Nell who stood silently at her husband's side.

Nell looked as if she had been crying for days; her eyes were slits between puffed and reddened lids; her lips were dry and cracked.

'My own lady-wife has taken it very hard,' James confided, drawing Margred aside. 'They were childhood companions, as you know.'

'I would like to see him.' Nell said in a clear, steady tone.

'He's upstairs in his own room. Would you like — ?' Margred glanced at James.

He had the peasant's instinctive fear of death, but said promptly, moved by concern for Nell, 'Shall I come up with you?'

She shook her head, and then, obscurely aware that she had hurt him a little, said, with difficulty, 'Later. Later, James.'

She had climbed these stairs so many times before, running up them to greet Lady Alys, coming down them to greet Robert just returned from a day's hunting with his father. She had known this house in every season and every mood, and only yesterday Robert had put his arms about her and asked her if she was happy.

The bedchamber was cold and already filled with the sweet sickliness of death. Nell went over and stood looking down at Robert. It was like gazing at a carven image of the man she had loved. Robert himself was gone and only this still and silent effigy was left. For a moment, desolation twisted her heart. To lose Robert was like losing her child again, for though Nell did not realise it, there was much that had been maternal in her love.

If he had not gone to London and met Catrin the two babes might have been her babes. But he *had* gone to London, and all

343

her hopes had run away like grain out of a sieve.

The room had been tidied, the shutters closed, the bed remade, the cradles removed, the fire extinguished. But Catrin's presence was still there. A book of rhyming couplets lay in the window seat, an ivory comb to which a few red hairs still adhered was on the table, an open chest held folded kirtles and stomachers.

A kind of madness possessed Nell at the sight of the bright, dainty garments. That silk had carressed her rival's pale skin, that brocade rustled about her rival's slender ankles. The perfume that Catrin used clung to the dresses.

Nell dug down into the chest, ripping and tearing, flinging them out over the rushes. She would have liked to tear Catrin to pieces as she now tore at a silken package that lay between the layers of clothes.

Four waxy, yellowed objects rolled to her feet. Her hands stilled she frowned down at them, and then she was on her knees, touching them cautiously, seeing the rusted pins glint dully in the light from the wake candles set about the bed.

Four figures, roughly approximating to human shape, one with a pin in its leg, two with pins through their middles, a tiny one with a pin jabbed through its blob of a head.

Sir Harry didn't die of the lung disease. He died with his face twisted in terror as if he had suffered some great and fearful shock. Catrin was with him when he died.

Her own words screamed into her mind.

Stared at me she did when I tried to speak up for myself. And next minute over I go!

That was John who would hobble for the rest of his days.

I supped with Catrin and my babe was never born.

The smallest doll had been that babe, destroyed before it lived.

Robert put his arms about me yesterday and asked me if I was happy. Catrin was watching us through the door.

Four figures, four people. And there were probably more hidden away, ready to be used if anybody offended Catrin.

We have grace before meals again now that Mistress Margaret has come, Lady Catrin never speaks the words.

Cook had confided that to Gideon. There had been an old woman at Maidstone two years before who had bewitched a herd of cows belonging to a neighbour with whom she had quarrelled. The beasts had yielded no milk and their calves had been born dead. The old woman had been arrested and searched for the witch mark. She had confessed too, Nell remembered. She had boasted of riding the wind on a broom-stick and of a black-faced man who came by night. They had strangled the old woman and burned the body, and killed the grey cat that was her familiar.

Catrin wandered about alone, taking no interest in the affairs of the village. She had not been to Sunday service for months, declaring she felt too ill and clumsy to ride there. She didn't like horses anyway, and Nell had never seen her pet any of the dogs. Gideon had told her that the mistress had a passion for small, wild creatures; for snakes and hares and mice and lizards. They had never had such rain and wind at the end of June before. The crops were ruined, and it would be weeks before the cottages were dried out.

Nell wrapped up the figures again and slipped them into the pouch that hung from her girdle. There was a metallic taste in her mouth, and bright light stabbed her temple. As she refolded the torn garments and placed them neatly in the chest, she held herself rigid, willing away pain. She would have to think very carefully and logically. Evil could not be destroyed by wild accusations.

There was already talk in the village, she knew, but she was not certain how easy it would be to turn talk into action.

Something dark and ugly had come into her plain face. Although she was never to know it she looked at that moment like her dead father, William, who had destroyed his paintings and his brushes and never thought of beauty again until he had seen a naked girl lying in the reeds on a sunny day.

Catrin must be destroyed. She must be rooted out before more harm befell Marie Regina and the people who lived there.

In all my life, Nell thought, I never had such an important task as I have now.

A glow of fervour suffused her. She was an avenging angel, a crusader, a protrectress of mankind.

She gave the effigy on the bed one last and meaning glance. Robert had failed her in life, but she would not fail him in death.

There were his sons to be saved from corruption, for who could tell what wickedness they drank in with their mother's milk? There were the drowned crops and ruined trees and cottages thick with mud and slime, and Sir Harry with the twisted horror on his face, and old John with his crutch, and her own babe that had never cried.

She closed the door behind her gently

and came down the stairs into the hall. The parson was talking to Catrin, their seated figures visible within the parlour. James came forward, squinting anxiously as he took her hand.

'Forgive me, but I am not well.' She spoke thickly, her fingers gripping at her husband feverishly.

'My dear, you must go home again and rest. I will give your regrets to Catrin.'

Margred spoke warmly, shook by pitying affection. The poor creature had truly loved Robert it seemed. She would have a lonely time, for it was obvious she felt no more than the mildest liking for her husband.

'You're very kind,' Nell said. She wanted to put her arms round the older woman and cry, *Beware! Your daughter whom you love is a monster who, one day, will turn and destroy you.*

'I'll come by tomorrow,' James said, intensely relieved that he had not been asked to view the corpse.

Moreover, he wished to get Nell home as quickly as possible, He had never seen such a fixed and wild glare in her eyes before.

18

Roger Aston reined in his horse and looked out across the mud and trampled grass of what had been lush pasture, From the bridge he could see the river winding behind the village street and then, before it swung away towards the tor, spilling into a muddy lake over broken banks of earth. From where he sat he could discern only the roofs of the cottages, gleaming wet under the quivering sun, and beyond them the spire of the church. In the sloping churchyard he could just distinguish, if he screwed up his eyes behind his spectacles, tiny black figures moving about like ants. A silence lay over Marie Regina, save for the tolling of the bell. Twenty-three sonorous tones, for the years of Robert's life.

Roger counted them mournfully. He had been fond of Robert, even though he was aware of the boy's selfishness, of the shallow, mercurial nature of his charm. There had been something of Harry in that grasping, greedy quality. But in the end Robert had been his mother's son, with Alys's love of the land and concern for the people leading him to lose his life in trying to help them.

James and Nell were at the funeral. Nell had looked ghastly on her return from Kingsmead as if she were sickening for one of her attacks, but she had evidently thrown it off for she had spent the two days since down in the village, helping the women to clean and salvage. Hard work would help the poor child, her uncle reflected. Certainly she seemed calm and busy, her grief no more than a veil laid lightly over her energy.

He had waited until they had left for the service and then had limped out of his room and down the stairs and through to the stable. The agony of mounting a horse had brought tears to his eyes, but wrestling with the pain gave him a subtle sense of achievement. He had not been out of the house for months, and the air was fresh and cool. He rode slowly, trying to ignore the painful throbbing in his leg.

Now he gave one final glance over the ruined landscape. His business lay neither in village nor churchyard. Instead he wheeled to the right, gritting his teeth as his mount plunged into the thick mud of the river path.

The trees were bent and broken and twisted out of shape. Branches and long trails of creeper were littered about the path. The reeds were swamped by still growling water and the current was running high and fast.

He reached the clearing and stopped, water lapping shallow at his horse's feet, his eyes fixed on the little house with its broken windows and swollen door and at the woman who stood staring at them.

He would have known her anywhere, he thought, and marvelled that she had changed so little. Then she turned and he saw that she was changed after all, that the wildness and sweetness had fled from her face to be replaced by something alien and strong. She was in black, her hair hidden, a pony tethered nearby. Her eyes, looking up at him, were clear and mocking.

'You guessed I would come here, didn't you?' she said.

'I thought you might.'

'I came to see if the Dower Cottage had been harmed,' she said. 'But the foundations were sunk deep and there's only the roof suffered. I suppose the windows cracked a long time ago.

'Have you been inside?' he asked.

She shook her head. 'The door is stuck fast,' she said. 'It will need to be broken down. Nobody kept up any repairs did they?'

'Nobody ever came here,' he told her.

'I'm glad,' she said softly. 'I don't like to think of another woman poking about here.'

She was thinking of Alys, he knew. Strange that two women who had never met should have feared each other so greatly.

'How did you know it was me; come back here, I mean?'

'I met Catrin. There was something about her, something in the way she held her head. It dawned on me slowly, and when you never called at Aston Manor, then I knew.'

'Nobody else remembered me, except old John,' she said wistfully. 'But I persuaded him to say nothing.'

'You took a great risk in returning.'

'Not so great. A long time has passed, and I will be leaving again soon.'

'Catrin is Harry's daughter, isn't she?' Roger said.

Margred drew a deep breath, but the mockery stayed in her eyes as she gazed up at him.

It was one thing to suspect, quite another to have a hideous suspicion confirmed. For a moment he felt as if he had looked down into some loathsome pit that crawled with toads and snakes.

At last he said, low and shaken, 'God

forgive you! but you have taken a terrible revenge on us all!'

'Catrin and Robert were happy. Their babes are healthy. And who will tell? Will you, Master Aston?'

At the direct challenge he flinched, and then shook his head.

Even if he denounced her he could never prove it, and even if he ever proved it, what good could ever come from casting a terrible shadow over the lives of two innocent babes, of hurting Nell all over again? And, more than that, there was his own nature to prevent his acting. Looking into her eyes he saw himself, mirrored and ridiculous and more clearly than he had ever seen himself before. All his life he had shrunk from action, letting them marry Alys to his best friend, remaining a bachelor not only out of loyalty to Alys but because it was easier to stand back and watch life flow past him.

'You must have hated him very much,' Roger said.

'Harry?' Something gentle and dreamy came into her face, making it young and vulnerable. 'I loved him. I always loved him from the moment I saw him. And what I have, I hold.'

Her face was smooth and hard again, her eyes like yellow stones. He was afraid of her and fascinated by her at the same time.

'And your daughter? Had you no care for her?'

'Catrin is a good, obedient girl,' she said calmly. 'She is as innocent as I once was, as sweet-natured as I could have been. I reared her to be a lady. She is mistress of *Kingsmead* now.'

Roger went on staring at her. Though he was on horseback and she stood below he was uneasily conscious of her domination and of his own powerlessness.

'I am no longer a young man,' he said pleadingly. 'I am fifty-seven years old, Margred, and my health isn't good.'

'I'm sorry for it,' she said tranquilly.

'I ought to do something, say something,' he muttered.

'But you won't.' She looked at him almost kindly. 'You are a good honourable man, and you will not bring dishonour upon the innocent.'

'Is Catrin well? James said she was most grieved.'

'She is at home resting. I could not allow her to attend the funeral.'

'And you are not there yourself,' he observed.

'Neither are you!' she flashed, and smiled again, her wide mouth curving over her pretty teeth. 'Let us agree that we neither of us like the trappings of death. We have more in common than you might imagine, Master Aston.'

She had moved to the pony and remounted as lightly as a girl. As she gathered up the reins she spoke with a quaint and touching shyness.

'I have never been inside Aston Manor. When I was a little girl I used to walk slowly past the lighted houses in the town and hope that somebody would open their door and invite me to visit.'

He had a sudden picture of a thin and lonely child forever shut out of lighted rooms.

'Perhaps you would like to ride back with me now for a cup of wine?'

He had given the invitation to a lonely child who had existed briefly in his mind. It was accepted by a small, hard-faced woman with a subtle smile. Yet, as they rode cautiously along the path up to the main road again, he felt almost as much pity for the woman as for the child.

There were people still in the churchyard, clustered there as if death held some fearful charm that drew them from their homes out to the hillside.

'James will ride back with you when he

and Nell have returned,' Roger said.

'I'm accustomed to riding alone,' she said, amused. 'But I'll not stay long. Catrin is resting, but I don't like to leave her and the babes for too long.'

'But you'll be going home soon anyway,' he said with a touch of alarm.

'As soon as I've found a good nursemaid for my grandsons.' Twisting in the saddle to look at him as they clattered over the bridge she said, with pleased surprise in her voice: 'Grandsons! Me with grandsons!'

The little figure toiling along the road saw the retreating riders and hesitated, but they went on towards the gates of Aston Manor. Catrin had slipped out of the house soon after her mother had left, and made her way down the sodden drive under the still dripping trees. She felt stronger than she had believed she would be, capable of walking miles with no more than a slight fatigue.

It was odd but she still felt no real grief for Robert. Her mind was numbed as if too much had happened too quickly for her to absorb everything. She had looked at her face in the mirror of polished steel and said to the dim reflection, 'You are a widow. The husband you loved is dead.'

And the words had no meaning, were no more than sounds spoken into the empty air.

It was not customary for widows to attend the funeral. They were supposed to sit at home, muffled in black crepe, and weeping. Catrin could not weep, could not believe this was happening. If she could see the fresh grave, if she could hear the people talking of the tragedy, it might become real to her.

She walked steadily, her feet squelching into the mud, a light shawl covering her head.

The street was empty, its cobbles still slimed from the night's storm, the river moaning behind the flooded houses like some beast held in check. She wondered briefly why her mother was riding with Master Aston, but she would probably never say. Often when Catrin looked at Margred she had the impression that her mother was carrying secrets behind her eyes. Once she had asked her, 'What are you thinking about?'

Her mother had smiled and patted her cheek and answered, 'Of your future, cariad.'

And something had warned Catrin not to ask again.

The grey church, built of stones from the despoiled monastery, stood at the end of the street. At its side the graveyard sloped down to the swollen village pond, now deep almost as the invading river. Bits of wood floated on the sluggish water, and a fallen elm lay at its edge.

Robert had died here, sucked down into the mud. Telling herself the fact brought it no nearer to reality. She pushed open the lych gate and went timidly up the slope between the dark yews.

The tomb of the Falcons was neither large nor elaborate. Robert's grandparents and parents lay within the angel-crowned sarcophagus, with its fine gold lettering and fringe of lacy stone. Catrin could see that it had been opened and closed; the empty pall lay on the ground nearby. Later in the week the stone mason would cut a new name into the stone and a goldsmith would inlay it with great care.

Practically everybody in the village was there, she noticed with pleased surprise. She had not realised Robert was so important, but then she supposed that such a sad and noble end would attract a large crowd.

The words had not originated in her own mind but were an echo of the words now being pronounced by Josiah Bewling. Balanced on a flat stone, his face gravely important, the parson was delivering a eulogy.

' — sad and noble end of the young

gentleman whose body we have just consigned to the tomb and whose immortal soul rests now in the hands of God. Sad because Sir Robert was young, in the promise of a happy and useful life, and noble because he laid down that life in the service of his fellow men. It is not our business to question the Will of God, but to accept — '

He paused, conscious that in some way he had lost the attention of his congregation. There was a shuffling of feet, a turning of heads towards the back of the crowd.

Then he saw her, a slight and pathetic figure in her black dress and shawl, walking slowly towards them, picking her way carefully through the wet grass between the headstones of humbler graves.

' 'Tis the widow,' someone said, not in compassion but as a kind of warning, for at the words folks began to move closer together as if for protection, clearing a little space near the tomb. Within the space Nell Fleet stood, a figure of sad and majestic dignity with white face and eyes pale with hatred.

'You are too late, my lady,' she said clearly. 'Sir Robert is safely buried. You can do him no more harm.'

'Harm?' Catrin paused, questioning, her puzzled eyes on the other's round, unyielding face. 'I don't understand.'

'Don't play the innocent,' Nell said heavily. 'It fools us no longer.'

'Fools?'

Catrin could only repeat what Nell said as if nothing remained of her but the sad echo of other folks' accusation.

'You fooled Robert,' Nell shouted, her voice breaking into the anxious muttering of the crowd. 'You tricked him with your honey ways into wedding you and bringing you here. And Sir Harry died, his face twisted with the horror of what he had seen!'

'He saw nothing! He saw — '

'You. You alone in the room with him. You watching him die. And my babe died too. My unborn child died because you could not bear to see another's happiness.'

'Nell! for the love of God!' James Fleet seized her arm, but she struck him away as if he were a gnat.

'My babe died for no reason save that you willed it so!'

'Mistress Fleet, you must stop these wild accusations!' Parson Bewling cried in distress. 'You are grieved at the loss of an old friend, but to say such things is wickedness. You have no reason!'

'Ask old John if I have reason!' Nell cried. 'Ask old John who will never walk properly

360

again! Ask the people here who saw their crops ruined and their homes made foul with mud!'

The villagers stood unmoving now, listening to Nell with an intensity they never displayed when Josiah Bewling preached. Occasionally their eyes flicked towards Catrin and then slid away again.

'Mistress, there must be proof of these matters!' the parson cried. 'It is monstrous to accuse an innocent lady in this fashion.'

'Innocent! Innocent, when she had these in her possession!' Almost beside herself, Nell plunged her hand into her pouch and drew out a silk-wrapped bundle, spilling its contents on the ground. 'Look at them! Hidden beneath her kirtles they were! Four images of wax, stuck with pins! Devil dolls!'

They lay on the ground, yellowed and flaking, unutterably obscene.

Only Catrin moved, her hands reaching towards them, indignation in her face.

'That was very wrong of you, mistress, to delve into my belongings!'

The silence was appalled. Even Nell was struck into a gaping dumbness, as Catrin stood there. Josiah Bewling could not take his eyes from her. A sensible and reasonable man, he had ignored the whispers concerning Lady Catrin's strange ways, but here was evidence and an admission that could not be denied.

'Witch!'

The word, hissed by somebody in the crowd, was like a spark to tinder.

'Witch! Witch! Witch!'

The cry, taken up and spreading to the edges of the mob, was like the sweeping sound of a hundred broomsticks.

Catrin backed away, the wax objects falling from her hands. She tried to speak, to tell them she had found the things in the abandoned cottage, but her throat ached and her mouth was dry. All the people had but one face, it seemed, and that face was fearful and brutish.

'You must let me question her at my house!' Josiah Bewling cried, but he had lost what little authority he had possessed over them.

Decent, law-abiding, humorous folk in ordinary times, there yet ran in them all the dark beliefs of their ancestors, a dread of the unknown that lay like bloodied bones under the green springtime of their Christian faith. Step by step, inexorably, they began to advance.

James Fleet had reached Nell and pulled her violently aside. She looked stricken and afraid, her mouth working, her fingers plucking at her skirt. She had unleashed something she was unable to control, and it was like inventing a nightmare that became life itself.

'Wait! You must wait!' the parson cried, but nobody turned to spare him a glance.

Suddenly Catrin began to run, swift as a hare, curving around the edges of the crowd, clambering over the graves, the shawl falling from her head as she clutched at stone and grass and projecting roots.

'Head her off! Head her off!' someone screeched.

Catrin twisted back upon her trail, her hair whipping about her shoulders, her breath coming in harsh and painful gasps. Her kirtle caught upon the projecting spike of a railed grave and she screamed in panic, ripping herself away from the iron, the silk of her gown tearing as she wrenched herself free.

For a moment she was poised in flight, one slender leg outlined through the rent in her black dress. There, glowing purple on her white thigh, a crescent moon arched across the smooth flesh.

'The devil's mark! God save us! she carries the devil's mark!'

It was Mistress Fiske who cried out the words. In her enormous wheel farthingale, her headdress askew, she should have been a comic figure, but her shrieking mouth and distended eyes were truly terrifying.

Catrin was running again, stumbling and falling and rising again, her teeth caught in her underlip, the world no more than a blur slipping past her terrified eyes. She was running in the wrong direction, not towards the road or the sanctuary of the chruch, but down towards the swollen pool of grey-green water that spread itself across the drowned green waiting to swallow her up.

Behind her the people ran and jumped and leapt and shrieked, fingers claw curved, faces pitiless with fear.

'Swim the witch! Swim the witch!'

The chant was like the baying of hounds. Their sense scarcely penetrated her frantic mind, but she had heard, dimly, of the swimming of a suspected witch, of the tying of left hand to right foot and right hand to left foot, and the throwing into the deepest water to see if the accused would sink or float.

If they laid their hands upon her she would die of shame and horror. So she made one last, desperate effort, turning to face them as they ran towards her, flinging her arms wide and then falling, like some doll dropped by a careless child, into the depths of the last, cold embrace.

She cleft the surface, water streaming from hair and face, her mouth opened in a silent plea.

'Mam! I want my Mam!'

The water claimed her again, dragging her down, mud weighting her full skirts. Her limbs threshed helplessly, a snake was twisted about her ribs, choking her. There were bright colours bursting into flower before her eyes and a pain in her lungs that was becoming a sweet pleasure as she surrendered to the dark mud that swirled up from the bottom of the pool.

She was treading the green water towards a light that was both bright and soft, tinting the peaks of the mountains, filling the air with tiny golden particles. The light lay across the field, haloed the barn and the stone cottage. She knew the place well, had grown up within the confines of marsh and sea and hill. Long ago her mother had forbidden her to speak Welsh because it was not a language for ladies, and Catrin must grow up to be a fine lady.

There had been a journey and a city with high walls that closed out the sky. There had been a panelled room and a young man in a gay doublet with blue eyes that smiled at her. There had been a big house with portraits of women she had never known on its walls and a man who clutched her wrist and died with twisted face.

But the bad times were fading and she was dwindling down into a barefoot child. Her feet made no impression on the grass as she began to run and the air was sweet with honeysuckle. There were beasts lying in the long couch grass, their eyes peaceful and dark, their heads raised to watch her pass. Little, trembling hares clustered around a rough-coated bear. A fox raised his sleek mask in greeting, and a snake coiled in love about a sparkling, jewel-eyed toad.

The door of the cottage was opening and an old man stood on the threshold, his shabby jerkin patterned in sunshine, his eyes creased in welcome.

'Prys? Are you Prys?'

But there was no need to ask the question, for he was speaking in the ancient tongue.

'So you are Catrin. Come in, cariad, and let me look at you.'

And she went in with him, into the little, whitewashed room where a fire burned smokily on a central hearth and the table was laid for supper.

A voice, loud and rough, intruded, thundering about the walls, shaking slates from the roof.

'She sank! God forgive us, she sank! Get

the water out of her!'

'I want to stay here with you,' she said to Prys.

And he reached out and closed the door, and silenced all the voices.

Epilogue

The birds were flying south again to the warm lands of Africa. Margred paused in the driveway and raised her head to watch the wings spread out against the sky. Some memory teased her mind and then was gone and the October wind blew chill again.

'You must forget this terrible tragedy,' Josiah Bewling had said.

'Could you?' She looked at him out of tortured eyes.

'It will be my lifelong regret that I could not prevent it,' he said sombrely. 'Master Fleet risked his own life to pull her out, but it was too late. If we could only have questioned her, but she fled so swiftly.'

' 'Death by misadventure.' ' She quoted the inquest verdict wryly and looked at him again. 'But you would not lay her within the churchyard.'

'There was — some feeling in the village,' he said awkwardly. 'She did say those — things belonged to her.'

'What happened to them?'

'I burned them,' he said at once, and took her hand in a firm, dry grip. 'Mistress, you

368

are not called upon to account for your daughter's nature. Perhaps it was no more in her than childish mischief, like a babe crawling too near to the fire. In time, her memory will fade from their minds.'

'Yes, of course,' she said with a grateful glance, and thought, with every word I betray my poor Catrin again, and there is nothing I can do.

People had been kind, so kind that she knew they felt guilty and ashamed. And yet their eyes slid away from her as they spoke, and under the regret in their faces moved doubts and suspicions.

Only Nell, her face unyielding, had said, clumsily and frankly, 'I am sorry for your grief, mistress, and for the poor babes, but I cannot forget that she was guilty.'

'We must remember there was no trial,' James Fleet said sombrely. 'She had no chance to defend herself.'

Roger Aston said nothing. Only his eyes blinked wearily behind their spectacles.

The river bank had been shored up with elm logs, the deep pool drained at its edges and confined within its normal span, the cottages swept clean. Those few crops that had escaped the worst of the rain were harvested, the fruit gathered from the broken trees, the root vegetables stored. The salting of the meat had begun. Marie Regina was settling down for the winter.

Margred had been to the Falcon tomb and stood, tracing with her fingers the names she had never learned to read. She had not visited the grave dug outside the churchyard wall. Catrin was not there, nor had Margred sensed her presence in any other place.

Our children are dreams we dreamed long ago, she thought, and for the first time a warmth glowed for Alys, for the woman who had borne Harry's other child.

'Nell is with child again,' James Fleet had confided shyly. 'We are very hopeful this time.'

'I shall pray for a daughter for you,' Margred said, pressing his hand.

She had reached the wall that shut the courtyard from the main grounds, and a desolation came over her as if the pieces of her life were scattered like leaves around her feet. Such a long road it had been, and nothing at the end of it but loneliness and despair.

I wanted so little. I would have been content with such a small part of your life. But you sent me away, and what I have, I hold.

Her fingers touched the smooth bark of a tree, and she leaned her head against it for a moment and cried in her heart for the eager girl who had once watched the birds fly south. Under her cheek the bark was warm, throbbing with sap. As she raised her eyes rusty leaves veined in purple spread themselves into a fan. Her grandsons were healthy babes, already thriving in the care of a young wet-nurse she had engaged.

Hal was the prettiest and the most demanding, roaring with rage if his feed were delayed. Robin was a neater, quieter babe with odd, light eyes that looked at her with an embryo greed. Hal would have *Kingsmead* and Nell Fleet's daughter. Margred was quite certain it would be a daughter.

Robin would have her farm in Wales and she would teach him how to scheme for more. Brother against brother, to please an ageing woman's jaded appetite.

Poor foolish Catrin, to be driven to death with the weight of another's guilt upon her soul!

Margred plucked a leaf, crushing it in her hands, holding it close to her nostrils. The scent of vinegar was drowning all other scents, and her yellow eyes had an ancient, evil beauty.

'We are not finished yet, you and I,' she whispered to the throbbing bark and shivering branches. 'Why for us it is only just beginning!'

McLEAN AT THE GOLDEN OWL
George Goodchild

Inspector McLean has resigned from Scotland Yard's CID and has opened an office in Wimpole Street. With the help of his able assistant, Tiny, he solves many crimes, including those of kidnapping, murder and poisoning.

KATE WEATHERBY
Anne Goring

Derbyshire, 1849: The Hunter family are the arrogant, powerful masters of Clough Grange. Their feuds are sparked by a generation of guilt, despair and ill-fortune. But their passions are awakened by the arrival of nineteen-year-old Kate Weatherby.

A VENETIAN RECKONING
Donna Leon

When the body of a prominent international lawyer is found in the carriage of an intercity train, Commissario Guido Brunetti begins to dig deeper into the secret lives of the once great and good.

A TASTE FOR DEATH
Peter O'Donnell

Modesty Blaise and Willie Garvin take on impossible odds in the shape of Simon Delicata, the man with a taste for death, and Swordmaster, Wenczel, in a terrifying duel. Finally, in the Sahara desert, the intrepid pair must summon every killing skill to survive.

SEVEN DAYS FROM MIDNIGHT
Rona Randall

In the Comet Theatre, London, seven people have good reason for wanting beautiful Maxine Culver out of the way. Each one has reason to fear her blackmail. But whose shadow is it that lurks in the wings, waiting to silence her once and for all?

QUEEN OF THE ELEPHANTS
Mark Shand

Mark Shand knows about the ways of elephants, but he is no match for the tiny Parbati Barua, the daughter of India's greatest expert on the Asian elephant, the late Prince of Gauripur, who taught her everything. Shand sought out Parbati to take part in a film about the plight of the wild herds today in north-east India.

THE DARKENING LEAF
Caroline Stickland

On storm-tossed Chesil Bank in 1847, the young lovers, Philobeth and Frederick, prevent wreckers mutilating the apparent corpse of a young woman. Discovering she is still alive, Frederick takes her to his grandmother's home. But the rescue is to have violent and far-reaching effects . . .

A WOMAN'S TOUCH
Emma Stirling

When Fenn went to stay on her uncle's farm in Africa, the lovely Helena Starr seemed to resent her — especially when Dr Jason Kemp agreed to Fenn helping in his bush hospital. Though it seemed Jason saw Fenn as little more than a child, her feelings for him were those of a woman.

A DEAD GIVEAWAY
Various Authors

This book offers the perfect opportunity to sample the skills of five of the finest writers of crime fiction — Clare Curzon, Gillian Linscott, Peter Lovesey, Dorothy Simpson and Margaret Yorke.

DOUBLE INDEMNITY
— MURDER FOR INSURANCE
Jad Adams

This is a collection of true cases of murderers who insured their victims then killed them — or attempted to. Each tense, compelling account tells a story of cold-blooded plotting and elaborate deception.

THE PEARLS OF COROMANDEL
By Keron Bhattacharya

John Sugden, an ambitious young Oxford graduate, joins the Indian Civil Service in the early 1920s and goes to uphold the British Raj. But he falls in love with a young Hindu girl and finds his loyalties tragically divided.

WHITE HARVEST
Louis Charbonneau

Kathy McNeely, a marine biologist, sets out for Alaska to carry out important research. But when she stumbles upon an illegal ivory poaching operation that is threatening the world's walrus population, she soon realises that she will have to survive more than the harsh elements . . .

TO THE GARDEN ALONE
Eve Ebbett

Widow Frances Morley's short, happy marriage was childless, and in a succession of borders she attempts to build a substitute relationship for the husband and family she does not have. Over all hovers the shadow of the man who terrorized her childhood.

CONTRASTS
Rowan Edwards

Julia had her life beautifully planned — she was building a thriving pottery business as well as sharing her home with her friend Pippa, and having fun owning a goat. But the goat's problems brought the new local vet, Sebastian Trent, into their lives.

MY OLD MAN AND THE SEA
David and Daniel Hays

Some fathers and sons go fishing together. David and Daniel Hays decided to sail a tiny boat seventeen thousand miles to the bottom of the world and back. Together, they weave a story of travel, adventure, and difficult, sometimes terrifying, sailing.

SQUEAKY CLEAN
James Pattinson

An important attribute of a prospective candidate for the United States presidency is not to have any dirt in your background which an eager muckraker can dig up. Senator William S. Gallicauder appeared to fit the bill perfectly. But then a skeleton came rattling out of an English cupboard.

NIGHT MOVES
Alan Scholefield

It was the first case that Macrae and Silver had worked on together. Malcolm Underdown had brutally stabbed to death Edward Craig and had attempted to murder Craig's fiancée, Jane Harrison. He swore he would be back for her. Now, four years later, he has simply walked from the mental hospital. Macrae and Silver must get to him — before he gets to Jane.

GREATEST CAT STORIES
Various Authors

Each story in this collection is chosen to show the cat at its best. James Herriot relates a tale about two of his cats. Stella Whitelaw has written a very funny story about a lion. Other stories provide examples of courageous, clever and lucky cats.